THE PROPHET'S RUIN

BOOK 2 OF THE CHRONICLES OF TALAHM

COLLEEN MITCHELL

COLLEEN MITCHELL WRITES, LLC

Edited by Halie Fewkes Damewood & Lauren Loftis
Cover Art by Angelique Modin
Interior Illustration by LeighAnn Lopez

First paperback printing March 2023.
Missoula, MT

Library of Congress Control Number: 2023900875
Paperback ISBN: 979-8-9850548-2-8
eBook ISBN: 979-8-9850548-3-5

For the mothers in my life whose steadfast
faith and encouragement laid the foundation
to pursue unbridled creativity.

God has planted eternity in our hearts.

Mom

A woman who never gives up on
her faith, values, family, or passions;
who finds the silver in rain and
gold in God's promise of forever.

&

Grandma Van

A woman who set the example
of faith, perseverance, courage,
and commitment through ninety-three
years of good times and bad.

The only way to live is to risk living.

N
W
E
S
MAIN GATE
HADRIAN QUARTER
GOLDEN QUARTER
TRIDENT GATE
STOREHOUSE
CATHEDRAL
STOREHOUSE
BLACKSMITH'S
KENNELS
CITADEL WELL
TRAINING GROUNDS
STABLES
INNER WARD
GARDENS
CHAPEL
STOREHOUSE
STOREHOUSE
OGWEN GATE
DRAGON QUARTER
TITAN QUARTER
VALON GATE
City of Camelot

KENNELS
CITADEL WELL
TRAINING GROUNDS
STABLES
INNER WARD
GARDENS
CHAPEL

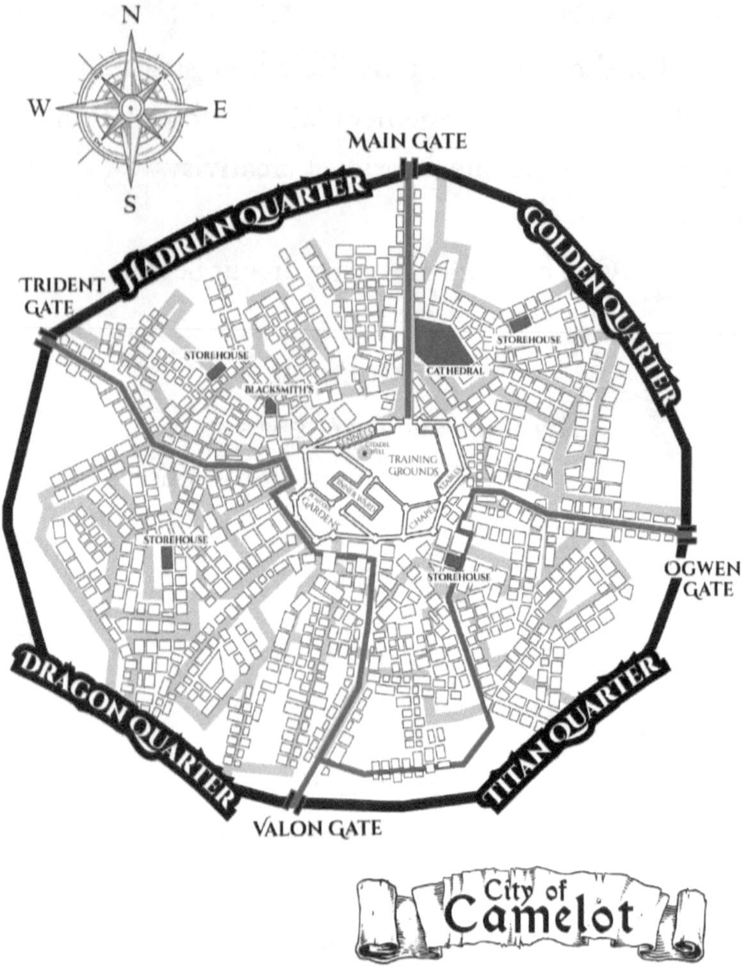

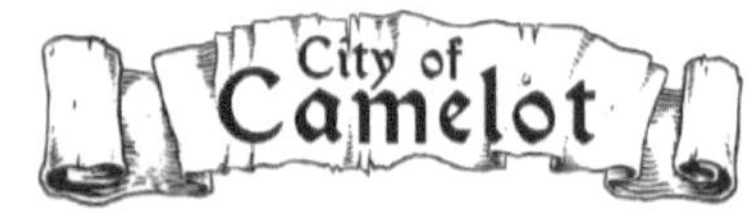

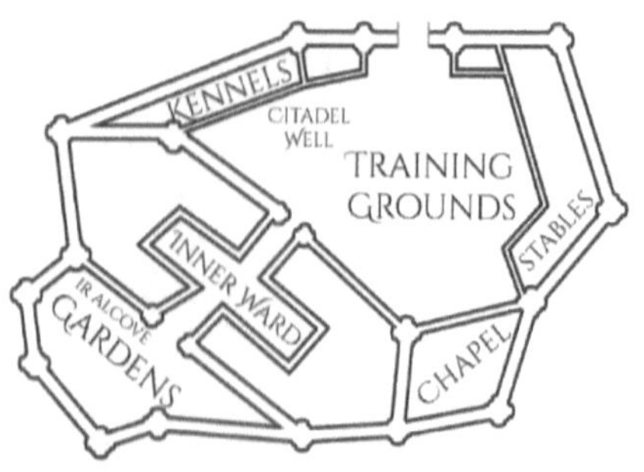

THE CITADEL

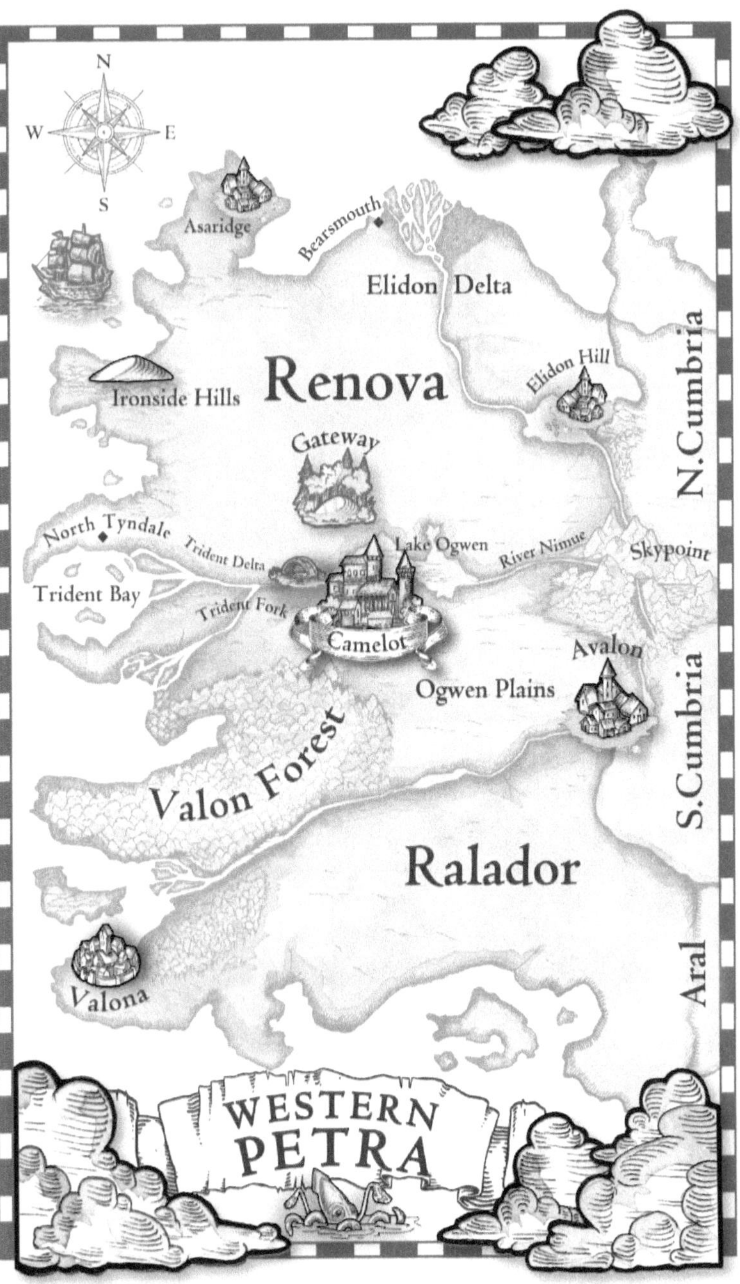

N
W E
S
Asaridge
Bearsmouth
Elidon Delta
N.Cumbria
Renova
Ironside Hills
Elidon Hill
Gateway
North Tyndale
Lake Ogwen
River Nimue
Skypoint
Trident Delta
Trident Bay
Camelot
Trident Fork
Avalon
Ogwen Plains
S.Cumbria
Valon Forest
Ralador
Aral
Valona
WESTERN PETRA

WHAT HAPPENED IN MARK OF STARS

Four years ago, Emma found out she has magic. On the eve of her 18th birthday, she received the last letter from her father written before he died—only to find out he's alive and waiting for her on another world. Talahm.

Her brother Luke, the next Prophet of Camlaan and Emma's Sentinel, escorted Emma and her best friend Bethany to Talahm. But the moment they arrived, he had a Vision of a terrible future: a curse spreading over Camelot, villages burning, and an arrow striking their father Tomás in the heart. The curse activated and encased the city as they crossed the gates, trapping citizens and killing two-thirds of those who touched it.

While Luke practiced defensive magic, Emma trained in elemental control and how to absorb magical energy. Their teacher, Ebony Reva, flirted with Luke to awaken Bethany's latent magic, and it worked—Bethany's first blast of fire injured Ebony, whose rune protection tattoos were damaged.

After visiting the Impossible Room deep beneath Camelot, Emma had ideas to break the curse. But when she absorbed too much energy, she accidentally electrocuted Bethany. Luke healed Bethany, and when she woke, they admitted their feelings for each other.

Sabotage thwarted their efforts to stop the curse as it crept closer to the citadel, forcing the surviving citizens into the tight confines of the training grounds and even into the crypts below the chapel.

Then, a shadowy figure shot Tomás—Prince Argent, possessed by Agamemnon Septim's spirit. Emma stopped him from killing King Aragon and released a powerful blast of magic. Before it could kill Argent, Ebony stepped in, sacrificing herself to save him and free him from Septim's hold.

In the infirmary, Luke and others worked to save Tomás from the poisoned arrow. Meanwhile, Emma and Renault made it past the curse and broke its anchor above the city gates, which crumbled the walls. Emma then used her Persuasion gift to stop the enemy army.

Before returning to Earth, Emma and Bethany received enchanted journals paired to ones with Tomás, Argent, and Luke. With the *Prophecy of the World's End* on Emma's horizon, she and Bethany used their last years on Earth to risk living.

PRONUNCIATION GUIDE

Agamemnon – Ag-uh-MEM-non

Amity – AM-itty

Aragon – AIR-a-gone

Argent – ARRGH-ent

Artair – ARR-tare

Cara – CARR-uh

Coventra – Coe-VEN-truh

Davan – Duh-VON

Doltev – DOLE-tehv

Hela – HELL-uh

Helcari – Hell-CAR-ee

Igraine – EE-grain

Langoth – LAN-goth

Le Fay – Leh-FAY

Magdalin – MAG-duh-lin

Nimüe – NIM-you

Olii – OH-lie (plural of Olis)

Olis – OH-liss

Petra – PET-ruh

Ralador – RAL-uh-door
Renault – Rehn-ALT
Renova – Reh-NOV-uh
Reva – REE-vuh
Richat – REE-caught
Rishon – Ree-SHAWN
Roque – ROW-k
Sargateth – SAR-guh-teth
Septim – SEP-tim
Talahm – Ta-LAW-m
Tomás – Toe-MOSS
Valon – VAL-un
Valona – VA-lone-uh

CONTENTS

CHAPTER ONE

THE LAST SCOUT

Emma Jackman blew at the wisp of jet-black hair escaping her knitted cap. She walked down the dark promenade through George Square Gardens, her cell phone pressed to her ear as she talked to her best friend, Bethany Hawkins. The University of Edinburgh felt quieter than usual this late winter evening, the fresh snow from that afternoon's storm crunching under her insulated boots. As the strongest witch to ever wield magic in Talahm, Emma could have worn a summer dress in the dead of winter and stayed warm, but on Earth, she had to at least pretend she was normal.

What a joke.

She'd wanted to be normal for her entire life, but the extraordinary, pure white tesseract birthmark on her right palm kept that out of her cards. The image marked her as a child of an ancient prophecy set in motion over seven hundred years ago by her ancestor, Sir Lancelot. Black and cobalt tendrils wove around the blemish, bleeding into her skin. Once small, the colored branches now spread across her chest and down the other arm.

The straps of Emma's backpack dug into her shoulders, the bag heavy with history books. "I all but proposed marriage," she whispered into the phone, glancing around the gardens. The only noise came from the thrum of traffic a few streets over, no one around to overhear her half of this strange conversation. "I basically told him that Renova couldn't handle me on the throne unless he was there too." She chewed on her bottom lip, anxious to hear Bethany's response.

"And?" Bethany demanded. "What did he say?"

Emma's breath caught, her throat tightening. She'd always hated how rejection felt, but somehow this seemed so much worse than all the previous rejections she'd experienced put together. Prince Argent's willingness to share hard things, his nightmares, and his dreams were like a balm to the bullying she'd faced in the past. After he was freed, Argent never spoke to her with disdain or as if he was better than her somehow. But now he wouldn't speak to her at all. "He never wrote back. It's been nearly a month, Bethany. A month! I thought he just needed time to process or figure out a polite way to say, 'no thanks,' but I asked why he's been ignoring me, and still nothing. He's never done this before."

Bethany sighed, the tinny sound sharp in Emma's ear. The low hum of other students at Washington State University filtered through the speaker. "What did your dad say about it?"

"Not much. They haven't gotten any letters since *The Sea Wolf* reached Doltev *two* months ago. I know more from the news you get from Luke than from what Dad tells me." She exhaled, watching the cloud of vapor rise into the harsh glare of the lamps lining the walking path. "It kills me that he's so quiet. I hope—" A soft crunch of snow to her left instantly drew her attention. She whirled to face it, darkness stretching in front of her.

"Em?" Bethany urged her to continue.

"I heard something," she said, automatically lifting her left hand to cup a ball of magical light in her palm. It let her see further across the otherwise deserted gardens, but eerie silence pressed against her eardrums. Then, a flash of gray fur streaked across the snow, deeper into the trees. "There's something out here."

"Em, wait—"

But Emma shoved the phone into her pocket, exchanging the ball of light for two handfuls of blue flames as she stalked after the intruder. She hoped it was just a dog, but whatever she saw had been as big as a person. Bethany's muffled voice vibrated against Emma's side.

Emma silenced her footfalls with magic, stepping into the fresh snow without a sound. She advanced into the trees, scanning through the darkness for something. Anything.

And then—

Ice blue eyes glowed in the darkness. A dark gray figure leaped straight toward her, easily four times the size of a wolf. Fangs jutted past its bottom lips, claws like a raptor's slicing through the air toward her face. Emma sent a ball of fire into the beast's maw, generating a thin golden shield with her other arm. The animal screeched in pain as it slammed against her, knocking her into the snow, her backpack digging into the small of her back. She scrambled to her feet, throwing as much fire as she could at it until it finally fled, vanishing when it reached the shadows.

Emma blinked, hardly believing her eyes. The silence lifted, noises from nearby cars hitting her eardrums. Hands shaking, Emma reached into her pocket for her phone, but found it empty. She spun around, looking at the ground, before spotting the phone in the snow. She picked it up and brushed off the screen.

"Bethany?"

"Oh, thank God," Bethany exclaimed. "You almost gave me a heart attack!"

"Sorry, I'll put you on hold first next time. We've got a problem." She described the encounter, and the creature itself, warily watching the woods for any sign of its return. Emma retraced her steps to the path, going back the way she came. "Remember what I told you about my history professor?"

"That he says stuff like he knows about *the other place*, and you think he's a scout who deserted? *That* history professor?"

Emma nodded before remembering Bethany couldn't see her. "Yeah, him. That wasn't a normal wolf. If anyone here knows what that was, or where it came from, it's Professor Ender."

As Emma approached David Ender's office, she rehearsed how she wanted to confront him. Though not a scout herself, she knew the rules Professor Ender was bound to if she was right. Don't talk about Talahm. Don't stay past the end of your mission. Don't fall in love.

Rules her father had broken decades ago.

Tomás Artair was a poor example.

Emma knocked on the door frame of Professor Ender's open office, watching her reflection in the dark bay of windows behind his wide cherrywood desk. Steam from the mug by his elbow curled into the air. One metallic corner of the laptop he usually carried to class peeked out from beneath an explosion of parchments, newspapers, and half-graded homework. True to his profession, bookshelves overtook every available inch of the walls, their contents neatly curated. In the center of the office, two fat leather armchairs sat on either side of a cherrywood coffee table piled with history books. At her knock, the professor glanced up, a beaming smile lighting up his clean-shaven face.

"Come in, come in, Miss Jackman!" he welcomed, shuffling the loose papers on his desk into a haphazard pile before standing up and stretching. Though middle-aged, the professor's short white hair and penchant for tweed jackets suited him. Emma had caught plenty of the girls in her Ancient and Medieval History class giving Ender appreciative looks during lectures. His grin drooped. "Are you all right? You look positively frightened."

Emma closed the door behind her, turning the deadbolt with a solid click. "Professor, I was attacked."

He rounded his desk, leaning against it, brow furrowed beneath his rectangular glasses. "Attacked? By whom? Are you hurt?"

Emma shook her head, getting a whiff of jasmine tea as she walked further in. "Just shaken up. But I think you can help me figure out what it was. It wasn't a *normal* animal."

Professor Ender swallowed, his Adam's apple bobbing as he stared at her, hands tense against the edge of the desk. "Animal, you say? Not a human?"

Emma nodded.

"Not 'normal' how?" he finally asked, with words Emma assumed he'd chosen deliberately. If she hadn't been looking for it, she would have missed the flash of apprehension that shot through his light blue eyes.

Emma described the creature, emphasizing its glowing eyes. "I was going to follow it, but it literally disappeared without a trace. Gone once it jumped into the shadows."

Professor Ender leaned forward, eyes wide. "You tried to *follow* it? After it attacked you? Good Lord, Miss Jackman, do you want to get killed?"

"I can protect myself," Emma said slowly, gauging his reaction. "Others can't."

But the professor seemed caught up in his admonishment, approaching her as he scanned her body for any hint of injury. "Are you sure it didn't hurt you?" Both hands hovered over her shoulders, as if asking for permission to touch her.

Emma sat, out of reach. "I'm sure, Professor. Do you know what it was?"

"Very sure?" he pressed, a vein jumping in his temple. "The bite of a Fenris wolf kills in mere hours without the proper treatment."

"A Fenris wolf?" Emma repeated, satisfied with her instincts. She hadn't imagined his Renovan accent or the Olii drawings left on his desk. She crossed her legs, leaning back against the cold chair. "You know, Renault Le Fay is going to have to answer a lot of questions the next time I see him."

"Renault—" Professor Ender took a step backward, his legs hitting the edge of the matching leather seat behind him. He slumped into it, panic clear on his face. "Who are you, really?"

Emma carefully unpeeled the glove from her right hand, showing him her birthmark. "You might know my father, Tomás Artair."

The professor's eyes fixed on the white tesseract, his face draining of blood. "You're her," he croaked. "The Seventh Sorceress. You're the Prophet's daughter?"

Emma couldn't stop her giddy laugh. "You have *no idea* how nice it feels to talk to someone else about this."

"I have more of an idea than you think," he whispered, reaching for her hand. "May I?"

She nodded, letting him touch the raised white ridges of the mark, the blue and black patterns swirling as his fingertips passed over them.

"You've been here under my nose the whole time," he breathed, a smile ghosting across his lips.

"You were a scout, weren't you?"

His eyes met hers, and she sensed his shared relief of not having to keep it a secret anymore. "I still am. *Davan* Ender, at your service."

"Professor, how could a Fenris wolf get here? I didn't even know they existed outside of Norse mythology."

Davan gently squeezed her hand before standing, pushing his glasses up the brim of his nose. He walked over to his desk, moving a pile of old newspapers from the corner. "Truthfully, I don't know. You said it disappeared when it reached the shadows? That's typical in the research I've seen on them. But this isn't the first time I've heard about this type of encounter." He handed her a paper he'd opened to a tiny article with the headline: *Centaurs in the Scottish Highlands?*

Emma's eyes widened. She scanned the minuscule article, barely finishing it before Davan handed her another. "'*Kelpie Spotted in Trafalgar Square Fountain*'? How was this not on BBC?"

Davan shrugged helplessly, taking back the papers and setting them on his desk. "Government cover-up? It wouldn't be the first. Creature sightings are happening all over the world, especially in the past two years. Though I'll admit, I've seen an extraordinary number of reports in the last six months."

"Where do they come from?"

"My first guess? Talahm. But if that's true, they must be coming through a portal. And they can't all be arriving at Goatfell."

Emma's stomach dropped to her feet. "Portals opening on their own? Is that even possible?"

"My dear, at this point, anything is possible."

She opened her mouth to ask another question when screams erupted from the promenade outside.

CHAPTER TWO

THE SEA WOLF

Perched on the prow of *The Sea Wolf*, Prince Argent Pendragon traced the leather edge of his journal, brows furrowing at the storm clouds roiling across the horizon. Cold seawater sprayed over the snarling figurehead of a wolf, stinging his bright green eyes and plastering brown hair against his face.

Heeled boots clacked against the forecastle behind him—boots belonging to Cordelia Roque, the acerbic captain of Talahm's most famous brigantine. Argent stiffened when she stirred the pot again. "If there's one thing I hate more than the bloody Artairs, it's having to ferry a weakling prince on my ship, possessed or not. I knew people who died in that wretched curse."

"Could be a ruse," another witch answered in a throaty whisper. "There's not a sacrifice out there powerful enough to free someone nobody loves. I think Septim's still in his head."

"He should help with the magic then," Cordelia groused.

A third witch chimed in, her high-pitched voice loud enough for the whole ship to hear. "Forget sacrifices. No magic lets a man's soul linger after death. I don't think Septim was *ever* there."

Argent swallowed and glanced behind him, the lump in his throat refusing to melt.

Cordelia peered over the forecastle railing with a wrinkled nose, scorn evident in her tight jaw. "And yet here we are, stuck with him as our next king."

Argent turned away from her, hugging the journal to his chest. Emma, the Seventh Sorceress, had been right. She'd told him that King Aragon's decree to keep the full details of what happened in Camelot secret would only lead to everyone filling in the details on their own. But his father had not seen reason. Argent closed his eyes, savoring the wind, his throat tightening again as he thought back to when Ebony Reva's sacrifice had freed him from Septim's twisted shade.

The lightness and hope in his soul, undone by the distrust on his father's face.

Relief that he was finally free after six years of captivity inside his own mind, shattered by the horror-stricken refugees packed inside the citadel to escape Septim's deadly curse.

The weight of what Septim had used him for slammed back onto his shoulders when he realized that they all blamed *him*.

What good is my freedom if no one believes I'm free?

He flipped the journal open to one of the many dogeared pages kept dry by Prophet Tomás Artair's intricate enchantments. A more complex enchantment allowed him to write to Tomás's daughter Emma, who was now in her last year of university on Earth, worlds away from where he sat as *The Sea Wolf* carved south through the Sleeping Sea on its journey home from the Helcari Isles.

The first few earthquakes had seemed harmless, rattling his father's battle trophies on their shelves in the Royal Apartments of Camelot. They'd had earthquakes before, and when the aftershocks diminished, King Aragon brushed it off as easily as he'd brushed off Argent's struggles recovering from possession.

But then the hawks came, bearing tidings of tsunamis from the northern port at Asaridge all the way to Helcari. Theirs had not been the only quake.

Then it happened again.

And again.

Without the grain and supplies *The Sea Wolf* had delivered, Argent doubted the Helcari Isles would make it through the rest of the spring and summer, let alone a winter without their own harvests.

Argent traced their conversations with his fingertips, his only link to Emma for almost two years—nearly four for her, thanks to how time flowed differently between their worlds. Her dry sense of humor jumped out at him—her curiosity, compassion, and staunch dedication to science were a welcome reprieve from the whispers of what had actually happened in Camelot. He admired her tenacity and, most of all, her willingness to share pieces of herself with him.

My birthmark made it to my shoulder today. Other students keep asking who my tattoo artist is, and what kind of ink makes it look like my arm's alive. It's funny—saying, "It's magic," makes them stop asking.

I got carried away practicing my sneak magic and almost got stuck inside Edinburgh Castle overnight. It turns out I can phase myself through solid matter, but it took so much power that I slept for fifteen hours and then ate more for breakfast than the entire football team combined.

Argent had no idea what football was, but he hoped to find out when Emma came back to Talahm—when she came back to *him*. He no longer felt silly thinking that way, not after their moments together in this journal.

I had that nightmare again last night. I wish Bethany understood, like you do, that Septim was in both our heads, using us, but I can't put that trauma on my best friend. I'm counting the days until I come back. Maybe when I see your face again, when I can touch you and prove to myself that you're alive—that I didn't kill you—then the nightmares will stop. I miss you so much.

Sometimes I wish I'd fought more for you to come to Earth with us. It's hard making friends here when I know I'll never see them again after I come home.

She considered Talahm her home. After all, her father and brother lived in Camelot. Only her mother remained on Earth. At the sudden thought that he could be part of Emma's reason, Argent blinked away the pressing tears.

He turned to their messages from a few hours ago. Not for the first time, Argent wished he could reach through the pages to hold the hand of the woman who'd penned those words into the journal's counterpart.

Think of it this way—your father is showing you what NOT to do when you take the throne. Keeping secrets, sending aid to foreign countries when Renova needs it more, not listening to his son.... It's less painful to learn from the mistakes of others.

In a moment of utter vulnerability, he'd finally written the words he'd wanted to write since the day she left. Words that revealed the depth of his self-doubt, his belief that no matter what, he'd never be good enough to rule Camelot.

You would make a better queen than I would a king.

And yet, as soon as he'd written it, a weight lifted off his shoulders. As if the mere act of sharing it with someone he trusted meant it didn't affect him as much as before. Now, Emma's beautiful script unfolded before his eyes on the parchment, finally answering him. His heart lodged in his throat as he stared at the message.

A clap of thunder startled him. Ozone filled his nose, the first droplets of rain beading over Emma's words. Dark clouds stretched over the ship, thin cracks of lightning threading across the sky like beacons of despair.

"All hands on deck!" William Pendragon bellowed from the sterncastle. Argent's great-uncle, the first officer on *The Sea Wolf*, seemed like his only ally on board.

Argent jumped to his feet, his stomach in knots over the fact he didn't have time to respond to Emma. And oh—how he wanted to respond. He climbed onto the main deck, stumbling backward with the pitch of the ship, and he hit the railing, knocking the breath out of his lungs. Wild waves churned around them—waves he hadn't noticed while sitting on the bowsprit. At William's command, witches streamed onto the deck, securing the rigging against the sudden snap of the wind, and they battened down the hatches, scaling the masts to tie up the sails. Rain poured down, drowning their shouts.

On the quarter deck, Captain Roque locked the wheel against the pull of the rudder, her dark, gray-streaked hair billowing in the wind. She showed no fear in the face of the storm, snapping orders with more confidence than an entire coven of witches. It was no wonder King Aragon had given her the mission to deliver the desperately needed food to Helcari.

"Princeling," William yelled at him, "get your sea legs under you! Your mother won't forgive me if I let you drown."

Argent tucked the journal into his jerkin. He pushed away from the railing, but a flash in the water made him peer over the edge again. Purple lightning crackled deep under the sea, creating a shockwave that rippled out in every direction. A colossal, dark form undulated below the surface. Icy dread trickled down Argent's spine.

He backed away from the edge of the ship in horror, hand on the hilt of his sword as the first tentacle slithered into view.

"Kraken!" he screamed, unsheathing his sword.

In the second between Argent's cry and the crew's response, blood roared in his ears. Sick, stale air swept across the deck. The Kraken's tentacles slid closer, wood creaking under the pressure. Argent sprang into action. He leaped forward, his sword coming down on the nearest fleshy limb with a strength he hadn't known he'd had. Around him, witches joined the fight, capturing tentacles with magical nooses, sending high-pressure jets of air and water into the vulnerable suckers holding the ship in place. The telltale *thump* of the ice cannons reverberated through Argent's feet.

His blade cut a thin, oozing slice in the Kraken's hide, but a moment later, the end of the tentacle twisted around his ankle, yanking him off his feet. It squeezed, and a lance of white-hot pain shot through his leg, tearing a ragged cry from his throat, his ankle snapping. Tightening his hold on the sword, blood drained from his fingers. Argent stabbed at the tentacle, twisting the blade until the Kraken withdrew.

Argent's chest heaved, heart racing, his hands shaking. Struggling to his feet, he hobbled to the railing, broken ankle dragging behind him. Tentacles seethed around the belly of the ship. Broken glass and splinters filled the maelstrom, and a high-pitched screech filled the air. The Kraken's gargantuan head rose above the deck, exposing hundreds of circular rows of sharp teeth.

Cordelia lashed a rope around the wheel and leaped from the quarter deck. A staff in one hand and a sword in the other, she jabbed them both toward the Kraken's maw without flinching. A storm of magic crackled between her and the beast. Three large balls of ice shot from the starboard cannons, slamming into its open gullet. It flinched backward, letting out another scream as its tentacles constricted around the hull and the mizzen mast, jolting the ship. With an almighty crack, the mast toppled across the port edge, crushing the railing and leaving a ragged hole in the deck. If they hadn't already unloaded the hold, their cargo for Helcari would've been lost in that one moment. Argent held his breath, trying not to whimper in pain as *The Sea Wolf* tilted, listing as water rushed through the cracks.

With determination etched into the premature lines on her face, Cordelia thrust her weapons at the Kraken again. While she distracted the beast, the witches around her cut through its limbs with sharp blasts of magic, working until the Kraken finally loosened its grip on the ship and slipped back into the swirling depths of the sea.

A slick sliding sound behind him caught Argent's attention. He glanced over his shoulder as the last tentacle slammed into his back, pitching him over the edge in a freefall. A rope of magic cinched around his broken ankle, and he screamed, the sudden rescue dislodging the journal from his vest and sending it tumbling into the waters below.

"No!"

Cordelia dragged him back onto the waterlogged deck, her face twisted in disgust. "If you'd rather drown, I'd be delighted to toss you back," she snapped, the rain plastering stringy hair against her thin face.

Despite the pain, Argent scrambled to lean back over the railing, bits of wood digging into his arms as he searched for the journal. He spotted it floating in the debris from the attack, now falling behind them as *The Sea Wolf* limped along. "Someone help! My book, please, someone get my book!" Frantic, he risked taking his eyes off the journal to beg the waterwitches, each of them more than capable of rescuing his only connection to Emma. "Please, help me get it back! I can't lose her!"

"Buy another in the Trident, little prince," Cordelia hissed, lifting a hand in warning before any of the witches could move. Her pale blue eyes cut Argent to the bone. "They don't answer to you."

CHAPTER THREE
FENRIS WOLF

Emma sprinted from Davan Ender's office to the side door down the hall. She heard him running behind her, but as the screams intensified, she didn't have time to tell him to stay put. She hit the crash bar so hard that the door slammed into the metal railing behind it. Winter air shocked her sinuses.

"There!" Davan exclaimed, pointing across the snow-covered walkways. A gigantic dark form crouched over a thrashing body. Two other figures slowly backed away.

Emma ran so fast she almost flew. The tesseract burned, warning her to avoid exposing magic as much as possible to potential witnesses. When she got close enough to counter-attack the Fenris wolf, she cast a charm to hide herself and her prey from the bystanders.

Then she held nothing back.

With a direct hit of telekinesis, her magic threw the Fenris wolf away from its victim, leaving a long red skid mark in the snow. As she closed the gap, Emma hoped the blood belonged to the wolf. She carefully stepped around the shuddering body, letting Davan do what he could to help the woman while Emma threw dozens of shining balls into the air. Light exploded into every corner of the promenade, chasing all the shadows away. Beyond her illusion, the two girls stopped screaming, clutching at each other with their eyes locked on the still form of their friend.

The wolf wriggled to its feet, snarling as it recognized Emma. Singed fur stretched across the side of its face, remnants from their first encounter in the gardens. It cringed in the light but stalked toward her anyway.

"How do I kill it?" Emma yelled, igniting her palms with crackling blue-black energy, the magic feeling like freedom. She hadn't been in a fight like this for almost four years.

"It's not a werewolf, Miss Jackman, you don't need anything special!" Davan shouted back.

Without wasting another breath, Emma attacked. Thankful for her college martial arts classes, she dodged the wolf's swiping paws and snapping jaw, blasting it in its face and barreled chest. Fire raced across its fur, and it retreated, rolling in the snow. Emma chased it, building the charge in her palm until she could wrap her fingers around a lightning bolt. She hoped she wouldn't cause a power outage by killing the mythical beast.

The wolf struggled to its feet, howling when the plasma struck. Thick globs of saliva dropped from oversized fangs, sizzling where they landed in the snow. Her muscles taut, Emma struck again. It took one more bolt of lightning before the wolf collapsed to the slushy ground, heaving once before stilling. Emma kicked its side with the toe of her boot to make sure it was dead.

Protected by Emma's charm, Davan had stripped off his tweed jacket to stem the bleeding from the girl's neck. One sharp edge of her clavicle pierced through the skin, and she took shallow breaths. Davan trembled, chilled and shocked. The girl's blood soaked the cuffs of his white dress shirt and stained the tips of her blonde hair.

Emma knelt on the victim's other side, meeting Davan's wild eyes for a moment before summoning a different kind of magic, meant for healing. Her hands glowed with golden light, not as strong as when her brother used it, but powerful enough to save the girl's life.

"You said the bite kills the victim within an hour," Emma said as she closed the wound, feeling the girl's bone knit back together under her hands. "What do I need to do to stop that?"

Davan wiped his brow with the back of one hand, leaving a streak of blood across his forehead. His white hair shone in the light. "You're already doing it," he said, smiling down at Emma's glowing hands. "Healing with magic."

The girl's breathing steadied. Her dark brown eyes fluttered open and, after a moment, she gasped. "Wolf," she croaked, her voice hoarse from screaming.

Emma helped her sit up, wordlessly extinguishing her lights and releasing the illusion distorting the other girls' senses. "It's dead and you're safe. It won't hurt anyone else." The two other women rushed toward them, falling to their knees by their friend.

"You killed it?" one of the friends asked, mascara running down her cheeks with her tears. "It came out of nowhere and grabbed her!"

Davan sat back on his heels, peering over at the body, now just a dark mound at the edge of the building's lights. "Miss Jackman?"

Emma left the girl with her friends, offering her professor a hand. He accepted without hesitation, and she leveraged him to his feet. "We can't leave it there."

"Can you... vanish it somehow?"

Emma frowned, walking back over to it. Her boots slid in the remnants of blood and snow, now slick from the heat of battle. It would ice over soon. Closing her eyes, she held her right hand toward the dead beast, imagining it melting into the shadows it had once been able to travel through. When she blinked, the Fenris wolf's body was gone.

"Incredible," Davan breathed. "I forgot how much I love seeing magic."

"Are you ever going home?"

"To Camelot? I dearly hope so. But I have work to finish."

"Pardon," the other woman interrupted with a thick Scottish accent. "Can we take Clara home now? I need a stiff drink to calm me nerves."

Emma quickly shook Davan's hand, promising him she'd come by his office again in the morning.

"Yeah, I'll walk you home." She helped lift Clara to her feet, steadying her. Emma hoped her healing had also fixed the blood loss, but she wasn't as good at it as Luke. She tried brushing the wet snow from Clara's shoulders, but it had already soaked into her peacoat.

"Thanks.... Hey, I know you," Clara said, gripping Emma's forearms, focusing on her face. "You're that American prodigy—the one with the wicked tattoo sleeve, right?"

Emma's face burned. Now a senior, she'd earned a reputation despite doing her best to keep a low profile. "Nice to meet you. I'm Emma. Can we get moving in case something else is lurking in the dark?"

She couldn't help but wonder. If portals could open on their own, who else might fall victim to other, more dangerous legendary creatures?

Emma owed Bethany another phone call—and a note to her father in Talahm.

In the privacy of her apartment three nights later, Emma dug her thumb into the tesseract, waiting for her mother to answer the video call. On the third ring, Julie Jackman's thin, freckled face appeared, framed by her long, wavy, dark brown hair. Emma had forgotten how little she looked like her mom. Behind Julie, the old workhorse refrigerator still had Luke and Emma's elementary school art projects stuck to the front with coin magnets. The sentimentality sparked another wave of guilt for not having done this sooner.

For nearly four years, she'd argued with her father Tomás across countless pages of their shared journals, pleading to tell Julie about Talahm. Determined not to disappear on her mother like he and Luke had, she'd finally teased out the truth. Even though he still wore his wedding ring, Tomás didn't believe Julie would want him back after what he'd done to her.

To them.

But now, faced with evidence of another world bleeding into Earth—with putting his family in the danger he'd tried to protect them from since the beginning—Tomás had finally cracked.

"Emma, it's good to see you," Julie said, the smile on her face so wide it startled Emma.

"Hi, Mom," Emma answered automatically. "Weird question, have you seen any strange animals recently?"

One of Julie's eyebrows went up. "What kind of strange animals?"

"Any kind? Listen, you still arm yourself whenever you're out, right?"

"Of course I do. You know I never leave the house without my gun. Emma, did something happen? Do I need to fly over there?"

Emma forced herself to take a deep breath, relaxing when it left her lungs. "Sorry. It's just...." She described the attacks, leaving out all the bits about magic. "Based on the newspapers, it seems like they can show up anywhere. I don't want you to get caught off guard if one shows up in Palouse."

Julie sat back in her chair, face serious but unreadable. The shadow of a tree branch waved across the window over the kitchen sink behind her. "All right, Emma, I'll be careful. Is... is that the only reason you called? Is everything else okay? I haven't heard from Luke in—" she cut herself off, jaw clenched.

Years. You haven't heard from Luke in years. "Luke's fine," Emma deflected. She glanced away from the camera at the open journal she shared with her father, his words a permission to speak. She hadn't realized how hard it would be to be the one to reveal this secret. Wet cement filled her throat, but she forced herself to swallow through the discomfort, hoping the non sequitur wouldn't startle her mother too badly. "You met Dad here in Edinburgh, right? Outside St. Giles Church on High Street when he was singing that Bryan Adams song for money? You thought he sounded like an angel."

Julie's jaw dropped, her face slack. "Who told you that?"

"And when you found out he also led tours, you went on three in a row and asked him out for scotch after the last one. Mom, am I right?"

"Emma, who told you all that?"

"Dad. He's alive." There. She said it. "He's alive, and I've seen him."

Julie's eyes widened, her mouth frozen in an 'O' of surprise. "*What?*"

"I'm going to tell you what Bethany and I really did when we came to Scotland after we graduated high school, but you can't steamroll me. Listen, please, for once, just listen and let me explain before you assume you know everything. It's too important."

Julie looked like she couldn't decide between anger and curiosity, so she settled for helplessness, gesturing for Emma to continue.

So, Emma told the strangest story of her life, wishing she could have brought her mother into the fold the minute she got back. But with the creatures and after almost thirty years in the dark, her mom deserved a chance to know the truth.

And the chance to come with them.

CHAPTER FOUR

CAN PARROTS BREATHE FIRE?

"Hi, Mrs. Jackman!" Bethany Hawkins greeted when she opened the front door, tugging the tail of her long, blonde French braid. Behind Emma's mom, twilight waxed with the promise of stars on the horizon. "Come in. Dad's starting a fire in the pit out back."

"Bethany," Julie said, unzipping her jacket as she stepped into the foyer, "how many times do I have to ask you to call me Julie?"

Bethany's eyes instinctively dropped to the holstered handgun Emma's mom always carried on her right hip, even at the corner store Julie owned. She'd always admired the older woman's courage and practicality about it. "Just be glad I'm not still calling you 'Mrs. Emma's Mom.'"

"You've got me there." Julie peered around the entryway. "Is your mother outside?"

The wafting scent of fresh-cooked pasta accompanied the sound of water pouring from a faucet. "She's in the kitchen. Did you want to talk to her?"

Julie straightened, matching Bethany's height. "Not yet." She lowered her voice to a near-whisper. "Did Emma tell you about our call?"

Bethany's lips split into a wide grin. "Right after it happened. It's about time, too. Luke's been upset that he hasn't been able to send you a message without spilling the beans. Plus, now you can help me break the news to my parents."

Julie's face spasmed at the mention of her son. "Is he okay? He's safe on this—in this other place?"

"As safe as you can get in a semi-medieval, post-war monarchy. The risk spices things up."

"Bethany—" Julie grasped Bethany's forearm. "I know we haven't always seen eye-to-eye, but if half of my family is on another *planet*, I need more than a token reassurance."

Bethany sighed, twisting her arm to mirror Julie's hold. "He's stressed. I can tell he's stressed, even though he's not telling me exactly what's going on. But he's alive, Tomás is alive, and we'll all be there before you know it."

She led Julie through the living room to the sliding door that opened into the backyard. On the left, a tidy garden was still wrapped up in cold-weather protection, the wild swings of early spring temperatures in Eastern Washington not yet conducive to growing. Past the garden, a chicken-wire fence with an open gate separated the dead grass of the backyard from the wide wheat field stretching to the edge of the main road into Palouse.

Jack Hawkins crouched over the fire pit, blowing on the smoldering coals beneath a tepee of kindling. "That you, Audrey?" Jack asked between breaths.

"Julie's here," Bethany said, gently kicking the sole of her dad's work boot.

He peered around, his graying hair nearly catching fire as the twigs ignited, whooshing into the air.

"Careful, Dad!" Bethany pulled him away from the stone ring around the pit. Ever since she first harnessed magic, Bethany had an affinity for fire. Holding a hand out, she willed the flames to behave. Julie's eyes sparkled with awe, a conspiratorial smile tugging at her mouth.

Jack got to his feet, brushing dirt and leaves from his knees. "Julie," he greeted, holding out a hand for her to shake. "It's been a while. I'm glad you could come over."

"I'll go help Mom with the food." Bethany left Julie and her dad in the back yard, butterflies in her stomach.

Bethany fidgeted with the enchanted friendship bracelet on her left wrist, twisting the cobalt blue charms until her fingers hurt. Disbelief radiated from her parents as they stared at her, the silence following her story only broken by the crackling fire. The bare hint of a smile pulled at Julie's lips. Finally, Bethany leaned down and picked up her empty plate, tossing it into the fire pit. As flames lapped the edges of the paper, Bethany curled her hand toward it, lifting the plate into the air by controlling the fire. As the plate disintegrated, Bethany drew a flame toward her hand, wrapping it around her fingers until it tickled.

"Holy Christmas crackerjack," Audrey shrieked, hands on her cheeks in shock. "You weren't kidding!"

"Bethany," Jack started, leaning forward with a frown on his normally genial face. He rested a hand on Audrey's knee. "Are you saying if you go back to this place—Talahm—you can't come back?"

"That's the catch," Bethany answered, finally coming to the part that hurt the most. Even though she and Emma had agreed to invite their parents, it meant giving up their entire lives on Earth. *What if they don't want to come?* "We only get to go through the portal four times. If anyone attempts a fifth... they disappear. No one's ever found them."

Audrey frowned. "But won't this next one be your third? You'll have one left."

Bethany sighed, threading the fire through her fingers like yarn. "I'm dating someone, Mom. He's on Talahm. If I used my fourth trip to come back here, I'd never see him again."

Julie laughed, the sound of it so unfamiliar that Bethany did a double take. "It's Luke, isn't it?"

Bethany's cheeks warmed, but she smiled, filled with love for Julie's son. "It's always been Luke."

"Well then, of course we're coming with you," Audrey announced, her hand clenched over her husband's knee. "I've always wanted to go inter-planetary house hunting."

Bethany almost choked on her relief. "We're going back right after graduation. The plan was always to bring you all with us, even if Emma's dad and the Royal Council didn't want us to."

A purple light lit the night sky in the meadow beyond their back yard. The quiet of the evening deepened, as if all the critters in the tall grasses sensed a threat.

"What was that?" Julie stood, right hand tightening over the grip of the gun in her holster.

Bethany held her hand out toward the house. In a rustle of wind, her staff flew across the yard from where she kept it stashed, slamming into her palm. She squinted into the night, the purple line suddenly disappearing. In the starlight, a dark shape streaked through the fields toward the highway. Realization dawned on her, and she exploded into a sprint, barely registering Julie running beside her with the gun now drawn at low ready.

Trampled wheat and grass marked the site where the shape appeared. Julie knelt, touching the damaged stalks with care. From the broken grass, she pulled out a long, sapphire blue feather. "This is too big for a parrot."

"Parrots can't breathe fire," Bethany answered, examining the scorch marks. "It moved like a snake, did you see that?"

Julie nodded, her grip on her gun never wavering.

An eerie tearing sound came from behind them, and before Bethany could pull her away, Julie lost her balance, teetering backward into the maw of a second rift. "Beth—!" The amber tear zipped itself back up, cutting off Julie Jackman's cry for help.

Bethany's heart hammered in her ears. *No, no, no, this is not good. NOT good.* She swore, running back to her parents as she tried to dig her phone from her pocket.

"What happened? Where's Julie?" Audrey asked from where she stood tucked against Jack's side, the fire flickering behind them.

Bethany swallowed past the gravel. "Talahm."

Emma picked up on what felt like the last ring. "Bethany, do you know what time it is here?"

"A portal sucked your mom out of my backyard into God knows where on Talahm," Bethany said, fighting the panic rising in her chest. The mysterious creature could wait.

"Mom's gone?" Emma's grogginess flipped to concern in an instant.

"That's what I said!"

"Shoot. I'll write to Dad. Send Luke a note, would you?" Sounds of rustling blankets came through the speaker.

"Already on it." Bethany turned to her parents. "Mom, go into my room and bring me the leather journal in the drawer of my bedside table. And a pen. Dad, there's something out there that could come back to attack us."

"I'll get the shotgun," Jack said, following Audrey into the house.

Bethany sat back in her camp chair, rubbing her eyes with one hand. Undulating spirals of smoke rose into the air from the fire. "Em, we can't wait. We have to go back right now."

"I know. So much for graduating, right? Did you tell your parents?"

Her eyes stung. "What a horrible way to leave them. Like, 'Hey, I'm going to a completely different planet for the rest of my life after college. Want to uproot your entire lives to come with? And oh—whoops, my best friend's mom got sucked into a magic portal. Sorry I can't stay longer.'" Her breath shuddered. "At least your mom had more than a minute to process the news that Talahm even exists. I'm going to strangle Renault when I see him. Sure, 'no other creatures.' And I'm the Easter Bunny."

"Just wrote to Dad," Emma answered. "I'm texting you Professor Ender's information. Give it to your parents. He'll be able to answer any questions and...."

"And guide them to the Gateway when they're ready to cross the universe?"

Emma gave a nervous laugh. "Exactly."

Audrey emerged from the house, handing Bethany the journal and pen.

"I'll talk to you later," Bethany murmured, fingers digging into the leather cover of the journal. She hung up, flipping near the end of the book, blank pages dwindling the more she wrote. She scribbled a short note to Luke, hoping beyond hope that Julie had landed someplace safe.

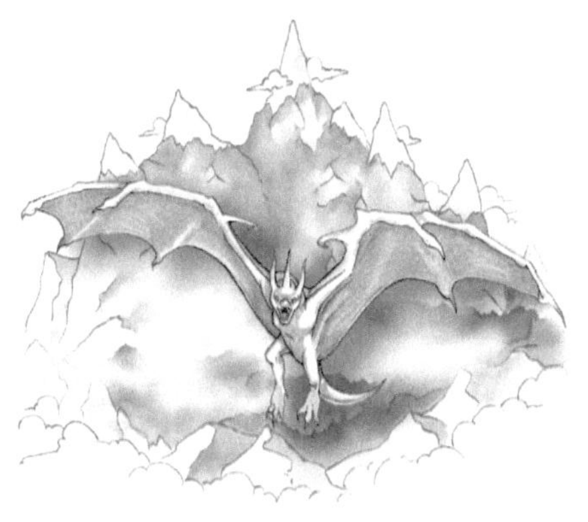

CHAPTER FIVE
A VISION OF DRAGONS

Luke hurried to his father's office, journal clenched in one hand. His long legs ate up the hallway, Prophet's robes swirling around his high leather boots, his sword heavy against his side. Panic pushed at his ribcage like a balloon. Of all the strange occurrences since the earthquakes began—close to a hundred catastrophes he'd Seen and dispatched relief to so far—he'd never imagined one of them being his *mother* coming to Talahm. Out of the corner of his eye, he noticed the paintings along the walls shaking again.

Before Luke rounded the corner, his father Tomás rolled himself into view using his wheelchair, looking as flustered as Luke felt. The two men shared the same heterochromia—one eye green and the other gold. As Prophets of Camlaan, men of Artair descent, white streaks of hair marked their temples on both sides. Sometimes Luke felt like a carbon copy of his father until he reminded himself that only one of them had dared challenge the assumption that their prophecies were set in stone.

Luke's tongue felt heavy in his mouth. "Mom got pulled through a portal."

Tomás held up his own journal. "I know. We must go to the King."

When they reached the War Room, situated behind the thrones in Pendragon Hall, Luke barged in without knocking. Luke spent so much time here, managing their response to the many problems caused by the quakes, floods, and fires across Renova, that he'd even left a stack of notes at his seat.

King Aragon looked up from the letters spread on the Round Table, stormy gray eyes demanding an explanation for the interruption. "Prophets," he said, leaning back in his gilded chair, his loose black curls falling over his furrowed brow. "What is it now?"

"My wife," Tomás said, voice tight. He and Luke summarized the events on Earth. "Let us send a search party for her. She knows little of this world, and without magic, she'll stand out."

The King glanced at the letters in front of him, twisting the eagle ring on his right middle finger. A tiny, green gem in the eagle's eye twinkled in the soft magical light. The scar on the back of Aragon's hand stood out against his skin. "Tomás," he sighed, "we have few resources available to search for your wife, especially if you cannot tell me where she came through. Luke knows better than I just how few witches we have ready. Didn't we recently send an earth coven to fix the cracks on the road to Avalon?"

"But—"

"Luke," King Aragon interrupted, picking up a parchment. "Since the hawks disappeared, I've had no choice but to send out letters using knights and other volunteers, and I am waiting for them all to return. Even if we had the forces to spare, where would you suggest we begin?"

Luke swallowed his retort, insides shriveling at the dismissal. Despite King Aragon's supposed confidence in him—he wouldn't have let him lead the relief operation if he didn't think him capable—Luke couldn't shake the thought that the King still didn't fully trust him. "The worst earthquakes are coming from Ralador, and the coven we sent a month ago still hasn't returned. If Mom's disappearance is connected to these disasters in any way, I would bet anything that we could start there."

Tomás picked up on Luke's train of thought, wheeling himself closer to the outer edge of the Round Table, rubbing at the corded scar that swept from his left ear to his collarbone. "There have been sightings of smoke to the south. Ralador's volcanoes haven't erupted in centuries. If these earthquakes stir them awake.... We are not prepared to face that magnitude of natural disasters *and* still defend against whatever threats Ralador's council of elders has cooked up."

Luke's vision swam. He stumbled forward, gripping the back of the nearest chair as the War Room dissolved into the ramparts of Camelot's citadel. Facing eastward as the rising sun blazed ahead, a massive shadow shot over the city. Luke didn't understand for a split second—but the wingspan and sheer size of the beast soaring over Renova could only be a dragon. It veered around the city, the high peaks of the Cumbrian Mountains an oddly appropriate backdrop. He stared at it for a heartbeat before the Vision ended, pulling his awareness back to his father and the King.

Worry deepened the wrinkles on the King's face. "What now?" Aragon asked, standing as he pushed back his chair. He came around to Tomás's side.

Mouth dry, Luke clenched his fists. "Dragon."

Aragon slammed his fist against the Round Table. "Damn it all. If we're to face a dragon, we must recall our battle witches immediately, including the ones in Ralador. Send a coven to retrieve them, Luke, but their primary mission is to withdraw our witches. The search for your mother must come second."

The door behind them clicked open. Sargateth Rishon, the Archmage and eldest of the Olii, slipped inside, scrolls tucked under his arm. His sharp green eyes swept across them, his normally friendly face tightening when he noticed the King. "Gentlemen," he greeted, his rich baritone stiff with tension. "Don't stop on my account. I'm just here to inform you we lost the Ogwen Gate tower, *again*, to that last tremor."

"Luke Saw a dragon, Sarg," Tomás said.

"That's a new one," the Archmage replied, eyes narrowing at King Aragon. "I haven't seen dragons in at least five hundred years." He tossed the scrolls onto the table, crossing his arms.

Unable to get the dragon out of his head, Luke pushed away from the chair, walking to the far corner where a fire crackled in the hearth. Could that be what Argent was up to? Of all Luke's orders, the only one the King had overruled was to send Argent with supplies for Helcari, an archipelago nation known for its darker uses of magic. Luke didn't think it was wise to send a royal—let alone a royal susceptible to mind magic—into a country that they were not allied with. *Unless there's something else going on I don't know about. Unless he's there to bring back something nefarious.* "Dad, have you Seen anything yet? Anything that might help us understand what's going on?"

Tomás sighed heavily, turning his wheelchair to face Luke. "Sometimes I wonder if the mantle has officially passed to you," he began, rubbing his bearded chin. "I haven't had a Vision since before Emma and Bethany first arrived nearly two years ago. Certainly not since I lost the use of my legs."

"Ah, yes," Sargateth said, still glaring at the King, "the Vision that drew my wife into a quest that could still kill her, given that I'm now forbidden from leaving the city to search for her."

Chills swept down Luke's spine. For the last year and a half, the Archmage and the King had been in perpetual disagreement, but no one would tell Luke why. He questioned when the people of Camelot, particularly the Royal Court, would start treating him with the respect his office deserved—especially since they all looked to him to minimize the damage from the catastrophes using his Visions. Even though he couldn't prevent the destruction, he could ensure relief arrived before a blacksmith's forge dislodged by an earthquake burned down an entire town. After the first few incidents had left Luke sleep deprived, the King had given him a star-shaped stone carved with runes to help him fall asleep and stay that way unless a Vision interrupted. Since then, he'd at least been able to function without feeling like a zombie.

"Tell him, Tomás," King Aragon finally said, pacing to the back of the room where the wall curved against the western citadel tower. He put the Round Table between himself and the Archmage.

"Yes, tell Luke why my wife is missing. Why our esteemed ruler believes her life is not worth rescuing." Firelight glinted off the silver circlet on Sargateth's brow, resting over feathery brown hair that reached his shoulders in soft waves.

Still Renova's sovereign, Aragon shot Sargateth a hard stare.

Tomás gestured for Luke to sit. "There were two Visions," he said. "In the first, I Saw the throne room of Skypoint, where the Olis council gathers."

"Olis council?" Luke asked, having never heard of this group before.

"My kin," Sargateth answered. "Twenty-four of us. No more, no fewer. Unless it's their season to stay in Skypoint, most remain in their home countries. The bulk of them meet every few decades to argue about who is the greatest and whether they should interfere in the 'petty lives of humans.'"

"Four thrones were empty," Tomás continued. "Three I understood. They belonged to Sargateth, Morgan, and Magdalin, the three Olii that the council shunned when they pledged loyalty to the throne of Renova. Ostracized for their apparent subservience to humans. But the fourth.... The fourth empty throne confused me until I heard what the others were saying. They desired to confront the strongest of the Olii about the disappearance of Magdalin's twin."

Sargateth sneered. "Cowards. They talk about showing their arrogant faces here but never sent a single ambassador."

"They're afraid of you." Aragon leaned against the wall, arms crossed over his broad chest. The muscles in his neck twitched.

"At least someone is," Sargateth snapped. "And yet, Magdalin was the only one brave enough to search for her brother." His eyes flickered back to Tomás, face relaxing a little. "Share your last Vision, my friend."

Luke leaned forward as his father spoke, his elbows digging into the stone table.

"I Saw him. An Olis in chains, one wing broken. I couldn't identify his surroundings, but when I described his markings to our council, Magdalin confirmed it. *Mountains Crumble Beneath His Claws* is being held captive."

Luke blinked. "That's his name?"

Sargateth actually rolled his eyes, finally moving to sit. He propped his legs up on the edge of the table, ankles crossed. "As an Olii purist, Mountains didn't *lower* himself to take a human name."

"And Magdalin went after him?"

"She did. And eighteen months ago, I felt our connection dim, right before that first tremor struck. For now, she lives, but tis a flutter in the back of my mind. If she dies, Pendragon, I will hold you personally responsible."

The tension in the room ratcheted so high that Luke wanted to crawl out of his own skin. He smelled the crackle of magic, evidence Sargateth felt far angrier than he looked. He wondered if he'd ever see the full power of Merlin on display, shuddering at the thought of it directed at him.

Bitterness warped King Aragon's voice. "I cannot give up the strength of your protection while Camelot rebuilds."

"Do not ask me to lose my mate for the sake of a vow I made to your ancestors," Sargateth retorted. "Every day I feel her less. The last time our connection faded like this, Septim's men broke her."

Bile rose in Luke's throat. His father had been there for the aftermath, slaying the men who had severed one of

Magdalin's wings and shattered the other. Emma had seen it too, trying to read Tomás's thoughts but accidentally falling into her father's nightmare instead. Luke wished he could ease the painful memories clear on his father's drawn face. "So now three people are missing," he whispered.

"Three?" Sargateth frowned. "Who is the third?"

Luke told him about his mother's disappearance from Earth. While the Archmage pondered that news, Luke continued thinking out loud, resolutely avoiding the King's gaze. "Everything I know about our history tells me this is right up Septim's alley—the earthquakes, the portals, the creatures on Earth.... But he's already been destroyed."

King Aragon twisted his ring again. "Unless he's found another way to come back."

CHAPTER SIX
WELCOME HOME

Emma watched Scotland's distant snow-crusted coast disappear as the sun set behind her. She couldn't do better for her last view of Earth, but she still felt uneasy about leaving in such a hurry, even if for a good reason.

It had taken a week to get everything in order and meet Bethany in Ardrossan at the ferry terminal. Emma hadn't come to the Isle of Arran since they returned from Talahm four years ago, not trusting herself to avoid asking the Gatekeeper to open the portal. She missed her father and brother so much, but Prince Argent's silence made her heart clench in fear. Had something happened to him? He still hadn't responded to her last message, which left her feeling vulnerable. She couldn't decide which was worse: Argent dead or Argent ignoring her.

Bethany circled the obelisk where the Gateway would open. She crouched by the marker, tracing the carved symbols with one finger. Dusk and cold had chased away the last hikers. "Are you ready? Luke should be waiting for us by now."

Emma nodded, resolute. She joined Bethany, grasping her hand. With one last glance at the horizon, she faced the obelisk. The tesseract on her palm burned. "Edorahana. I am Emma Vala Jackman, the Seventh Sorceress, daughter of Tomás Artair, the Prophet of Camlaan. Open the way."

A moment later, amber light split the air, the seams wrenching open when it reached the ground. The empty void stared back at them. Without hesitation, Emma thrust her arm into the darkness, feeling an armored hand wrap around her wrist. With a jolt, she fell through the universe, leaving Earth behind for good.

"Hi, Rowan," Emma said, now in the Dome, the stone enclosure protecting Talahm's obelisk. The Gatekeeper helped steady her. "Bethany's coming too."

"I know," Rowan said, her lilting voice muffled by the golden helmet. She reached her hand back into the tear and gripped, muscles straining as she pulled.

"Hey Squirt," Luke greeted from the wall, relief spreading across his face. Grinning ear-to-ear, he strode forward, pulling Emma into a tight hug.

"Did you get sexier while I was gone?" Bethany asked when she arrived, voice shaking. She gripped her staff so hard her knuckles turned white.

Luke gave Emma one final squeeze, but she couldn't blame him for leaving her standing there while he reunited with his girlfriend.

Not interested in watching her best friend and brother kiss, Emma reoriented herself. Closing her eyes, she reached out with magic to feel the land beneath her feet, the air around them, the trees and grasslands in the distance. Back on this ground, she felt more connected to her magic.

The earth rolled beneath her feet, a tiny ripple at first, before the entire Dome shook, the stones loosening from their mortar.

Rowan let out a cry, lunging for her staff on the weapons rack. Off-balance, Emma stumbled to her brother, and Luke held Bethany against his side, blossoming a golden shield above them with his hands. Emma looked around wildly, chunks of stone hitting the ground as Luke's shield held against it. Rowan held her staff over her head, the wood barely protecting her.

"Rowan!" Emma yelled, stretching out one hand. The loose stone that had been about to hit Rowan in the head stopped in midair, hovering as Emma controlled it. She willed her magic outward, holding the rest of the Dome back from crushing them under thousands of pounds of stone.

When the Gatekeeper made it to them, Luke carefully backed them out through the entrance. Emma and Bethany steadied him against the unstable ground, stray rocks bouncing off his shield. "Clear!" Luke said, and Emma let go, the entire Dome collapsing in a cloud of dust.

"What's going on?" Emma demanded, adrenaline pumping. The roiling finally diminished, the Dome's rubble settling in the stillness.

"Another earthquake," Luke said, worriedly checking everyone for injuries. He pressed a fingertip to a cut on Bethany's cheekbone, his golden healing magic knitting the flesh back together. She hugged him fiercely, squashing her face against his chest. His arms snaked around her shoulders. "I've lost count of how many we've had."

"*You* lost count of something?"

"The first was one too many," Rowan said, pulling off her helmet. "We can't afford this kind of damage, not with the wall still unfinished."

"I'm sorry, *what?*" Emma exclaimed, head swiveling from her brother to the Gatekeeper. "It's been four—I mean, two years! How are the walls still down?"

Rowan started down the path to the city, forcing the rest of them to follow. A copse of trees budded with new leaves, evidence of the turning seasons, and produced a fresh, sweet scent. "It's hard to make progress when the quakes undo work, and most of the remaining covens are either helping the damaged villages or forced to play peacekeepers where wicked men see opportunities for thieving," she answered. "Even the Ancients cannot work fast enough."

"I've had to get creative with who we send to put out fires now that most of the waterwitches are dealing with floods along the entire coast." Luke sounded drained. He even had new worry lines on his forehead.

The cobblestones in the road to the castle had shifted, creating tripping hazards every few feet. The smell of fresh-turned earth combined with the lack of birdsong sent prickles down Emma's spine. They hurried around the bend to where the valley opened up, Lake Ogwen to the east with the River Nimüe flowing west toward Trident Bay. Camelot sat on the far side of the lake, the collapsed bridge over the river making her heart drop. "Luke," Emma said, voice tight, "why didn't Dad tell me about any of this?"

Luke sighed, running a hand through his dark hair. "We thought we could handle it. Your education was more important, considering you can't go back to Earth now. Dad didn't want you returning earlier than planned."

"Great plan, now that Mom's gone!"

Luke told them what had elapsed so far. "Without the hawks, we have no way of knowing if *The Sea Wolf* made it to the rest of their stops in the Helcari Isles or if there have been any more storms." He glanced at Emma, a calculating look in his eyes. "You've been talking with Prince Argent through your journals, haven't you? Did they ever make it to Borna or Stedrov?"

Emma almost tripped over her feet. *The hawks are gone?* "He hasn't said," she hedged, not wanting to tell him that Argent had stopped writing to her. Telling Bethany was one thing, but her brother? Her birthmark tingled, as if it wanted her to keep that detail to herself for now.

Luke's face tightened, eyes flinty. "Well, ask him. Even if Cordelia Roque has more sailing experience than Captain Jack Sparrow, the King will want to know if the supplies made it to the rest of the Helcari people. Last we heard, they were leaving Doltev."

Emma couldn't believe the state of Camelot's walls. The southern side, closest to the Valon Forest, was the most complete, lacking only the top level of stones that made the ramparts and a safe place for soldiers to patrol. The rest of it, though, lay in mostly the same ruin Emma had caused when she broke Septim's curse over the city. A temporary gate stood where the main gate should be, conscripted citizens out of place in their ill-fitting armor.

"Where are the real guards?" she whispered as they entered the city. Despite the pleasant spring breeze that blew through the streets, it felt colder and emptier than she'd expected.

"King Aragon hasn't been able to bring the numbers back up after what happened with Septim," Luke muttered back. "Many were dispatched with the knights and soldiers to keep the peace with all the natural disasters... and the unnatural ones. Creatures are appearing here, too."

"I'm going to murder Renault," Bethany announced.

The man in question descended the cathedral steps, his towering frame made larger by his broad shoulders and the shield protecting his back. A short baton peeked over his right shoulder, a weapon that extended into a full-length amethyst staff. "Careful, Miss Hawkins, or someone might take that as a threat against me," he said, his scratchy voice startling them.

"You!" Bethany exclaimed, breaking away from Luke to stomp toward Renault.

Renault's chiseled face flickered from surprise to amusement, his eyes sharpening from light blue to green as he focused on Bethany. He crossed his thick, muscled arms, enchanted bracers glinting with vibrant colors. "Yes, me. Why do you want to kill me?"

"I had to chase a feathered, fire-breathing snake from my parents' backyard, and all I could think about was that you said there weren't other creatures besides the Olii!"

Renault reached the last step, still several inches above Bethany. He peered down at her, face unreadable. "Did I say that? Or did I care more about bringing you and your little friends to safety in light of what happened the *last* time you walked into this city? Pray tell that something similar isn't about to happen." His gaze turned to Emma. "Is there?"

The tesseract tickled on her palm, cords of blue and black undulating in response to Renault's magical presence. "How would I know?"

Renault didn't answer, raising one eyebrow. His beady eyes landed on Bethany again. "You must have small minds indeed if you thought the Olii were the only creatures the Lord made. You do know what a horse is, don't you?"

Bethany stared at him, jaw dropped, before he swept toward the Hadrian Quarter without a backward glance.

Emma's eyes tracked him as he disappeared down a side street. "Looks like you'll have to reschedule your premeditated murder plans," she said, continuing toward the citadel at the center of the city. "I want to see Dad."

Luke's shoulders hunched as he drew ahead by a few paces.

Emma eyed him, wondering if Renault wasn't the only one keeping secrets.

When they crossed the threshold of the citadel's gate, Emma couldn't help but fall into the memory of Septim possessing Argent and shooting her father with a poisoned arrow. She blinked, the vision of Tomás's slumping body dissipating, replaced by the wide, smooth stones of the courtyard, now free from refugee tents—but also free from any witches or soldiers practicing their crafts.

Here, Emma noticed the dearth of Camelot's forces the most. Citizen soldiers did their best, but in this state, Camelot wouldn't be able to defend itself from crop blights, let alone if another kingdom decided to attack.

All thoughts fled when she saw her father, Tomás. He wheeled himself toward them through the tunnel that led to Camelot's keep, his claymore in a new sheath across the back of the chair and his mechanical bracer folded over his left forearm. She let out a cry, rushing to him.

"What—how—why are you still in this?" Emma gestured helplessly to the wheelchair, throat closing over the rest of her words.

"It's not so bad," Tomás replied warmly, attempting to ease her concern with a smile. "I've gotten used to it." He opened his arms for her, and Emma hugged him as much as his restrictions allowed. "Welcome home," he murmured into her ear, stroking her hair. "Are you all right? That quake seemed closer than the last ones."

"The Dome collapsed. So did the bridge over the river."

Tomás tensed. "And the obelisk?"

"I'll find out."

"Dad," Luke interrupted, holding Bethany to his side, "could the earthquakes be tied to portals opening? There was one right around when we got the news about Mom."

Their father frowned, as if he too had lost track of how many times the earth had shaken beneath their feet.

"Speaking of Mom," Emma started, "have the covens found her yet? It's been a week already."

"For you, yeah, but it's only been a few days for us. The last coven only left three days ago, and it's at least a four- or five-day journey on foot to Valona." Frustrated, Luke ruffled his hair. Bethany reached up to smooth it back down.

"There hasn't been enough time. We need all the help we can get. Now that you two are back—"

"Patience," Tomás said softly.

It fell on deaf ears. Nothing but time had passed, not just for her mother but also for Argent. Once more, Emma's thoughts zeroed in on the Prince's silence, questioning her decision to write those vulnerable words. Would she ever get the chance to take them back? Did she even want to? She went into a spiral, the world around her dulling more with every second.

Tomás patted her hand where it still rested on his arm. "I know at least one witch who wants to see you both."

Emma started. *The Grand Mage. Morgan Le Fay.*

CHAPTER SEVEN
THE ROYAL COVEN

Neither Bethany nor Emma had been to Morgan Le Fay's office before. They followed Luke deep into the coven barracks until they came to a rich mahogany door engraved with tiny Celtic knots. Luke knocked, pushing the handle down at the Grand Mage's invitation to enter. Beautiful, dark wood panels lined Morgan's office, giving it the feel of an old English librarian's study. Stuffed bookshelves took up both sides of the room, books stacked on top of each other in every available space. Several staffs lined the wall behind her desk, each capped with a different colored gem. Four life-sized portraits hung behind the staffs, depicting witches controlling each of the core elements: water, earth, fire, and air.

Bethany smirked, knowing that, like Emma, she could control all four simultaneously. She thanked her ten-year-old self again for making that blood pact with Emma—the only reason she could do magic.

"We've been expecting you," Morgan said, seated behind her desk. She reached up, tucking her short black hair behind her ears. A thick gold ring with a purple gem caught the light from the magical sconces on the ceiling. Beside her, a witch tall enough to meet Bethany eye-to-eye stared at them, wild red hair not helping the contemptuous pull of her lip and the hardness in her pale blue eyes. That look alone could melt steel, and Bethany didn't even know her name. But something about her was familiar.

"It has to be now," Luke said, closing the door behind them.

"You're sure it will work?" Morgan asked.

"Of course not, but we have to try."

"Luke?" Bethany asked, nerves jumping in her stomach.

He rested both hands on her shoulders, mismatched eyes full of worry. "I'm sorry I didn't say anything sooner, but none of the witches we sent to Ralador have used their Coven Marks to report back. I only suspected a trap after we sent the second coven out. I want you to join the Royal Coven."

Bethany's brain short-circuited. "Me? What about Emma?"

"Emma's the Seventh Sorceress. She and I work best as a unit, and we can't do that if she's in the Royal Coven. You have all her abilities, Bethie. You'd be the most powerful witch in the Royal Coven other than Morgan. If you pass the trials and take a Coven Mark, we might be able to re-establish contact with the coven that's missing before the second even gets there."

"Hang on, *trials*?" Bethany interrupted, digging into one ear to clear the wax out. She hadn't even dropped off her backpack stuffed with things from Earth, and Luke was talking about trials?

"Nothing you can't handle," Morgan answered, folding her hands. "And before you ask, as an Olis, I cannot take the Coven Mark. Otherwise, we would have already tried this plan. You, however.... You've trained for four years already without a tutor. And with great success."

Bethany narrowed her eyes. "Does anyone ever fail these trials?"

Emma bumped her with her shoulder, making that expression that Bethany read as *stop looking for all the hard parts*. But Bethany succeeded because she found the hard parts before the hard parts found her. And so far, that had worked.

"Anything is possible," Morgan answered, sitting back in her chair. The skirts of her dress swished as she crossed her legs. "But Luke has full confidence you can pass them with—how did you say it?"

"Flying colors."

Morgan's hands curled over the ends of the armrests. "Ebony Reva believed in you, Miss Hawkins." A wistful smile flashed across her lips, her shoulders dropping against the back of her chair. "The other Coven Mages made it clear that, should you return, your power would be a welcome addition to our ranks."

Bethany pointed at herself. "Me?" She glanced around the room as if another Bethany was hiding beneath a table about to jump out and take the praise for her. The redheaded witch's lip curled in contempt, the heat of her anger palpable from across the room. A memory of that mane of red curls forcibly dragging a grown man away from Septim's curse down in the chapel crypts sprung into Bethany's head. *One of Ebony's Coventras from before! I knew I recognized her. What is her deal?*

"You'll be fine," Luke reassured, gently touching her shoulder. "I wouldn't do something insane like send you to Ralador, Bethie. I just want you to use the Coven Mark."

The Coventra finally spoke. "Can we get this over with?"

Luke worried at his bottom lip, and Bethany momentarily forgot about her impending doom. "Hela's right. We need to do this right now."

Bethany could think of a thousand malicious jokes about Thor and Loki's sister, but this Hela had a gleam in her eye that made Bethany wary. Instead of cracking a joke, she squared her shoulders, her hands white around the staff in front of her. The ruby glinted in the soft, magical lights along the ceiling. She'd traded her emerald one for this on their way up through the armory, already feeling like the emerald was holding her back somehow. The itch to cast something built under her skin until she felt her fingertips combust.

Luke looked her up and down in a manner she could get used to. "Let's get you into some coven armor."

When they left the armory an hour later, Emma wished Bethany luck, peeling off with a young earthwitch to help repair the bridge, the Dome, and make sure the obelisk hadn't been destroyed.

"I should have practiced more last week," Bethany muttered, twisting at the leather cuffs around her wrists. Her arms were bare up to the shoulders, the coven armor stripped down until she passed the trials and earned her battle witch chevron. She held her staff under one arm, barely conscious of its arc as she moved, trying to get the cuff to sit right over her pulse point.

"You're more than good enough to handle this," Luke said as he jumped out of the way of the staff's swing.

Bethany shrugged the shoulder not responsible for the staff, bringing her wrist up to her mouth to tug on the leather with her teeth. It finally rotated correctly, the runes lighting up like they were supposed to. She shook her enchanted friendship bracelet over the cuff, hoping it would help against whatever she was facing. Bethany shoved open the door to the inner ward tunnel, right next to the armory entrance, where the midday gleam illuminated the courtyard to their left. A portion of the grounds and the guardhouse were visible on the other side.

Luke stumbled, staggering to press his back against the stone wall of the tunnel. He gripped his head with both hands, eyes squeezed shut. Bethany's stomach dropped, and she went to him, hovering until he came out of the Vision. When he did, the dark circles under his eyes spoke to the weight of his duties.

"Another fire—this one up the River Nimüe toward Sutton Peak. I'll have to find a waterwitch after we're done here."

"Renova needs all the help it can get," Bethany said softly, pressing a hand to his stubbly cheek. She drank in his broad shoulders, his rough jawline, and the grand streaks of white at his temples. "Send me if you need to."

His hand came up to cover hers, its warmth on par with her penchant for fire. His gold-colored eye caught light from the courtyard, making it shine in the gloom. "If I could avoid putting you through the trials right now, I would. You deserve a better 'welcome home' than this."

Bethany's eyes flutter closed, wishing she could throw her staff aside and drag him to the Artair Apartments, trials forgotten. But she'd already received sour looks from some of the few remaining witches in the barracks and armory who recognized her as the one who'd snagged Luke. "I haven't forgotten what you told me all those years ago, before we first came here. Witches take the pain as a lesson on what not to do next time. I'm a witch, Luke, and I'm taking all the pain that's offered to me."

Luke leaned in, capturing a searing kiss before they headed to the training grounds, Bethany's cheeks flushing.

Morgan stood speaking with Hela and two other battle witches along the stable colonnade. As they approached,

Hela moved like a cat across the courtyard, disappearing into the stable. Another witch with deep brown hair and a squashed nose like a pug dog scurried off to the chapel narthex. That left Morgan standing with a woman who had four chevrons on each pauldron and a beautiful ruby staff in one hand. She looked barely thirty, but the short, choppy gray hair complemented her sharp cheekbones and the slant of her almond eyes. She glanced up and down at Bethany with disdain.

"Miss Hawkins, meet Ordinal Coven Mage Evie Watson. In past years, we would have a proper trial course laid out beyond the city walls," Morgan said. "But the principle is the same. Most battles are against other witches or Royal Covens, and there is no fighting fair in war. To mimic those conditions, you will fight two Coventras and Mage Watson at full strength. Do not hold back. The trial ends when you have proved your skill."

Bethany set her face, sizing Evie up. "Are you waiting to hit a tiny gong before we start?"

The first warning was her instinctual dodge away from the jet of ice that flew from inside the stable doors. *A ginger waterwitch? That's new.* Bethany responded, using the muscle memory from her solo practice sessions out in the wilds of Eastern Washington, finding her stride about thirty seconds into the trial. She dodged and struck, hissing when the other witches landed shots and taking risky chances with other branches of magic she hadn't practiced as much as fire.

Using the leather cuffs as a focus, Bethany created a thin golden shield between her and the circling witches. Swinging her staff overhead, she formed a long whip of fire that trailed from the ruby gem. She snapped the whip at Hela, who had been the most trouble so far, willing the flame to explode when the crack sounded. The attack forced Hela to throw up a water catch, steam billowing when it made contact. Bethany used the cover to move out of range while dealing with the other two battle witches. Her fire whip snagged the brunette's ankle, leaving a thin, angry burn when Bethany yanked her off her feet.

But Watson had clearly earned her rank. Bethany barely managed to get close enough with an attack to leave anything worse than a blister. Strategizing, she fell back on her old standby of chattering incessantly until it distracted them enough for her to land a hit.

"Three against one is so cliché," she quipped, dancing away from a crackling energy bolt, sweat forming on the small of her back. They must have been fighting for at least ten minutes by now, and even though it felt like hours, she felt so alive. "I got suckered into playing rugby in college and let me tell you, getting tackled by ripped chicks with anger problems made it way easier to learn my other powers." Mid-swing, Bethany changed the fire whip to a whistling cord of wind, the pressure high enough to cut through wood. Morgan had said not to hold back, so Bethany took her word for it.

Watson hastily erected a shield, but the wind sliced right through it, catching her on the shoulder and shearing off half of her pauldron down to the skin. Blood welled up, rivulets feeding into the grooves of the rest of her armor. Her staff clattered to the ground, but Hela and the brunette picked up the slack with coordinated jets of tiny, razor-sharp ice spikes and shrapnel from the damaged flagstones. *Ah, so pug-nose is an earthwitch.* In the confines of the citadel courtyard, earthwitches couldn't do much with the dirt beneath the stones without earning the righteous fury of the city architect, but they could manipulate pebbles and shards of broken rock.

Bethany wished Renault was there to watch her vaporize the ice-and-shrapnel counterattack with a controlled web of plasma, another gift courtesy of her blood pact with Emma. Bethany, too, had the abilities of the Seventh Sorceress with about a third of the power. But a third of a lot was still *a lot*, and Morgan finally called the trial to an end by stamping her amethyst staff against the ground and casting a shield to separate the fighters.

"Well done, Miss Hawkins," Morgan congratulated, her skirts billowing as she marched toward the four panting, sweaty witches. "Time to get your Coven Mark."

CHAPTER EIGHT
FIREWHIP

Bethany couldn't stop stroking the spot on her throat where Morgan would tattoo the Coven Mark. She'd contemplated getting a tattoo while in college, but she couldn't decide what she wanted or where she wanted to get it. It was just as well that her first one would be magical anyway. She thought of Ebony's *algiz* rune tattoos. They had been a net of protection against magic she couldn't absorb, burst and rendered useless by Bethany's fire. It hadn't been fair, but Bethany's guilt circled that drain for four years, finally sucked down into the pit of acceptance after her thousandth talk with Emma about their combined traumas.

She could *help* here. She had magic and not any garden-variety strain of power like that belonging to the three witches she'd fought. Bethany had *Seventh Sorceress* level magic without any of the weight of that world-ending prophecy given by Lancelot Artair. She might not be able to take any of the Olii in single combat, but she could best the best of the Royal Coven with spells she'd practiced by herself on Earth.

She could already tell Hela didn't like her and had an inkling as to why. One of Ebony's lieutenants, probably forged in the fires of the Valon War, was bested in fifteen minutes by a cocky twenty-two-year-old who lacked the rigor of having trained with magic her entire life.

Luke opened the infirmary door for her, ever the picture of medieval chivalry. She couldn't wait to get him alone for more than a minute. Morgan waited for her by a table with a squat inkpot, a pointed stylus glowing with teal runes, and a vial of clear liquid. Bethany hoped it was vodka, but it was probably a potion. Pity.

She lay on the bed, exposing the left side of her throat to the Grand Mage. "All right, stab me," she said, clenching her teeth. She gripped Luke's hand in a vice, but he gently extricated it.

"I have to organize a response for the Sutton Peak fire. I'll be back as soon as I can," he said, glancing at the door they'd come through. "Morgan, normally I'd ask Hela—"

"Send Dakota. Earth can smother fire just as well as water. I need Hela here when Bethany tries contacting the missing coven."

Luke gently kissed Bethany's knuckles and strode back through the infirmary doors as Morgan bent over her neck with the stylus. Bethany forced herself to relax.

"Do not speak or move until I finish," Morgan said evenly. The tip of the stylus pressed against Bethany's skin, and she hissed, doing her best not to tense the muscles in her neck. She didn't open her eyes, instead forcing herself to run through the list of commands she could use her Mark for, including the communication between battle witches that Luke expected her to achieve.

She endured the poking, scraping, and scratching of the stylus against her throat for the better part of an hour. She compelled herself to keep an even keel on breathing, making herself relax when all she wanted to do was jerk away from the needle's sharp tip. It was probably a good thing she'd never gotten inked in college. If she'd known what awaited her, she would have refused to join the Coven on principle instead of getting rewarded with a hundred thousand needle jabs in her neck.

Morgan dropped the stylus on the table, sitting back to stretch. Bethany cracked an eyelid. "Done?"

"With the part that hurts, yes."

"Finally!" She got to her feet, stretching both arms over her head as she asked Morgan for a mirror. The Grand Mage conjured one, and Bethany inspected the work with interest. The black triquetra shimmered on the left side of her throat, her skin still tender. "Do I have to let it heal naturally?

"No," Morgan answered. "I still need to enchant it to connect with the rest of the Coven. Please sit back down." The Grand Mage dipped her fingers into the clear potion—not vodka—and brushed it across her aching skin. She placed a palm over the new tattoo, chanting under her breath in a language Bethany didn't understand but suspected was her natural Olis language.

The space between her hand and Bethany's skin glowed bright teal, shining through Morgan's fingers until Bethany had to squeeze her eyes shut again. When the light faded, Morgan's soft fingertips withdrew.

"Welcome to the Royal Coven," Morgan said with a soft smile. Behind her, the infirmary doors opened again, Luke and Hela returning to find out if the gamble had paid off.

Morgan took a few minutes instructing Bethany on how to reach out through the link to Hela, who was leaning against the wall across from them. It took a concentrated effort, but Bethany felt her way into the magic of her new mark, and Hela stood out like a bright blue spot in an ocean of darkness.

Hela's hand flew to her own mark, surprise on her face.

"Well done," Morgan chuckled, clearly amused at Hela's shock. Bethany fist pumped in triumph.

"Don't celebrate yet," Hela hissed. "The true test has yet to begin."

Thanks for the bundle of nerves, girl from hell. Bethany took a deep breath, sitting back on the pillows. She closed her eyes, feeling into the magic of the Mark again. In her mind, she zoomed far above Camelot, pinpricks of light signifying far too few witches present within the city limits. All around Renova, sporadic clusters of light moved toward Camelot, evidence that at least some covens had received the King's order to come back. Bethany concentrated to the south, finding covens out doing the work Luke had assigned.

But she found nothing beyond the border to Ralador—not even the second coven of witches he'd sent. Disappointed, Bethany came back to herself, doing a double take when everyone seemed both relieved and on edge. "What?"

"You were out for hours," Luke whispered. His hair stood on end, probably from running his hands through it too many times.

Hela glared at her, seated like an agitated bird across the room. "Well?"

Bethany swallowed past the lump in her throat. "I couldn't sense anyone beyond the border."

"Not even the second coven?" Luke asked in dismay. "They would have crossed into the Deadwoods yesterday. That's not close enough to Valona that it should even be a problem—"

"A failure *and* a liability," Hela seethed. "Can you do anything besides disappoint your betters, or destroy things with that fire whip of yours?"

"It's not Bethany's fault," Luke said hotly. "Something must be wrong if she couldn't pick up on *anyone* in Ralador!"

Hela sprang to her feet, magic crackling in her hair. "Something *is* wrong," she pointed at Bethany, "with her. She couldn't do the *one thing* we needed her to."

Bethany's shoulders slumped.

One sharp look from Morgan closed Hela's mouth, but the damage had already been done. "Coventra, mind your temper. As Bethany will be joining *your* coven, I suggest you pray for guidance on how to consider Firewhip an asset instead."

The nickname made Bethany glance up. "Firewhip?"

Morgan led her to her room in the witch barracks, where a new set of coven armor lay on the bed, a single chevron on each pauldron with etched runes on almost every piece of leather. Bethany could already see ways to make the narrow room her own. She'd spice up the plain stone walls, double bed, and chest of drawers at its foot. A simple wood desk was pressed against the wall by a short bookshelf, a few volumes on fire magic stacked in a little pile.

"Make yourself comfortable," Morgan said. "I expect Hela will introduce you to your battle sisters soon."

When she left, Bethany felt thrown adrift, wondering what she'd gotten herself into by joining the Royal Coven and getting assigned to a Coventra who clearly hated her.

Fortunately, that mystery didn't remain a mystery for much longer.

Barely five minutes after Morgan's exit, Bethany's door clicked open again, and Hela slipped inside. She slid the lock shut, and any hope of her new battle sisters joining them took a steep nosedive.

"Cocky, arrogant, *liability*." Hela's sibilant description felt like the spines of a cactus pricking at Bethany's relatively thick skin. "I'm beginning to wonder if Morgan has a peg loose to trust you after that pitiful performance upstairs."

"It's nice to meet you too," Bethany deflected, forcing the wave of anger away as she picked up the armor from the bed. The magic felt the same as the enchantment on her bracelet. "Did Mr. Artair make this?"

Hela sneered, ignoring the obvious bait to change subjects. "Insolent, aren't you?"

"That's my middle name." Bethany dropped the armor and rubbed both of her hands across her face and into her hair, massaging her scalp where her braid pulled on it. "What do you want from me? I barely know you, and you were ready to rip my throat out the moment you saw me in Morgan's office."

Hela wrinkled her nose. "I want nothing from you. I thought I made that clear to Morgan, but nothing short of treason can break her trust in someone."

"*Treason?*" Wide-eyed, Bethany stared at her, all defenses gone.

"A battle witch strong enough to burst protection runes in a single blast *is a liability* to any coven's safety," Hela snarled, her curly red hair growing in size with every word.

Does every witch have a bad hair day when they get mad? At least Bethany now understood the basis for her Coventra's animosity.

"Killing one of your own is treasonous, wouldn't you say?"

"You're talking about Ebony." Bethany said softly, her shoulders dropping.

Hela held herself like a drawn bow, ready to snap. "I grew up with her, bled with her, mourned our Prince and our sisters with her. That Ebony Reva is dead because *your fire* damaged her *algiz* is an insult to the sacrifices she made during the war."

Bethany didn't know what to say because it was a hundred percent true. She grasped for the right words for a solid minute, trying not to wilt under Hela's fierce gaze. "Look," she began, steamrolling right through Hela's indignant expression. "I've had four years to come to terms—"

"If you try to tell me her burst runes were *not your fault,* we *will* have a problem," Hela interrupted.

"No," Bethany insisted, "those were definitely my fault. I burned her with my first grasp of magic. I'm not denying that. And I'm sorry about it, really. If I hadn't damaged those runes, I don't know if they would've stood up to Emma's onslaught any better. But it all happened so fast after that, you know? You were there. I saw you in the crypts toward the end. I didn't know Ebony hadn't fixed her tattoos when she brought me down to help keep the perimeter."

She paused, thinking of all the possibilities for danger now that she *was* fully inducted into the Royal Coven. She touched the triquetra on her throat, still warm under her fingertips.

"I don't know what I can do to make you like me, so all I'm left with is being myself. But if you're my commanding officer now, I need to trust that we have each other's backs."

Hela's face relaxed, but only just. "Do you?"

Bethany pulled the fishtail braid over her shoulder, fidgeting with the end. "I don't want to die on whatever missions we go on, so yeah. I have your back."

"Not because you want to be my *friend*, but because you're worried for your own life," Hela assessed, one eyebrow raised as she appraised her. "You may yet last this fight, Firewhip." She paused, the silence dragging between them for far longer than Bethany was comfortable. "Come to the armory after dinner. You need more gear than just those leathers. How good are you with knives?"

"Hurry up, you rule-breaker," Emma groaned from the front door.

Bethany stole one last kiss from Luke before picking up her things scattered across the Artair common room. After her visit to the armory, she'd technically broken Coven curfew by canoodling with Luke into the late evening hours, tucked under his arm as they read together like an old married couple. Every time she'd thought to leave, she couldn't pull herself away. It was only when Emma emerged from her bedroom near midnight to use the bathroom that Bethany finally realized her conundrum.

Getting back to her barrack room without alerting Hela.

"If Hela didn't like you before, she'll hate you now."

"I know, I know," Bethany muttered, finally slipping on her coat and grabbing her staff from the weapons rack. Despite the urgency, she felt lighter than a balloon. "All right, I'm ready."

"You're lucky I practiced invisibility at school. Did you forget about that one?" Emma waved one hand around them both with a flourish, disappearing from view, though Bethany could still sense her presence. The magic tingled across her skin, tickling as it hid her. "Let's go."

They tip-toed down the hallway toward the witches'
barracks, cutting through the wing where the King and
Queen lived. While not off-limits, Bethany felt like an
intruder nonetheless, as though she were walking through
Buckingham Palace without anyone knowing she was
there.

Finally, they approached the stairwell that led to
Bethany's new room, when they heard low voices from an
open doorway. Emma threw her arm out to stop Bethany
from moving.

"What happened to the child I helped raise?" Sargateth
said, his deep voice filled with accusation. "What happened
to the man who led us through the worst war in Renova's
history?"

A boot scuffed against the stone stair. "Watch your
words, Rishon," King Aragon replied tightly.

"You're not the man you were before your father died,"
Sargateth pressed. "King Hadrian would not have kept me
here at my wife's expense."

"Death changes people. So does war. Are you the same
Olis who fought with me in the forest, or are you regretting
your vow to my ancestors?"

Emma seized Bethany's wrist, creeping into the stairwell
just enough to see the two men on the first landing between
floors. The King's arms were crossed, and he bristled with

anger and agitation. The sconce of light by Sargateth's head cast them both into shadow.

The Archmage's eyes gleamed. "The vow I made to Arthur bound me to him as much as it bound me to your father and to you," Sargateth said slowly. "But never has a King of Renova kept me chained to the city like a dog."

"Is that what you think of me?" Aragon snapped, tilting his head back. "A cruel master too weak to let his best chance at protecting this city slip through his fingers?" The light caught the gold sheen of his crown, drawing Bethany's attention. She'd never seen him wear the crown outside the throne room despite his position. In fact, the only person she could remember wearing any kind of crown on the regular was Sargateth, and his silver circlet was now obvious in its absence.

Sargateth stared at him, his mouth falling open in surprise. "Have you learned nothing from Septim using your son against us? I had no part in breaking that curse. If anyone is your best shot at protecting Camelot—or Renova—it is the Seventh Sorceress."

Bethany twisted her wrist in Emma's grip until she found purchase, digging her fingers into Emma's palm. They crept another pace forward.

"A witch whose only ties to this kingdom are the Prophets of Camlaan," King Aragon replied, a sneer on his lips. Bethany had never seen such an out-of-place expression.

"What's gotten into you?" Sargateth demanded, crossing his arms as his gaze hardened. His eyebrows squished together. "Since when do you doubt the veracity of Lancelot's prophecy? Since when do you doubt *me*?" When Aragon didn't reply, Sargateth continued, voice grave. "Respectfully, sire, I must question why you let your son, your *heir*, go on a dangerous voyage while forbidding me to even render aid to the Ironside—let alone *my wife*."

The King drew himself up and pulled his lips into a contemptuous frown. "I don't answer to you, Rishon. Pray I do not shorten your leash any further." Emma flattened herself and Bethany against the wall as he strode up the steps toward them, sweeping past without seeing either girl.

Sargateth's shoulders slumped with a sigh. Eyes closed, he pinched his nose and leaned back against the wall. He looked crumpled in the shadows.

Bethany didn't dare move a muscle. She'd never seen the Archmage look so broken.

Sargateth pushed away from the wall, slowly coming up the steps into the main hallway. He took one long glance toward the Royal Apartments, shook his head, and disappeared down the corridor toward the infirmary.

Emma finally let out her breath. "Come on," she muttered, pulling Bethany down the stairs.

They made it to Bethany's room unscathed, silent the whole way as she pondered the overheard argument. If Sargateth couldn't leave... could they?

CHAPTER NINE

LORD OF THE TRIDENT

Every cell in Luke's body hummed with a lightness he hadn't felt since Bethany's first trip to Talahm. As he got ready for bed, pulling down the blankets and pressing the rune switch on his sleeping device, he did not expect a Vision. He fumbled for his notebook on the bedside table, dropping it when the Prophecy transported his perception into an unfamiliar circular stone room.

Knowing the Vision would only last seconds, Luke cataloged the details. A long, horizontal window was cut into the wall at eye level. Through it, the Sleeping Sea shimmered with the setting sun, a purple tint cast across the choppy waters. A brigantine bobbed in the waves with its sails up, the flag of Renova snapping in the wind.

A crash drew his attention, and his stomach jolted as a woman with long, gray hair wearing a deep purple dress knocked over several potion flasks from a small wooden table on the far side of the window. Clearly using magic, her hands stretched out in front of her.

Then he saw Argent.

The Prince dangled in midair, hands frantically scrabbling at his neck as the woman—witch—held him captive against the rough stone wall.

Luke took a step closer, blood rushing in his ears, chest tight. Had he stumbled across someone who also believed Argent Pendragon still posed a threat? Ignoring Argent's fumbling movements, Luke tried to identify the witch, memorizing the details of her face, hoping he could find her after he came out of the Vision. Something about her dark, glittering eyes seemed familiar.

And then it was over. Luke blinked, his unlit room in the Artair Apartments coming into focus despite the darkness. He slumped back against the wall, his foot accidentally kicking the notebook askew on the floor. After a heartbeat, he bent down to retrieve it, quickly scribbling the details of what he witnessed.

Luke didn't trust many people anymore, not after Septim's curse. He trusted Argent least of all—hadn't from the first time they'd met during Luke's first visit five years ago. Even after the tragedy with Ebony, even after watching Emma grow close to Argent once she broke the curse.... He couldn't shake the feeling that something wasn't right.

Naturally, Luke kept his suspicions to himself. Even if Septim wasn't inhabiting the Prince—if he'd possessed him to begin with—Luke couldn't risk the possibility that Argent was pretending to be a changed man. The library's volumes on possession were sparse, and he suspected the tomes that went in depth about it were locked in Morgan's office. If *The Sea Wolf* made it through Helcari, what would Argent bring back? His imagination had run wild, cataloging everything he knew about Septim and the Helcari Isles. The sleeping device would keep him asleep long enough to form new connections. And with every new catastrophe, his paranoia increased.

The woman, though.... Luke's Visions always came true unless Emma was emotionally invested enough to invoke a precipitate prophecy. That magic had saved their father's life, and Emma definitely cared whether Argent lived.

Luke clenched his jaw. Emma couldn't know about this Vision.

No one could.

Dawn arrived with yet another earthquake. Luke rolled out of bed, landing on all fours on the thick carpet. He pushed protective magic away from his core and through the walls, keeping everything in the Artair Apartments stable while the rest of the citadel shook around him. Through his shield, he sensed both Emma and his father waking up. When the rumbling ceased, he got to his feet, the Vision from last night at the front of his mind.

"Luke!" Emma banged on his door.

"Give me a minute." Luke nervously shoved his prophecy journal beneath his mattress, fixing the blankets and pulling a shirt over his head. He cracked the door. "Yeah?"

Emma yawned. "Are earthquakes happening daily? One yesterday, one just now…. I can't believe you haven't tracked down the source yet!"

Brows furrowed in consternation, Luke opened the door all the way and padded past Emma to the common room table, where Tomás had wheeled himself from his bedroom. "It's not for lack of trying. King Aragon won't permit an investigation when the aftermath is more than our resources can handle."

"And," Tomás added, "the King recalled all available covens thanks to Luke's Vision of a dragon."

Emma's jaw dropped. "You Saw an actual *dragon*?"

Luke rubbed the back of his neck. "Flying over the city. I don't know when it will happen, just that it will. That was right after you sent word about Mom."

Emma shoved both hands through her hair, pacing back and forth like a crazy person. "Does it attack?"

"I didn't See enough to be able to tell. You know how my Visions are. Enough to know what's coming, but not always enough to know for sure what happens as a result." Luke shoved away the tiny voice in the back of his head questioning the Vision of the woman and Argent. "In any case, there's plenty of work to do here, especially once the covens return. Maybe we can actually get the walls rebuilt before that dragon arrives."

A flurry of expressions crossed Emma's face before she turned on her heel, going back to her room. The door slammed behind her.

"I'm going to assume she's getting dressed to help with the wall, not going back to sleep," Tomás said from the table. He folded his hands on the smooth wood, peering up at Luke with piercing, mismatched eyes. "Is there anything you want to share? I know well the burden of Visions in difficult times."

Luke dropped into a chair, rubbing his face with both hands. He almost admitted what he Saw in his Vision last night but swallowed it back down. *It's just until we figure things out. But Lord, it's hard to do this on my own.* "I always knew this would be my job eventually. I didn't expect your Visions to stop for this long."

A flash of grief spasmed across Tomás's face. "I don't know if they'll ever come back. Luke, yours may be all we have now."

As the sun reached its zenith over the city, Luke climbed the rubble around the Trident Gate. To the west, the distant edge of the Valon Forest stretched from the river to the Ogwen Plains where farmers tended to their spring crops. Emma and Bethany were helping rebuild the Ogwen Gate tower again on the other side of the city, but it was slow work. Sargateth or Morgan had to enchant runes on each stone block before it could be moved into place, and though their power surpassed most of the coven, the repetitive work drained them. He wondered if Emma had a chance to find out if *The Sea Wolf* left Helcari and, more importantly, when they could expect Argent to ride back into the city... if he made it back at all.

The distant clip-clop of hooves on cobblestone echoed from the west. A lone horse trotted toward the gate, its rider's armor dull but still catching the sun. The edges of the man's cloak draped over the packs secured to the horse's rump, billowing with each trot forward. The rider slowed as he approached, head tilting up to watch Luke on the rubble.

The man's shoulders were too broad to be Argent. "Identify yourself," Luke demanded, ready to shield. It wouldn't be the first time bandits wore armor to appear more trustworthy.

The man reached up to pull off his helmet, the trident on his breastplate coming into view. "Elijah Cade, Lord of the Trident," the man called back, thick blond hair plastered to his head. "My people need help."

"Show me your signet," Luke said, picking his way down the chaotic heap of rocks and ruin. Luke had seen the Lord of the Trident's signature and seal on several letters sent before the hawks disappeared but had never met the knight in person. He kept one eye on him, magic ready just in case, and stopped on a block of stone a few feet from the horse.

Cade's stormy blue-green eyes tracked his progress, flicking to the white streaks at Luke's temples. He tugged off his left gauntlet, holding his hand up to Luke. The silver signet ring featured a dragon curled around a trident's staff, the three prongs touching the raised circular edge.

"Welcome to Camelot, Sir Cade," Luke greeted, his face relaxing. He jumped the last three feet, dust billowing around his boots at the impact. "What kind of help do you need?"

Cade tugged the gauntlet back on, urging his horse through the broken gates. Luke walked beside him. "Earthwitches. The Trident won't survive another tidal wave if we don't block the bay."

"Won't that prevent ships from making port?"

"Not if the witches can leave a protected channel." They passed several empty houses formerly owned by permanent victims of the curse. Elijah Cade surveyed the dismal dwellings. "Even the crew of *The Sea Wolf* cannot do what we need."

Luke's stomach jumped. "*The Sea Wolf* is in port?"

Cade nodded, rubbing his beard. Spots of rust marred his dull gauntlets. "Made berth right before I left. Most of Captain Roque's witches command wind or water. What use is an earthwitch on the open sea?"

Luke turned left, the street looping around to the front of the citadel, thoughts racing. If *The Sea Wolf* was docked in Trident Bay, that meant Prince Argent was there too. And if the pieces fit.... "My sister could help."

"Your sister?"

Down the street, Emma and Bethany came into view, both waving. Luke waved back, a half-smile on his face tempered by the flood of thoughts revolving around his Vision. "Emma Jackman, the Seventh Sorceress."

"That's me," Emma agreed, appraising the newcomer. "Who's this?"

Luke introduced the knight, watching Emma's face. Her eyes lingered on Cade like Bethany's gaze sometimes lingered on him.

"It is truly an honor to meet you. The stories of you saving Camelot from the curse have spread far and wide," Cade said. His smile crinkled the corners of his eyes.

Emma's smile grew fixed, her cheeks turning pink. "Thanks."

Cade dismounted, pulling the horse's reins over its head. He glanced at Luke. "If the Seventh Sorceress is your sister, that means you're—"

"Luke Artair, Prophet of Camlaan."

"Since when did you change your last name?" Emma demanded, gaze bouncing between Luke and the knight.

"Since the Prophets of Camlaan have all been Artairs," Luke answered simply. "You don't have to change yours, if that's what you're worried about."

Bethany slipped her free hand into Luke's. "I'm Bethany," she introduced, shifting awkwardly, still uncomfortable in her Coven armor. "Her best friend, his main squeeze." She gestured at Emma and Luke with her ruby staff.

"'Main squeeze'?"

"Only squeeze, technically. I'm his girlfriend."

The confusion written on Sir Cade's face gave way to mild embarrassment. "I see. Miss Jackman—"

"Please, call me Emma. And let's get to Pendragon Hall. I'm starving. Lifting and placing those massive stones is no joke."

"Emma, Luke said you can help the Trident." Cade explained his situation, and Luke watched with satisfaction as Emma drew herself into the conversation, her questions revealing a keen sense of strategy.

"Where are your earthwitches? Or those with energy manipulation?"

Cade inclined his head. "We have fishermen, sailors, and farmers. Too weak, poorly trained, or simply unskilled. Most of our witches control the waters, and the few who till the ground are not strong enough to raise rocks from the depths."

Luke could see the gears in her head turning. Most coastal cities on Earth secured vulnerable facilities from floods with berms tall and thick enough to withstand the force of a tsunami's impact.

"Terraforming," Emma surmised. "Raise stone pillars across the mouth of the bay, obviously with enough space for ships to get in and out. It'd be a tight squeeze, but doable...." By the time Emma seemed confident in their plan, they'd arrived at the citadel gate, ill-dressed guards on either side.

"We should leave in the morning," Luke said, peering across the courtyard to the stables.

"We?" Emma snapped her head around as Cade led his horse away. "Don't you need to stay here to direct relief?"

Luke shoved his discomfort deeper down, making a mental note to deal with it later. "I'm your Sentinel. Now that you're back, where you go, I go."

"Yes!" Bethany pumped her fist in the air. "Road trip!"

Luke's insides twisted again. "Bethie, you'll have to talk to Morgan first. If that dragon comes while we're gone, someone needs to help the Olii contain it."

"It's not that I don't want to talk to her by myself. It's that I haven't seen you in four years and—"

Luke cut off Bethany's ramble with a kiss. "Okay, I'll come with you to talk to Morgan."

She grinned. "You're the best."

When they got to Morgan's door, Luke placed a calming hand over the hand on her staff, stopping her from running a thumb over the carved patterns. She relaxed, knocking on the door a moment later.

"Come in," Morgan said, her lilting voice like music. Luke still couldn't figure out her accent, and by this point had stopped trying.

Bethany looked around, zeroing in on a painting on a low shelf behind Morgan's desk. In it, a young woman with long brown hair curled over one shoulder sat with hands folded on her lap, her expression flat and haunted. She pointed at it. "Who is that?"

Luke's stomach jumped. Those were the same dark, glittering eyes of the woman in his Vision! She wore a lavender dress in the portrait. A gold chain with an eight-pointed star hung to the middle of her chest.

Morgan glanced over her shoulder. "A former apprentice." She drummed her thin fingers against the wood, purple eyes piercing Bethany. "Tell me what you've come to ask," she said.

Bethany flexed her grip on her staff. "Emma and Luke are going to the Trident tomorrow to help fortify the towns there against more tsunamis. I want to go with them."

Morgan regarded her, expressionless. "Why?"

Luke suppressed a shiver in the face of Morgan's quiet power, commanding authority without speaking much at all. Morgan drew the answer from Bethany without effort.

"I can help them. Sir Cade talked about how hard it's been to dry some things out, and I can use my fire powers to do what they can't."

"Why else?"

Bethany opened and closed her mouth, briefly glancing back at Luke.

The Grand Mage leaned back in her chair, hand on her chin. Her probing gaze flickered to Luke momentarily, the eye contact shaking him. "Bethany, my witches may have relations with whomever they wish. Sometimes they even fight side-by-side with lovers in battle. But Luke Artair is not a soldier, and you are my newest witch. It's not against any rules to accompany him and Emma on this journey, but you have your coven sisters to consider."

Luke's heart sank, but he couldn't say he was surprised.

"Is that a yes, I can go... or a no, I can't?"

Morgan stood, rounding the edge of the table to sit on the other side. The corners of her lips pulled into the slightest smile, inviting them to relax. "You may do whatever you wish. It is difficult for those outside the Royal Coven to truly understand how I operate it, though Luke's recent involvement gives him a better idea than most. I am asking you to think about how your position has changed. Instead of requesting my permission, which you do not need, I suggest you speak to your fellow battle witches."

Bethany's lips thinned into a tight line. "Including my Coventra?"

"Especially your Coventra," Morgan agreed. "I know Hela is not the easiest witch to work with, but she cares deeply for all her charges."

"She hates me," Bethany said, then cringed. "Sorry. It's hard to talk to her when she blames me for what happened to Ebony." She told Morgan about the accusations and Hela's malice after the trials. Even their excursion to the armory for knives hadn't done much for Hela's attitude toward her. "Are you suggesting I get her permission to go to the Trident?"

Morgan shook her head. "No, you still misunderstand. Your Coventra cannot give you permission for anything. After talking with your sisters, you must decide whether you want to give *yourself* permission to leave. Hela may lead your coven, but she cannot force you to do something. The

Royal Coven relies on the respect shared for one another as humans, not on arbitrary measures of authority."

Bethany frowned, staring past Morgan at the paintings of the four elemental witches. A moment later, she nodded, turning on her heel and sweeping past Luke to the door. He followed, silently thanking the Grand Mage for her guidance.

Luke sensed the battle in Bethany's head, reaching for her arm to stop her march down the corridor. "No matter what you choose, I will always love you."

Bethany turned, sinking into his embrace. "I never thought I'd be more than a minute or two away from you and Em," she whispered thickly. "While I really, really want to go with you... I know I should stay here." She sucked in a deep breath. "Not only in case the dragon shows up like you were saying, but also so I can get to know Hela and my battle sisters better. I don't think they would like me traipsing off with you two right after joining. Besides... Emma's the one Sir Cade needs."

"Promise me you'll stay safe," Luke whispered, nose pressed against the non-tattooed side of her neck. She smelled like home.

"I think part of the job is to go looking for danger."

"I mean it. Stay safe." He squeezed his eyes shut, worrying she'd find some way to get injured or, worse, killed.

She rubbed circles across his back. "You come back to me, okay?"

"Always."

CHAPTER TEN

THE RIVER ROAD

"**I**'ve never ridden a horse," Emma admitted, staring dubiously at the pitch-black mount named Crescent. The rest of the stalls were empty since even the King's charger was loaned out to support relief efforts. Stale hay and dust made Emma want to sneeze. Ready to trot from the stables, Luke and Elijah sat on their horses as if they belonged there. She should have learned horseback riding growing up in rural Washington. "Seeing it done and getting on for real are two different things."

Elijah dismounted Ashfall, his dappled gray and white horse with expressive eyes and a thick black mane. Elijah's traveling cloak swung around his shoulders. The sight gave her flashbacks to the medieval movies she'd watched growing up. The knight crouched, threading his fingers into a makeshift stirrup, much closer to the ground than the real one hanging from the saddle. "Step here and let me lift you," he said, tilting his head to meet her eyes.

Emma placed her foot in his hands, bracing herself against his shoulders as he lifted her closer to the saddle. Seizing the saddle's horn, she swung her other leg over the leather until she found the other stirrup. Embarrassed, heat crept up her neck. "Thanks."

"Here," Elijah pulled the reins over Crescent's mane, showing her how to hold the thin leather strips and putting his hands over hers to demonstrate how to make the horse change directions.

Elijah's callouses brushed against her birthmarked skin, a stark contrast to her memory of Argent's smooth hands. Now knowing that the messenger hawks had disappeared along with countless other birds, Emma couldn't help but think something had happened to Argent. If he couldn't use his journal *or* send a letter....

Elijah's breastplate pressed against her leg as he leaned closer, still explaining how to ride a horse. Unbidden, a shiver raced down her spine.

"Ready?" Elijah asked, corners of his blue-green eyes crinkling with a smile.

She flexed her knees, tapping Crescent's flanks with her spurs. "Ask me again when we get to Trident Bay."

Luke smirked at her, urging Richat from the stables into the courtyard. Few people congregated to see them off, but Emma only had eyes for her father. Tomás sat in his wheelchair by the guardhouse, Bethany standing by his side.

"Be safe," Tomás called to them.

Three miles of open field stretched between the Trident Gate and the dark edge of the Valon Forest that butted up against the River Nimüe. The River Road followed parallel to the rushing waters.

They rode in silence until they came to the juncture, taking one last look at Camelot rising high above the surrounding village, new grass pushing through the spring dirt.

"You'll be back soon enough," Elijah promised, pointing Ashfall down the River Road. A cloud passed over the sun, sending another shiver down Emma's spine. The path was wide enough for their three horses to ride abreast, Emma sandwiched between Elijah and Luke. To their right, the river gurgled as it flowed west toward the Trident. Boulders lined the shore, most likely deposited by an ancient, violent flood. Trees grew at an angle over the water, shading the banks.

Luke reached behind him, placing a hand on his horse's rear. He whispered a quiet word, and a shimmering shield formed in place of the chain mail. Richat jumped at the magic, forcing Luke to pull back on the reins.

"We're safer in a group, right?" Emma asked, watching how Elijah's cloak swept from his broad shoulders to cover Ashfall's rump. "Three days alone must have been hard." Despite the fact that Luke trusted him, she hadn't enjoyed how Elijah had greeted her when they met. Camelot's survivors welcomed her back as one of them, not as a legendary hero. *If only they could see Argent as he truly is. Lord, I hope he's okay.*

"I've had worse," Elijah replied simply, urging Ashfall forward. Darkness increased the further they went, even with the sun rising behind them. "But yes, we are safer as a group. It will make night watch easier." They rode a minute more before he added, "But safer is not safe. Indeed, even with three of us, we're the odd ones out. Anyone else we meet on the road will likely be an enemy."

That evening, they met the first promise of trouble. In the distance, a figure stepped out from behind a tree, a hood hiding his face.

"Emma, quick—" Luke reached over for Crescent's reins, "—kill him! There's only one way this ends if we don't—"

"Excuse me?" Emma cricked her neck to stare at Luke.

"I don't have time to explain—"

"Well, well, lookie here," the man said with a guttural voice, pulling daggers from two sheaths at his waist. He lifted one blade, picking at his teeth with the point. "A witch, a knight, and a man ride down the river.... It's the start of a terrible joke." Behind him, three more figures stepped into view, two of them females with fire crackling in their hands.

Luke stiffened. "They're bandits, Emma, *kill them*—"

"You can't be serious," Emma blurted, fingers tight over the reins.

"Emma, now!"

Emma threw Luke a look of pure disgust, unable to comprehend his command that she kill these people *on purpose*. He knew how hard it had been for her to come to terms with accidentally killing Ebony. She rose, feet pushing down at her stirrups as her hair billowed around her face. She drew crackling blue-black magic into her palms. Clapping her hands together, she produced a concussive wave that knocked the bandits down. Her tesseract thrummed, charged with anger toward Luke, and she used her Persuasion. "Forget you ever saw us. Stand in the trees until we are out of sight, then remain for another hour. When your time is finished, return home."

The first bandit blinked, slowly re-sheathing his daggers, his eyes glazed over. The others followed suit, clumsily getting to their feet and walking backward into the trees until they were nothing but shadows in the forest.

She urged Crescent into a canter past them, and Elijah and Luke hurried after her.

"I wasn't joking, Emma," Luke snapped when he caught up to her. "People like that are profiting off the catastrophes—robbing houses, holding up travelers, accosting covens, killing our citizens. They don't deserve to live!"

"The Luke I know doesn't order me to kill people carte blanche," she retorted, her anger reaching its peak. "Who are you, and what have you done with my brother?"

"You haven't Seen what I have. I'm the one sending covens to clean up after those troglodytes when they've had their way with vulnerable towns. You don't know what it's been like for the last two years." Luke kept glancing behind them, agitated, his cheeks flushed, and eyes narrowed.

Emma frowned. "Bethany never said you were this upset."

"What makes you think I told her? I didn't want her sacrificing her education to come back before she was ready just because I'm having a hard time."

Emma almost threw the reins away, and Crescent jerked beneath her in response. "A hard time? This is more than a hard time, Luke, if you're telling me to kill random people on the road before we even get close enough to know who they are or what they want!"

"They would've taken any opportunity to slit our throats and steal our supplies."

"We're only a day from Camelot!"

Elijah urged his mount forward, increasing his pace to a trot and forcing Emma and Luke to match him. "Times like these make it easy for them to get so close," he said over the rushing waters to their right. "We cannot afford to waste mercy on those who would see us dead."

"Renault would say the same," Luke said. "I would rather have blood on my hands than see us get hurt."

You mean my hands. "Renault also says stuff like 'drink the blood of your enemies.' He's not exactly a dazzling role model." She rode in silence for several miles, angry as she mulled over the battle's outcome. Septim's faceless men hadn't seemed human when they filled the city after she broke his curse over Camelot. She remembered watching Renault tear through them, leaving blood in his wake and giving her time to reach the keystone and save the city. But other than the witch who taught her magic, Emma hadn't taken a life. And that one was enough to fuel her nightmares.

Luke pulled forward to talk with Elijah, their horses drawing closer as the path narrowed. Luke's drastic swing toward outright violence scared her. Despite his reasons, despite whatever things he'd Seen to drive him to demand she kill without discretion, in her heart, she knew she could never be that person. *What's happened to Luke? Argent wouldn't talk like that.*

Her stomach dropped. *But the King would.* Even though she hoped it would be decades before Argent had to take up the mantle as King of Renova, she suspected his gentle soul would struggle with wartime decisions like the ones Aragon made. As glamorous as the books and movies made it out to be, she'd seen firsthand how heavily the crown weighed on the Pendragons. Emma suddenly felt uncertain that she knew Argent as well as she thought she did. *Do I even know myself anymore?* So much had changed. Argent's camaraderie through the journal had kept her grounded during college. In her nightmares, his death had been the worst to bear.

And now she couldn't even use the journal to prove he was alive.

Out of earshot, Elijah said something to Luke that made him chuckle, and the tension in Emma's stomach eased. She missed the solidarity she'd had with Luke during her middle and high school years, their easy conversations, and his keen ability to make her laugh during her darkest moments, even if he didn't know the truth about them. She valued his opinion, but…. A prickle crawled down her spine. Had the exposure to high stress and expectations changed his personality?

A while later, Elijah led them about twenty yards into the forest, close enough to see the road through the dense trees but under enough cover to avoid any more trouble—at least from humans. As night fell, wolves howled, branches snapped, and Emma wondered how anyone could sleep through such danger. The men piled dry sticks and twigs together for Emma to ignite, and soon a crackling fire warmed them, assisted by Luke's heat charm. The horses nickered nearby, tied to a tree within Luke's protective circle.

"This is definitely more comfortable than before," Elijah commented, stretching out his legs while he rested against a tree. "Enchantments only go so far." He lifted the hem of his cloak for them to inspect. Tiny, stitched runes followed the frayed edge, not quite glowing but not blending in either.

"What would you have done if you'd faced those people alone?" Emma asked, refusing to call them bandits. She picked up a rock to fidget with, using earth magic to mold it into different shapes.

"Defeat the men in combat and hope to block the magical attacks until I could get close enough to strike the witches." He said it so bluntly that Emma's mouth fell open. He caught her eyes, expression softening. "I don't seek out enemies, Emma. Out of necessity, I killed many in the war." He paused, his Adam's apple bobbing. He looked around their camp, the fire casting long shadows. "I remember all their faces even now."

Luke rolled out a blanket and sat cross-legged on it. He dug in his bag, withdrawing a star-shaped stone covered with runes. "Did you know Ebony Reva?"

Elijah's face lit up with recognition. "Fearless, that one," he said, a fond smile breaking through his gloomy war memories. "I'd wager more than half the battalion survived thanks to her skills. I lost track of her after I became Lord of the Trident. How is she?"

Emma's throat tightened. "She died during Septim's curse."

Surprise flitted across his eyes. "I'm very sorry to hear that."

Emma cast a glance at her brother, wondering why he'd brought up Ebony. But Luke wouldn't meet her eyes, fussing with his stone. "When you arrived at Camelot," she said to Elijah, "you already knew me. What stories are people telling about me? About us?" She gestured to her brother.

The knight laughed. "You know how bards are. They embellish almost everything if they can get away with it."

Emma raised an eyebrow. "There's not much to embellish. By itself, it was pretty wild."

A beat of silence washed over them, broken only by the crackling fire. Elijah met her gaze, the intensity in his eyes locking her in place. "They say you walked through a curse that killed or incapacitated every other living creature who touched it. That you singlehandedly tore the magic from its anchor and stopped an entire army with a song."

Emma's face flushed. "Oh. None of that's embellishment."

"That's all true?" Elijah exclaimed.

She nodded, holding her right hand toward the fire. A flame spiraled to her palm, wrapping around her fingers like thread.

Elijah's fascinated eyes fixed on her, unblinking. "I thought for sure the bard had made *some* of that up."

Emma shrugged, not sure how to respond. Instead, she released the flame from her hand, getting to her feet. "I'll take first watch," she said, walking over to the horses, her chest tight with discomfort at the attention.

A child of prophecy on another world, Emma never thought she belonged with a man born on Earth. She'd rebuffed every college student to ask her on a date, knowing she would have to break it off before returning to Talahm. Her kinship with Argent made those rejections easier, though it took a couple of years before her thoughts toward him turned romantic—if unmentioned, until that last message in their journals.

Her heart twisted. Crescent nudged her shoulder for attention, and she rubbed her long face, desperately trying to squash the unwelcome thought that something had befallen the Prince.

CHAPTER ELEVEN
CRACKS

Luke woke from his restless sleep with a jerk. He hadn't roughed it like this in years, and was grateful that he'd remembered to bring his enchanted runestone, even if it didn't smooth the rocky ground. Emma slept while Sir Cade kept watch, and Luke studied him for a moment without moving. The Lord of the Trident didn't look at him, his eyes gentle as they rested on Emma's still form. Luke realized he didn't mind the idea of Cade and Emma together, but he knew better than to say that to his sister's face.

Luke rolled, sitting up.

"Did you have a night terror?"

"No," Luke said automatically, startled by the question. The woman in purple filled his dreams, each one urging him to get Argent into her presence. After a moment, Luke crawled over to Emma and nudged her awake, handing her a waterskin when she sat up.

She took a long, greedy drink, glancing around their camp as if searching for eavesdroppers. In hushed tones, Emma told them what she and Bethany had overheard in the barracks stairwell. Her eyes landed on Elijah for a long moment before she turned back to Luke. "We're far enough away from the castle now that I can say it out loud. I think something's influencing the King. Even with resources already stretched thin, he sent the first two covens out of the city. He let Prince Argent go on a dangerous voyage with a captain who wouldn't care if he died." She swallowed, eyes shining in the low light of dawn. "Doesn't it seem odd to you that Aragon would do *all that* but stop Sargateth, Morgan, and Renault from leaving the city?"

"I agree with you." Luke took a deep breath, thinking through his words as Argent's face popped into mind. "I have a bad feeling that I can't shake. King Aragon has been making erratic decisions since before you broke Septim's curse. Something wasn't right with Argent, and something's not right with the King. You should be careful with what you tell Argent in your journal."

Emotions fluttered across Emma's face at lightning speed, culminating with a furtive glance toward Cade. "What's Argent got to do with it?"

Everything! The knight's clear interest and Emma's cagey responses about the Prince fueled Luke's confidence. *Maybe things aren't so great between her and the Prince after all.* "I've never had a good feeling about him," Luke admitted as he began gathering his supplies, ignoring the pit in his stomach. "From the moment I met him when I first came here. That didn't change after you broke the curse."

Her eyes narrowed. "Say what you actually think, Luke."

"Are you sure you want to hear it? Nobody else does." He cinched his pack to Richat's rump, his fingers trembling.

One eyebrow crawled up her forehead, almost disappearing beneath the sweep of her jet-black hair.

In Luke's head, Argent appeared, thrashing, suspended in midair. "I told the King that Argent shouldn't go to Helcari. Any other regent would have sent a delegate instead of an heir. It was the only time he ever overruled me about managing the disasters, and what happened?"

Emma's eye twitched.

Luke plowed on. "No one knows. The hawks all disappeared, so we can't send a letter and haven't received one after Doltev, and you never said if Argent told you if they'd made it to the rest of the islands. From what I saw, the Prince couldn't wait to leave Camelot."

"You'd want to leave too if you were in his place," Emma muttered, fingers curled into fists as magic arced up her arms. "Get to the point."

"Helcari has a dark reputation, Emma. Did he or did he not tell you why the King sent him or what he's been doing on the islands besides delivering supplies?"

She slowly shook her head, her face expressionless. "He did not."

I knew it. He's hiding things from her. Luke's lips felt too dry. "I'm sorry, Emma, but I have to ask—why wouldn't he tell you any of that? What if there's still something wrong with him? What if the King is under the same influence?"

"I know where you're going with this, but it could be anything," Emma burst out, gathering her things. "A magical artifact, a witch, the weather, genetic paranoia—at least it's not Septim."

The question fell from his mouth as he recalled the King's words. "Who else could be that powerful?"

Emma's face crumpled. "Luke—"

The half-truth formed before his rational brain could stop it. "I had a Vision. A woman—a witch with the power to break whatever's controlling Aragon. I think she's in the Trident but can't be sure until we get there."

"Prophet," Cade's soft voice interrupted, "I told you there wasn't a witch powerful enough in Trident Bay to help protect against the tsunamis. I doubt there is a witch there capable of doing what you hope."

Luke had almost forgotten about the knight. "Not all magic works the same," he countered, watching his sister's face for any hints of suspicion. All he saw was a blank slate. "Emma... I only want you to be careful around Argent in case it's affecting him, too."

Emma shoved her bedroll into the straps that hung down over her saddlebag and got to her feet, hauling the pack to Crescent. "With everything else going on, I'm surprised King Aragon even agreed to let us help the Trident."

Luke extracted the waterskin again, taking a long draw. "I didn't ask his permission. Unless Morgan told him, he doesn't know we're gone."

They doused the fire and untied the horses, carefully scouting the road for signs of trouble before trotting west, nibbling on their meager breakfasts. Luke drew in a deep breath, savoring the dewy morning air. Further down the road, the scent of death lingered just beneath hints of moss and dirt. He drew his fingers across his chest, creating a bubble of warmth to keep out the chill.

The horses started jerking at their reins, spooked by whatever lay ahead.

"What's going on?" Emma whispered, struggling to keep Crescent from bolting. "And what is that awful stench?"

Elijah wrinkled his nose, forcing his spurs into Ashfall's flanks. "Ditch of the dead." He pointed to the forest where a deep trough cut into the far side of the road, flies buzzing over vague shapes Luke could only assume were decaying corpses. "Wasn't this bad earlier, but things change fast in these times." He frowned. "Something isn't right."

Beyond the ditch, a chasm blocked their way forward, cutting across what was left of the River Road.

"That wasn't here before," Elijah said, urging Ashfall closer. "Must've happened with that last quake after I came through."

Luke scanned their surroundings. "Make us a bridge, won't you?" he asked Emma, but it sounded more like a command even to his own ears.

Emma didn't hesitate. Stretching out her hands, she pulled dripping wet earth and stone from the abyss. She forced it to pack together in a hasty but solid bridge, the pressure driving water to stream back into the river.

Elijah stared in astonishment, his face betraying awe at Emma's power.

Emma took the first steps across, leading Crescent behind her and digging her toes into the dirt to make sure it stayed put. Luke could see the whites of the horse's eyes, reflecting his roiling sense of wonder at his sister's power.

"Did she just—"

"Yep," Luke replied. "She'll do more than that to change the Trident's coastline."

A beat of silence passed between the men, the river gurgling in the background. "Of course," the knight said, shaking his head and leading Ashfall closer to the brand-new bridge. "I know I should not be so impressed... but she formed this with hardly any effort."

"I can still hear you," Emma called over her shoulder, her cheeks flushed. Luke made a note to tease her about her embarrassment later. For now, he wanted to put as much distance between them and this blatant reminder of the danger they were in if they didn't find the source of the earthquakes... and take measures to protect the vulnerable people of the Trident.

CHAPTER TWELVE

A TRICK OF THE LIGHT

Emma's head pounded as she, Luke, and Elijah plodded up the narrow, winding path from Trident Bay to the little village of North Tyndale. Dusk had long since melted into night, the bright stars burning overhead. Hanging in the sky, both crescent moons sent shimmering tracts of light across the deceptively calm sea. Three of Emma's magical orbs lit their way. All Emma wanted to do was sleep, knowing the next day she would tax her magic more than she had in the past four years combined.

Her horse stumbled, and she instinctively squeezed her thighs together to keep balance on Crescent. Butt sore from so much sitting, she leaned forward to ease the climb. "How much farther?"

"Less than a mile," Elijah replied from where he rode ahead of her. Ashfall picked her way around broken branches strewn across the trail, remnants of the last earthquake and tsunami combination that had left most of Trident Bay in shambles. North Tyndale couldn't be much better off.

That last mile felt like an eternity, but as the ground leveled, bonfires illuminated a sea of tents. Collapsed buildings littered the backdrop. A tall stone cathedral stood out as the sturdiest building left standing, the cross at the top of its iron steeple barely visible against the night sky, candles flickering in a few of its windowsills. Luke's eyes lingered on the church's western tower, face indecipherable.

Elijah stopped for a moment, apparently deciding where they could pitch camp. He turned his reins to the right. Near the edge of the camp, they found a gap big enough for three horses and some bedrolls. A bonfire roared nearby with several villagers crowding around it. He dismounted, coming over to help Emma get off her horse.

Emma peered around her, eyes landing on a slim figure she hadn't seen in over four years. Despite his shorter hair, she would recognize Argent Pendragon's silhouette anywhere. The ache in her chest swelled, memories of the moments she'd shared in the journal with Renova's Prince drowning out her fears about his silence. Almost as if he sensed her gaze, Argent looked up, his burning green eyes meeting hers across the desolate land. Electricity raced down her spine.

Her foot caught on the stirrup and tore her attention away from the Prince. Off balance, she fell, hands grasping for the saddle but missing the horn. Before she could call on magic to soften the landing, Elijah's strong arms caught her.

"Careful," he said quietly, setting her back on her feet. His hand lingered on her triceps. "Are you okay?"

"I—" words stuck in her throat. She frantically scanned the crowd, searching for Argent. But he had disappeared, almost as if he'd never been there. The black maw of rejection swallowed her hope. *Did I imagine him?* "I'm fine." She patted Elijah's armored arm, moving to undo her saddlebag. Her heart thundered in her ears as she resisted the urge to search through the camp, unsure if it had been a trick of the light.

"You look like you saw a ghost," Luke said, his own bag tucked under one arm.

"I fell off the horse," she replied, not wanting to give Luke any more reason to shut her out.

Luke brushed a lock of hair away from her face, his smooth fingertips startling her. "I know you're tired. Let me take your things. I'll set up for you."

Her shoulders sagged, guilt and gratitude fighting in her chest. She had stubbornly forgotten how much Luke cared. "Thank you. Are you going to look for the woman from your Vision tomorrow?"

He undid the remaining straps, heaving Emma's saddlebag over his other arm. "Yes. I think I know where she's *going* to be. I hope the *when* is while we're here." He gave her a tight smile, then joined Elijah by the fire without another word.

Heart in her throat, Emma turned back toward the bonfire. Her eyes roved the crowd once more for any glimpse of the Prince. A hand rested over the pack strung across her body, comforted by the familiar outline of her journal against her hip. Despite Argent's silence, she couldn't bear to leave the journal behind.... *Just in case he decides to finally answer me. Just in case he wants to break my heart.*

But he didn't appear again.

Disappointed, Emma trudged over to her bedroll, collapsing on it with a huff. She glanced over at Luke, who took out his own journal, paired with Bethany's. The hole inside her heart widened.

Luke flipped toward the end, only a handful of empty pages left after two years of near daily messages. He froze, eyes glued on the ink.

"Everything all right?" Elijah asked, untying his breastplate.

Luke cleared his throat, glancing away from Emma so quickly she almost missed the fear in his eyes. Her heart sped up again. "King Aragon sent Bethany's coven to Ralador. They're searching for the missing witches and our mother." He passed the journal to her, and she stared at the words, ignoring the rest of their back-and-forth.

"I'm surprised," she admitted. "Bethany should be near the top of the King's list of magic-users to keep under lock and key. That being said, if anyone besides us can find and rescue the covens and Mom, it's Bethany."

The frown on Luke's face deepened, but he kept quiet.

Emma cast a warming charm on herself and pulled a blanket over her legs before curling up into a ball, abruptly ignoring Luke and Elijah in order to chase sleep.

She tossed and turned for hours, drifting in and out of a restless sleep, her mind still wired by the split-second glimpse of Argent Pendragon. Finally, when she realized there was no hope of finding rest, she quietly got up, making sure Luke and Elijah were asleep before she tip-toed to the bonfire. A few people still milled around it despite the late hour.

Two men sat on the far side of the blaze, their features obscured by the dancing flames. When Emma got close enough to make out their details, she stopped in her tracks again.

It *was* Argent.

She stared at him for so long that her eyes began watering, afraid that if she blinked he would disappear again. When she couldn't bear it for a second longer, she squeezed her eyes shut, and when she refocused a moment later, Argent stared back.

He'd filled out in their time apart. His shoulders were broader, his face thinner yet more mature. A thin, curving scar marred the right side of his chin, a new companion to the one that ran from his left cheek to his hairline. Emotions flitted across his features so fast she could barely keep up: relief, surprise, guilt, judgment, anxiety....

Rooted to the dirt, she couldn't move.

She had missed him *so much*. The gentle way he spoke to her, his curiosity to know *her* and not just the Seventh Sorceress, the raw vulnerability they showed one another in their journals.... She wished she'd stayed behind to grow with him in person instead of through the pen.

Argent held her gaze for another second before turning to his companion and speaking a few quiet words. Then, he got to his feet, making a subtle gesture inviting Emma to follow.

She finally made her legs move, trailing him at a distance as he led her through the camp to the rocky outcrop over the bay. Her chest and throat remained tight as she picked her way after him, trying to decide what to say.

Glittering moonlight sent reflections across the water. Three ships were moored at the pier, one with a wolf's head at its prow. A light breeze mixed the scents of pine trees and salt, ruffling Argent's hair where he stood at the ledge, his posture somewhere between relaxed and nervous.

"Emma—" His voice cracked, and Emma felt like a rug had been pulled out from under her.

Her heart jumped. "You're alive," was all she could think to say, her nightmares finally put to rest. She hadn't quite believed it until he'd spoken.

Confusion spread over his face. "Didn't your father tell you I lost my journal? In the Kraken attack?"

Stunned, Emma took a few more steps toward him. "*What? A Kraken?* No, Dad didn't tell me anything! This whole time I've been afraid you were ignoring me—or worse, dead." In a rush, she closed the distance, throwing her arms around his solid body.

He froze for an instant before returning the hug, crushing her against his chest, nose pressed to her neck. He smelled of salt water and smoke, cloves, and the forest. While they held each other, Argent quietly explained the ordeal, his voice catching when he described the journal falling into the sea.

"Did you read my last message?" Emma asked quietly, not sure if she wanted to know.

"It's burned into my memory," he breathed. "I missed writing to you so much. You were an anchor of hope on that blasted ship. Even at sea, I couldn't escape the whispers."

She pulled away to search his eyes. "Your father didn't stop the rumors," she said. It wasn't a question. Of course, he hadn't.

Argent's cheek muscles spasmed, and he turned away from her. "Everyone has a different theory. But none of them think I'm innocent."

"I do."

A sad smile flickered at the edges of his lips.

"Argent," she grabbed his wrist, the cold leather cuff a shock to her warm fingers.

He cleared his throat. "The knight—Lord of the Trident, isn't he?"

What does Elijah have to do with anything? "He came to Camelot to ask for help, since the hawks have all gone missing. That's why Luke and I are here." She explained her mission, the dearth of witches, and how Bethany had joined the Royal Coven and almost immediately gotten dispatched to Ralador. For now, she left out her and Luke's concern about whether Aragon was in his right mind.

Argent frowned. "No hawks? I sent my letter to your father from Borna, where we stayed for repairs. It should have arrived shortly afterward. The hawk must have been among the last to disappear."

"You think it never got to Camelot?"

He shrugged, rubbing his chin in thought. "It would explain why you never heard about my missing journal."

Emma's heart sped up again.

"Emma...." His brilliant green eyes shone in the moonlight. "If you and Sir Cade—" He couldn't finish the sentence. When he took a breath to continue, a rustle in the bushes distracted him. His eyes zeroed in on something over her shoulder, and Emma spun around.

The knight in question stood at the mouth of the game trail, one hand on the hilt of his sword. "Emma, you left so suddenly—"

Argent stepped to one side, and Elijah's easy expression evaporated into wariness the instant he recognized the Prince.

"Your Highness, my apologies. I did not mean to intrude." The knight gave a short, half-bow, but he didn't remove his hand from the hilt. Alert, his eyes darted between Emma and the Prince.

"You're forgiven, Sir Cade," Argent said stiffly.

Emma saw the knight's questioning glance out of the corner of her eye, but she couldn't believe he'd had the nerve to interrupt them.

Without another word, Argent left before Emma could reach out to stop him.

Elijah waited until the Prince was out of sight before he approached, glancing behind him as if checking for other intruders. "I apologize for not following sooner. It must be difficult to be near the man who crippled your father."

It took a split second to register his words. "Excuse me?"

"I heard Prince Argent was behind the curse and shot the poisoned arrow—"

Emma shoved him hard in the chest. He stumbled back a step, mostly unaffected thanks to their size difference. "How *dare you*—" she snarled, anger clouding her vision.

"You trust him?" Elijah sounded so astonished that Emma actually laughed.

"You don't even know the whole story, do you, Cade? How Agamemnon Septim's disembodied spirit possessed Argent for *six godforsaken years* before all that went down?

How Ebony Reva sacrificed herself for Argent when I was *this close* to killing him?" She held up two fingers a hairsbreadth apart. "And you have the audacity to accuse the Prince of hurting my father?"

Elijah lifted both hands in a placating gesture, backing away a few paces. He glanced at her hands—she'd conjured hazy blue-black energy without realizing it. "I heard it from bards in taverns, Emma."

"And you believed them?"

"I had no reason not to. After all, you told me the things they said you did were true."

She flashed back to their first night on the River Road, the embarrassment of his awestruck praise washing over her again. "Yeah, *me*. You didn't ask about anything they said *Prince Argent* did."

"My mistake," Elijah said softly.

Emma breathed hard through her nose, adrenaline finally subsiding. "I'm more than just the tesseract, Sir Cade." Unclenching her fists, she extinguished her signature flames. "There's more to us both than what the bards could ever tell you. If you really care, at least give Argent a chance. He's your future king."

She didn't give him an opportunity to argue, pushing past him and down the rocky path, hoping Argent hadn't gone far.

CHAPTER THIRTEEN
BUT A FOOTNOTE

Argent heard Emma storm down the trail toward him. He slid behind a tree, his heart thundering, anxiety tight behind his eyes. He didn't know how to thank her for standing up to the Lord of the Trident for him. *As if I deserved it.*

"I learned how to hunt in college, Argent. You can't hide from me in these woods." He peered through the darkness, shielding his eyes when a light blossomed from Emma's palm. She stepped off the path, joining him behind the thick trees crowding the available dirt. "How much did you hear?"

"All of it," he admitted before he could stop himself, unable to look away from her vibrant cobalt eyes. "You didn't have to defend me," he continued, but his words felt hollow.

"Yes, I did," Emma insisted, coming closer to him. The light revealed black and blue tendrils creeping above her collar toward her neck. "You'll have a hard time ruling a people who think you're a liar," she huffed. "Or worse, that you *helped* Septim do all those horrible things."

Argent stared at the lines on her skin. "Your birthmark—"

"It's not crawling up my face, is it?"

He shook his head, taking the opportunity to study the rest of her. The coven armor fit well, hugging her curves, the glowing white tesseract on her shoulder a beacon of hope for those who knew what it meant.

"Good. Hopefully it'll stay that way."

Argent swallowed, his heart rate increasing as he thought about what he wanted to say. "I saw when you arrived," he murmured. "I couldn't believe it, seeing you back here after so long. I thought—" He cut himself off, lost in her presence.

"What did you think?" Emma's beautiful blue eyes pierced him to the bone, sharp and warm all at once. He'd forgotten how much he'd missed her face.

"I thought I was dreaming. I don't know what's real and what's my imagination anymore." She certainly looked real now and had felt real on the outcrop, but crushing doubt remained. Maybe he'd *imagined* her last words in the journal.

Emma's cheeks turned pink in the cold morning air, the antithesis to her frown. She drew close enough that he could smell the honeysuckle in her hair. She said out loud the words he'd seen her write a thousand times, drawing them together like moths to lanterns. "Tell me."

Fearing he would cry if he kept drinking her in, Argent squeezed his eyes shut and forced the words out. "You say I'm stronger than I know, but I have never felt weaker. Not even under Septim's thrall." The weight in his chest lifted a fraction. "The crew of *The Sea Wolf* is just a symptom of the sickness my father has done nothing to cure. You heard Sir Cade—the governors of Renova listen to the exaggerations of bards, casting doubt into the hearts of Camelot." Finally, he opened his eyes again, blinking back burning tears. "You, your father, and my Great Uncle William are perhaps the only souls who believe that Septim actually *died* that day. I thought leaving Petra would allow me to outrun the furtive looks, the whispers, and the stares that followed me whenever I walked the streets of my childhood." It felt good to release his tension. Venting his frustrations to Emma in person was more cathartic than writing them to her. "But no distance took me far enough."

"I know," Emma whispered, her face full of compassion. He did not deserve her, a strong witch more than capable of commanding respect, and she didn't even have to try. She took another step, now just a couple of feet away. The light in her hand created shadows across her face, freckles flickering in and out of view. "Why did you ask about Elijah?"

She's on a first-name basis with him.

Emma's eyes widened, suddenly excited. "Oh—Argent—"

"What?"

"Just because I call him by his first name doesn't mean anything," she breathed. "But that's not the point. The point is I heard your thought!"

His knees buckled, blood draining from his face. He stumbled backward, tripping over a root and slamming into the nearest tree. He scrabbled his hands against the bark to keep from falling. Eyes still fixed on her, he shook his head in denial. "That's not possible—"

She gingerly approached, holding out her hand for him to take. "It happens with family... or those I feel close to, who also feel close to me."

"I don't understand," he said, his head spinning, still not sure if he could trust himself.

"Luke, Bethany, Dad... my mom." Her voice caught on the last word. "And now, you. But not Elijah."

Argent grasped her hand, now close enough that he could hug her again if he wanted to. "But why? Why me? What makes me so special that you would even want to be my friend?" He hadn't realized how much his experiences continued to hurt him until now. His voice sounded quiet and hoarse, filled with the pain of how much he hated himself for being the pawn of a too-powerful man.

Emma extinguished her light, her hand cupping his cheek, tilting her head to one side as she studied him. "He was in both of our minds. I didn't even sense him there, and he made me feel like a worthless failure. I only know what he did to you because you trusted me enough to tell me only hours after he'd died, and you kept telling me for nearly the entire time I was gone. You're one of the most courageous people I've ever met, Argent. You survived six years of personal hell and woke up in a world that still can't look past the charade they thought they knew."

His bottom lip trembled. "I fear he's still here with me, and I can't sense it."

"I promise you, he's not." Her warm fingers stroked the smooth angles of his jaw. "You don't have to believe me, but I'll die before I call you a coward or a weakling."

He drew a ragged breath, which turned into a sob. His forehead pressed against hers, finally processing some of the pain he'd buried for so long.

"You were an anchor for me, too," she whispered, her lips nearly pressed against his ear. "Every morning after a nightmare, I had to re-read our messages to remind myself that *I didn't kill you.*"

His arms tightened around her, pressing their bodies together. "I don't deserve you."

Her breath shuddered. "That won't stop me from loving you."

Argent swore his heart stopped. "What?"

"Are you going to make me explain what love is? Because there's this really corny song from Earth that I do not want to get stuck in anyone's head." Emma rested her temple against his shoulder and smirked.

Argent searched for the right words. "Tell me what it means to you," he asked, scared that she would change her mind and leave him standing alone in the pre-dawn silence of North Tyndale's grove.

Her smirk disappeared. She righted herself, now face-to-face with him, cobalt eyes shining. Her fingers found the dragon head etched on his breastplate, the ancient symbol of his ancestors. "Protection, laughter, and support," she started, looking at his chest. "It's holding each other up. Comforting each other through hard times. And it's unconditional. Sometimes, I think it's the best feeling in the world."

"And other times?"

"Other times it hurts to love so much, but that only happens when I think I've lost someone. When that happens, I know it's not the love that hurts, but the grief. I went through so much grief waiting for you to write back." Her gaze flickered up to meet his again. "There's a saying on Earth. 'It's better to have loved and lost than to have never loved at all.' The bigger the grief, the bigger the love."

His throat tightened, thinking of Ebony. He never had the chance to tell her his feelings without Septim's influence. "Is it possible to grieve the love you couldn't express?"

"Ebony will always have a place in your heart," she told him, nodding. "And she won't leave it."

The painful truth finally spilled out, his voice ragged. "Losing the journal ripped me apart," Argent choked. "I thought because I never had a chance to reply, that you would never want to speak to me again. That you would be so angry at me for making you believe I didn't care, and—" He sucked in a breath. "—and when I never got a hawk back from you... I didn't think you wanted to even *see* me again. I know now that you never heard about the Kraken, but that doesn't take away the misery I've been living in. When I saw you with Sir Cade... I thought you had moved on. That I was but a footnote in the story of your life." His tone had grown bitter, filled with self-loathing. His hands trembled against her back and shoulders, as if his admission would make her averse to his touch.

"Why didn't you stay when I first saw you? To ask me what—or *who*—I want instead of assuming?"

Dawn lightened the sky, and Argent could see the details of Emma's face without her magic. He traced the curve of her face with a gloved hand. "I've dreamed of your return since the moment you left. After all the things we've shared with each other.... I didn't want to feel the pain of hearing you say a name that wasn't mine."

"Argent Pendragon," she said, deliberately drawing out his name. A shiver swept down his spine. "Argent Arthur Pendragon, I want *you*. Not a Lord Knight of the Realm or another man who can't see past the power of the Seventh Sorceress. You."

His chest felt so full it might burst. Not knowing what else to do, he leaned down, closing the distance between them to kiss her. She responded immediately, gripping his shoulders and pulling herself even closer to him, his armor presenting the only impedance. He savored the sensation of her lips on his. The tension of her strong muscles as he ran his hands over her arms. Hope rekindled deep within him, brought to life by the incredible witch kissing him back.

Finally, he broke the kiss, pressing their foreheads together once more.

"I missed you so much," she breathed. "You're alive. You're here."

"I'm alive," he repeated, unable to think of anything else to say. "I'm here."

Peace settled over him like a warm blanket, his soul reassured and strengthened by the promise of Emma's love—for him. In that still, calm moment, nothing else existed but them, standing alone in the dense woods overlooking Trident Bay.

CHAPTER FOURTEEN
SKY'S HEART

Luke wiped his brow, taking stock of his work so far. Several villagers with lingering injuries from the tsunami were healed, a mountain of broken wood from destroyed houses sat near the forest at North Tyndale's eastern edge, and somehow, the town seemed a little brighter. Most of the Trident's people, once they got over their shock from seeing a man performing magic, asked him for news from Camelot. Once they learned who he was, they also asked him if he'd Seen anything else coming. Their weary, fearful faces tugged at his heart. Seeing death and destruction in his Visions was one thing, but encountering it face-to-face, *smelling it*, was entirely another. Elijah had been right. The people of the Trident needed help, and the fact that it took this long to get it made Luke feel like he'd failed somehow. He hadn't Seen the Trident's tsunami coming.

North Tyndale's cliff looked over the entirety of Trident Bay and across the vast Valon Forest to the south. Somewhere beyond the deep green that swallowed the horizon, Bethany would be traveling with her coven into Ralador. Luke's heart clenched. The one place he didn't want her to go, and King Aragon sent her there almost as soon as Luke departed. *If Aragon didn't know we left before, he certainly does now.*

Closer to shore, at the edges of the Trident Bay village, remnants of trees that snapped under the force of fifty-foot tsunami waves stuck through the dirt. Boughs lay across pathways, crushing what was left of houses and leaving great tracts in the earth. He couldn't call it anything but utter carnage.

No buildings had survived. Waterlogged wood littered the ground, and stone remnants of fireplaces and forges sat half-buried in silt and mud. Ragged, weary villagers picked through the remainder of their homes, and salvaged food from torn-up gardens and cellars as they tried to clean off mud-caked mementos. If they didn't stop the earthquakes.... How many more villages would end up like the Trident?

I have to find the woman from my Vision. Morgan's apprentice. I know she has the answers, and this must be the place. The stone cathedral's western tower window matched what he remembered from his Vision, cut horizontally across the curve facing the Sleeping Sea. A ship would need to leave the bay and point north for it to pass in front of the window at the right time. He closed his eyes, trying to recall the details, but he'd been more captivated by the woman choking Argent against the wall.

When he woke that morning, Emma was already gone, starting her work of pulling massive stone pillars from the ocean floor to tower across the mouth of the bay. A crowd had gathered by the rebuilt pier leading to the moored ships, peering across the rippling waters to where Emma worked. They watched as she first pointed both of her hands palm-down at the water's surface before slowly turning them back up and lifting them like the conductor of an orchestra. The water's surface bubbled and frothed until, one pillar at a time, the stones breached the surface, and Emma would jump across to raise them seventy feet high. As the sun dipped closer to the western horizon, she was almost finished with the ship channel.

Not having seen her perform such magic for a couple of years, Luke tried to bury the pit he felt in his stomach warning him that if Emma knew what he was doing, even his Sentinel powers could not stop her.

Shouts filled the air. One of the ships lifted anchor, two airwitches filling the sails to coax it toward the new entrance. A spike of adrenaline coursed through him. *It's time.* Luke scanned the remnants of North Tyndale for the Prince, finally spotting him standing by the cliff's edge, one hand resting on the hilt of his sword while he watched Emma work. *If he's already talked to Emma, I have to get him into the cathedral without her knowing.* It was the first time all day he'd seen Argent without the tall, older man who could only be William Pendragon, the King's uncle.

He approached quietly, shoving his anger, paranoia, and fear down deep. If Argent suspected anything.... Luke had kept the secret of his destiny from his family and friends for years. Lying to the Prince of Renova shouldn't be hard.

"Prince Argent," he said stiffly.

Argent glanced over his shoulder. "Luke. I'd wondered if you'd come with her. Your healing skills are certainly needed."

"How long have you been here? We never received word of *The Sea Wolf's* progress past Doltev."

Argent wrinkled his nose. "Right. No hawks. We arrived about a week ago."

Luke glanced back across the sea of tents, eerily reminiscent of the refugees in Camelot's citadel the last time Septim caused problems. It bothered him that the Prince hadn't immediately returned to the capital. "Of all the missions I've sent in response to these disasters.... The only time the King overruled me was to send you to Helcari. He never told me why."

Argent turned away from the cliff with one last look toward Emma. He opened his mouth to answer but hesitated, expression hardening.

Luke followed his gaze, spotting Cordelia Roque staring at them from one of the clusters of tents, her eyes narrowed. So far, he'd managed to avoid crossing paths with his irritable great-aunt who held a grudge against her sister's entire family, and he didn't want to tempt fate. His heart sped with adrenaline. "Let's go to the cathedral. I don't trust Roque as far as I can throw her."

"Nor should you," Argent muttered, walking toward the church. "I know my father doesn't, even if she was the only captain mad enough to sail north despite the threat of more tsunamis."

"Luke?" Emma landed behind them in a great whirlwind as they climbed the steps to the cathedral's entrance. Sweat dripped down her temples, her hair soaked. "What's going on?"

Luke swore viciously inside his head, heaving open the heavy cathedral door. "Inside, now," Luke said curtly. He would have to figure out how to deal with Emma's presence later and could only hope the woman in purple wouldn't waste time.

Emma tried to hold her ground, but Luke yanked her into the narthex, Argent darting in behind her. He pushed the door closed, scanning the large stone chamber lit by the setting sun. The double doors that led into the darkened nave were propped open, one lopsided on its hinges.

"Luke Artair, you explain right now—" Emma's hiss evaporated when Luke covered her mouth with his hand, all but dragging her over to the staircase.

Certain that his heart's staccato would betray him, he whispered, "I don't want that harpy overhearing."

Emma slapped his hand away, eyes blazing. "What harpy? Overhearing what?"

"Captain Roque," Argent answered, as quiet as Luke. "You remember what I wrote about her, don't you? Just because my father trusted her to ferry supplies to the Helcari Isles does not mean he trusted her to be a diplomat."

Luke led them up the staircase lit by candles in iron brackets, trying to keep his bearings as they twisted up the tower. The floor above the narthex had a room with a window matching the one from his Vision, so he exited on the first landing, making a beeline for the wooden door he was now positive the woman in purple was behind. *This is it. This is my chance....*

He held his breath as he turned the handle, pushing in to reveal a cozy stone room bathed in the setting sun.

"Oh, thank Christ—help me!"

Luke froze for an instant, during which his world completely crashed around him. *She's not here. This isn't the place.* Out to sea, the ship crossed in front of the window, but the rest of the room didn't match. Instead, a dark-haired man wearing a disheveled cassock looked up at them, face frantic, sleeves stained with dried blood.

"I can't leave her, not even to call a healer—"

The pastor of North Tyndale's cathedral held a reddened rag against a large, unmoving animal. As big and fluffy as a snow leopard, with ocelot markings and a long, thick tail, it could only be an Olis. One wing splayed awkwardly against the flagstone floor. A thick lump of scar tissue covered the joint where the other wing should have been.

Magdalin Skyheart.

Sargateth's missing wife.

Emma crouched at her side while Luke gestured from head to tail, creating a shimmering projection of the Olis's body in the air. Luke studied it, frowning.

"What happened?" Emma asked the pastor. She gently shifted the awkward wing, but at her touch, Magdalin shuddered.

"A witch found her in the waters last night and brought her here," the pastor answered, collapsing into a chair beneath the window. He buried his face in his hands. "I can treat minor wounds, but nothing like this. The witch left before I could ask her to find someone more qualified. It's only by God's grace I've kept her alive."

Luke moved his healing hands slowly over Magdalin's neck, ribcage, and lower body, pausing wherever he saw something odd or wrong in the projection. After he finished helping with what he could, sweat beaded Luke's brow. Not all her wounds would close. He rested a hand on Magdalin's head, a soft white glow shining between his palm and her fur. After a minute, Magdalin's large golden eyes blinked open.

"Water," she croaked, her tongue rasping over long incisors.

Argent handed Emma his waterskin, and she brought it to Magdalin's mouth. When she'd drunk her fill, she tried to move, but couldn't.

Luke sat back on his heels. "We need to get her to Camelot. I can't do anything else for her here."

"Wings," Magdalin said, her voice so soft they strained to hear her. "Worlds. Doors... to Langoth." Her eyes rolled to the back of her head as she fell unconscious once more.

Emma, Luke, Argent, and the pastor stared at each other, confused.

"What's Langoth?"

Against his better judgment, Luke left Emma and Argent alone with Magdalin to retrieve their things from the camp while the pastor excused himself to clean up. His thoughts raced during the short trip down the tower and across the narthex. *If the Vision doesn't take place here... where could it be? How did Magdalin end up in the Sleeping Sea? When did Emma and Argent meet up?* He pulled the door open, twilight barely illuminating the village. Luke darted between the roaring bonfires to their camp, quickly gathering their things.

"Artair," a harsh voice spat behind him.

Luke winced, slowly pivoting to face Cordelia Roque.

Her flinty blue eyes moved from his heterochromia to the white streaks at his temples, sneer deepening. "May God curse every man who can wield magic. I should have known you were Tomás's spawn."

"You're not the first to mistake me for my father," Luke replied evenly, calculating how to escape.

Cordelia leaned in, her air magic generating eddies that lifted the dirt and leaves around them. "Your precious sister is little more than a royal puppet, unworthy of the mantle she wears—"

Luke's temper flared, creating a halo of light around him that disrupted the wind. Sticks and pebbles clattered back to the ground. Tomás had warned him about how Cordelia had pined over Jesse Artair before her younger sister Elaine won his heart. "We didn't ask for this, and neither did our grandmother. God chose Elaine to be the Sixth Sorceress, and you're hanging onto decades-old anger that you didn't get the same roll of the dice for your magic or your love life." Luke's chest filled with disgust. "You must be so heartless to alienate your entire family because you didn't get what you wanted."

"You know nothing of this world or what I've borne in my life, boy—"

Luke took a single step forward, his shoulders back. "I've Seen enough to know that I'd do *anything* to protect my family. Even from you." He shoved past her, generating a thin shield across his back in case she decided to attack.

By the time he slipped into the cathedral, his magic felt more drained than it should have. *I'm dealing with way too much right now.* Luke climbed to the second level again, not bothering to knock before entering Magdalin's room.

"Did you bring my bag?" Emma asked, still sitting by the Olis's furry head. Argent leaned against the wall beside her, expression unreadable.

Luke tossed it to her, dumping the rest of their things in the corner to set up later. He knelt beside Magdalin, trying to fold the broken wing against her body, but it wouldn't move correctly. He cast the projection again to double-check her stability. Satisfied, he released the spell. "Now, Argent, why did your father send you to Helcari?"

"Because I asked. It would not have occurred to my father on his own, so my mother coerced him into letting me represent the crown rather than Great-Uncle William. I didn't realize she didn't tell you."

Luke frowned when Argent didn't continue. "That's it?"

The Prince's lips thinned. "William abdicated the throne for a life on the open sea. He's of royal stock, yes, but in terms of diplomatic relations, he is not my father's first choice. What more did you expect?"

Luke opened his mouth to answer, but closed it again when Emma glared at him, giving him a subtle shake of her head.

She cracked the journal paired with Tomás', clicking her ballpoint pen a few times. Argent watched her with a fond smile that sent a wave of anxiety rolling through Luke's body. "I'm going to let Dad know we found Magdalin." When she finished, she closed her journal with a snap. "How are we going to get her to Camelot?"

CHAPTER FIFTEEN
LANGOTH

The next morning, Argent recruited William Pendragon's help to take Magdalin back to Camelot while Emma stayed behind to raise pillars in front of North Tyndale's promontory. In her absence, Argent's heart keened for her even more strongly than it had during their years apart.

The men stopped thirty miles from Trident Bay, moving off the path and into the trees. Luke started a fire while Argent and William tied up the horses. Luke had barely spoken to him the entire journey, though Argent had to admit it took a lot of concentration to levitate an Olis and ride a horse at the same time.

Sighing, Argent sat on his bedroll by his uncle, alternating between watching William stoke the fire and looking out into the trees, hoping for Emma. Twilight waned into dusk, the visibility to the road decreasing with every minute.

Luke busied himself with Magdalin, laying her on one side and fussing with her limbs. Her limp wing still wouldn't fold back, and eventually, Luke gave up trying to make it cooperate.

The fire sputtered as a rush of wind blew through the camp. When Argent blinked, Emma stood at the edge of the circle of light, looking more worn out than Argent would have liked. He closed the distance between them before anyone else noticed her arrival. "Tell me what's wrong," he asked gently, taking most of her weight as she collapsed against him.

"I'm just really tired." Dark circles painted the skin below her eyes. "Turns out that raising enough stone barriers to protect an entire cliffside village and then using air magic to fly all the way here uses a lot more energy than I thought."

"Come and sit. You must be starving." He helped her to the ground by the fire. While Argent fussed with the blankets to make her more comfortable, Luke tracked them, face unreadable but for a hint of worry. *He's always been hard to read unless Bethany is nearby. Speaking of which....* "Why did Bethany not come with you to Talahm?"

"She did," Emma said between bites, explaining her best friend's quick initiation into the Royal Coven and subsequent mission to Ralador. "I haven't had a chance to tell you this—our mom somehow got sucked through a portal here, but we don't know where she ended up. Part of me had wondered if she was in the Trident, but now I hope Bethany finds her in Ralador since it seems like most of the problems are coming from there."

Argent's brows furrowed. He didn't like the implication that Ralador was once more the source of his kingdom's problems. A warm touch on his knee pulled him back to the present.

"You're you," Emma whispered, eyes boring into his. *I promise Septim's not coming back.*

Argent's heart fluttered from hearing her thought in his head.

Emma devoured the food in record time. When finished, she snapped her fingers for Luke's attention. "Will you wake Magdalin up? We need to find out what Langoth means."

Luke knelt by the Olis, a stasis field still active over her body. One moment later, the stasis disappeared. Luke touched three fingers to Magdalin's skull, and after a second, her eyes blinked open.

"How are you feeling?" Luke asked.

Magdalin tried to stretch but only managed to move one front leg. "Pain," she whispered, voice low. "Better than before."

"We're taking you to Camelot," Luke told her. "What happened? You've been missing for a year and a half."

"What?" Magdalin assessed them one by one with her wide golden eyes. "That's not possible. I haven't been gone longer than three months!"

Emma and Argent scooted closer to her, not wanting to miss a single word. William leaned against a nearby tree, face inscrutable.

"Sargateth has been fighting every day with the King to search for you," Luke said. "Do you remember me?"

"You're Tomás's son. Luke," Magdalin whispered. Her eyes found the tesseract mark on Emma's shoulder. "And you—you must be Emma. The Seventh Sorceress."

Emma shifted uncomfortably, moving from her knees to sit cross-legged. "Yes, that's me. You said something about doors to Langoth. What did that mean?"

Magdalin tried to roll to her belly, sighing when Luke helped her. The wing complicated things, but finally, the Olis rested like a sphinx with her head on her front paws and her eyelids drooping in fatigue. "Surely you've seen that the fabric between the worlds has become so thin that doors have started opening on their own, at times with great shaking," she said.

Emma told her about Julie's disappearance and the beasts she and Bethany had fought. Argent mentioned the purple lightning before the Kraken, as well as his encounter with a strange animal on the Isle of Borna, a stop on the way home. Knots formed in his stomach when Magdalin huffed out a deep breath.

"I went searching for *Mountains Crumble Beneath His Claws* after Tomás shared the Vision of him in chains. I was perhaps a month into my journey before a portal opened right in front of me. The force that pulled me through...." She shuddered. "It stretched me beyond my wits. The agony made me lose consciousness. And when I woke, I woke in this form." Her voice trembled. "I have not been like this since the war."

"I thought the portals only connected Talahm to Earth," Emma said, confused.

A chill swept down Argent's spine. "The creatures. They must come from this other place."

"The Fifth Travelers named it Langoth."

Luke's jaw dropped. "You found the Fifth Travelers?"

"They fought off the creatures that would have devoured me."

Luke ran both hands through his hair, clearly shocked. "There hasn't been a Fifth Traveler in at least a century," he stuttered. "Maybe two. No scout now would risk going between worlds five times."

A jolt thundered through Argent's chest. Emma's hand found his, and they laced their fingers together for mutual comfort and support.

"Tell us more," Emma urged. "Maybe there's a way to rescue the Fifth Travelers."

Magdalin shook her head, the motion tiny. "The doors are unpredictable... but some seem planned. At first, they told me many creatures were taken. Then, the travelers began disappearing. They learned how to tell an intentional doorway from an accidental one, and they've been jumping through the unintentional portals hoping they'll appear somewhere safe on Talahm. Or... I suppose they could have returned to Earth. I do not know their fates for certain."

"Why are they so desperate to escape Langoth?" Argent asked. "Besides the creatures?

"Those terrible beasts are not what scares them. Langoth has no sun."

"*What?*" Emma yelped. "How is anything alive if there's no sun?"

Argent remembered Emma's obsession with science, wishing they'd had the pages in their journals for her to explain it more. Now, though, they could talk for hours without worrying about using too much paper. His heart warmed.

Magdalin shifted, pain spasming across her face. She briefly closed her eyes. "The sky is nothing but a mottled disk, eternally locked in red twilight. There's barely enough heat to survive. I saw the strangest ocean, the waves so tall that if the encampment hadn't been on such a high cliff, it would have been destroyed many times over. My body felt so heavy it took more effort to move than I could spare."

Argent could almost see the gears turning in Emma's head as she stared at the Olis.

"No way," she breathed. "No freaking way."

"Share with the class, Emma," Luke demanded.

"Oh, come on, you're an engineer," Emma said, now excited. "A red disk in the sky? Tidal waves larger than regular tsunamis, but without the earthquakes? Increased gravity? Magdalin thinking she was only there for two months. Luke, for you, it was eighteen."

Luke frowned.

"Langoth must be orbiting a black hole," Emma announced, breathless. "And it sounds like it's close enough to feel the tidal and temporal forces."

Surprise melted Luke's frown in an instant. "You're kidding."

Emma gestured at her own face. "Do I look like I'm kidding? I studied black holes in my astrophysics classes. Magdalin, it's supposed to be impossible to escape that. How did you or the others do it?"

"It felt impossible," she said, golden eyes turning to Emma. "When I was finally well enough to roam, I watched for the tears. After a while, I could tell when one was created on purpose, by whom, the Lord only knows. Those... I avoided. Whoever is capturing the creatures or the Travelers...." She shuddered. "I hope I'm wrong that my brother is their pawn." She extended a single claw from her paw, scratching at the dirt with its razor-sharp tip. "Long ago, the only way to cross between Talahm and Earth was for an Olis to find the weak threads in reality and tear open a door. It has been millennia since I performed such a feat. The effort taxed me so much I would have drowned if that witch hadn't rescued me from the Bay. If any of the Travelers followed me, I doubt they survived."

Emma bit the tip of her thumb. "If your brother—Mountains, can we just call him Mountains?"

Magdalin nodded.

"If Mountains is being forced to open portals to Langoth, what could the reason be?"

Luke's face darkened, and Argent got a sinking feeling in his gut. *Don't say it. Don't say—*

"It could be Septim, or someone trying to bring him back. Rebuilding an army more powerful than any human has built before."

Emma's eyes flashed, and without a word, she rose to her feet and dragged Luke into the woods. Either she didn't take him far enough away, or Luke neglected to put up a silencing ward, because Argent heard their whole argument.

"Would you stop bringing up Septim?" Emma demanded, frustration clear in both her voice and stance. She crossed her arms tightly over her chest, her shoulders back and chin jutted out defiantly. "He's gone. He's dead. And you know exactly what killed him!"

Luke matched her, equally incensed. "What proof is there? Feelings aren't *proof*, Emma. Even if Septim *was* in Argent's head, we don't know that the Wraith didn't find some other host to infect, like the King!"

Argent wished the ground would swallow him whole. He didn't know which was worse—Luke suggesting he'd never been possessed, or the possibility that the Wraith of

Valona had cheated death once more and now had his hooks in the King of Renova. Unable to bear looking at either his uncle or Magdalin, Argent continued tormenting himself by staring at Emma and her brother.

"Everything happening is right up Septim's alley, Emma," Luke pressed, voice hard as flint. "Who else could it be if not him or someone serving him? Who knows whose loyalties he twisted while bodiless? What if this is all a lead-up to another attack against Camelot? Against *us?* The city is still in shambles; our forces stretched thin. We are not even remotely prepared to handle another invasion. If I don't find the woman from my Vision—"

"Wait—she *wasn't* in the Trident?"

Luke's face pinched, clearly feeling his failure. "No. But if we don't find her soon, I'm afraid it will be too late to save the kingdom."

Emma held up a finger, her face set but trembling. "I don't believe Septim could have survived Ebony's sacrifice. But... if you think the woman you Saw has the power to break whatever's influencing King Aragon, then I need you to trust me enough to help you find her."

"What did I miss?" Magdalin asked, puzzled.

Everyone looked at her, including Emma and Luke. Luke's face paled, perhaps realizing their fight had not been private. He stormed further into the trees while Emma sat heavily on her bedroll. Since Magdalin had not been present in Camelot at the time, Emma gave Magdalin the short version of the events from her first visit to Talahm, and what she knew of Luke's Vision prior to them going to the Trident.

Lost in his thoughts and sick to his stomach, Argent barely heard Emma tell the tale. *Septim could have survived.* His brain latched onto the thought, playing it on repeat until he couldn't even see the crackling fire beside them. He jumped when Emma slipped her hand into his, threading their fingers together again. She must have cast a warming charm over herself with how much her skin burned.

A foreign thought filled his head, pushing out his circling anxiety. *Something else is going on because we both know Septim's dead. You're not a monster. You're brave, kind, compassionate, and courageous.*

He stared at her, overwhelmed with gratitude for her projection into his mind, while she related the story to Magdalin and William.

"I'm sorry," Magdalin said when Emma finished. "I wish I could have been there to help."

"If you were, Septim would've done whatever he could to destroy three Ancients instead of just two," Argent objected, relishing the feeling of Emma's hand in his.

"We have enough problems right now, anyway," Emma said with a sigh. "Starting with finding your brother and my mom."

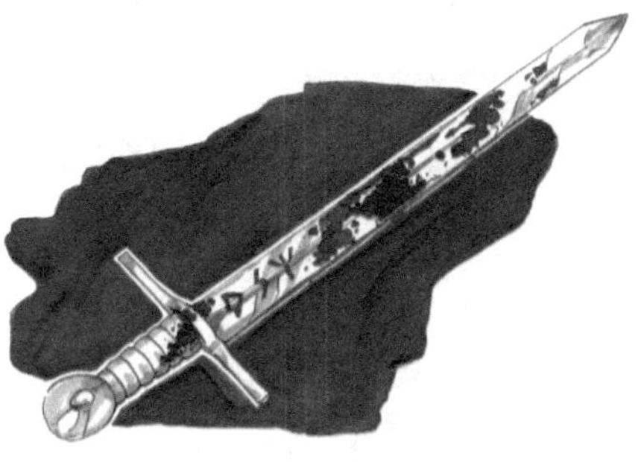

CHAPTER SIXTEEN
THE HUNTED

Luke woke to William nudging his feet with one boot, sword out, a finger over his lips in the universal gesture to be quiet. The dim light of early dawn filtered through the trees, hints of blue promising another clear spring day.

Silently, Luke deactivated his sleeping stone and peeled off the blanket, moving to his knees as he scanned the camp for trouble, hands ready to cast a shield. He did a double-take at his sister, curled into Prince Argent's side, a blanket pulled over their lower bodies. Luke's jaw clenched.

Twigs snapped under heavy weight, the low branches of nearby trees whispering against something large. The horses stamped their hooves against the dirt with soft nickers of concern, the whites of their eyes showing. Magdalin slept like the dead, and Luke watched her for a moment to make sure her chest was still moving.

William's head snapped toward another rustle.

Noises circled them, the only silence coming from the direction of the River Road. As quietly as possible, Luke rolled up his things, stuffing it all into his saddlebags in record time. He glanced at Emma and Argent, then locked eyes with William.

William nodded, understanding.

Keeping his back toward the road, Luke crouched near Emma's and Argent's heads, ignoring his bitterness toward the Prince while he clamped his hands over their mouths.

Emma writhed, scratching at his hand before sagging back to the ground, recognition in her eyes. Her rapid heartbeat thrummed, visible in the lines of her neck. Argent woke without fighting, shaking his hand free from the blankets to reveal a razor-sharp dagger. One of the Prince's eyebrows raised, and Luke freed their mouths. He tapped his ear, pointing to the sides of the camp where the noises were coming from. Another rustle filled the campsite. Argent curled into a crouch, priming his knife to throw it, but it didn't look like he could find a target.

They all kept one eye on the forest, silently gathering their things and soothing the horses while they reattached their saddlebags. Soon, they just needed to wake Magdalin. Luke knelt in front of the Olis's still form, gently resting both hands on top of her head. He bent forward, a soft white light filling his palms. When Luke sat back, Magdalin's eyes were open, her ears twitching backward. She slowly got to her feet, stretching. Her wing dragged along the ground, her first few steps on her own wobbly. Luke let her lean against his side as he looked around the camp, his heart in his throat. The noises hadn't stopped or grown. They stayed constant, but the hairs on the back of his neck prickled, a sign they were not alone—and not with something friendly.

Argent and William led the horses, Emma circling behind Luke and Magdalin, her fingertips twitching. The snapping twigs followed them to the edge of the River Road, the source remaining hidden.

They moved slowly, their pace set by the injured Olis.

Luke focused his attention on his sister, projecting a thought to her. *We'll never make it back to Camelot if we don't speed up.*

But she didn't reply.

Brushing aside the concern that her lack of reply raised, he whispered the thought out loud.

"Can you levitate her again?" Emma whispered back.

"We're being hunted. I'll need all my strength to raise a shield."

Emma frowned. "I have strength to spare. Let's put some distance behind us."

Luke whispered in Magdalin's ear, her resigned nod giving him permission to pick her up with his magic. He mounted Richat, Magdalin floating beside him. Even on the horse, the magic pulled at his core. Luke dug his heels into Richat's flanks, urging him down the path at a trot, the others close on his tail.

Almost two hours after their tense wakeup, Luke finally felt safe enough to get answers. "What's out there?" he asked William, whose brow shone with sweat.

But William didn't answer.

Argent did. "Direwolves," he whispered, sounding like he was trying to hide his terror. "I've never heard so many at once."

Luke frowned at him. "You've encountered them before?"

Argent swallowed hard, glancing behind them. Luke followed his gaze, landing on Emma, who twisted in her saddle as she protected their rear. "When Septim possessed me—" Argent floundered for words. "He would sometimes walk through the Valon Forest, where my father destroyed his body. Direwolves usually hunt in pairs, and I—I mean

Septim—killed the ones who attacked us. If he hadn't had magic, we wouldn't have survived."

Luke's opinion of the Prince dwindled even further with how he talked about the Wraith of Valona, as if they had been cooperative spirits in one body. *How can Emma trust a man cooperating with evil?* His lip curled in contempt, almost without his noticing it. But as soon as Argent's eyes flickered to his face, he knew the Prince had seen.

"Direwolves aren't your everyday city dogs," William interrupted, voice quiet but gruff. "You say there's more than two?"

Prince Argent nodded, his head on a swivel. The whispers followed at a distance. "I heard five."

William cursed, spitting on the ground. "Son," he said to Luke, "can your sister handle five direwolves? We can fight, but we have to protect Magdalin."

"And ourselves," Luke added. "Emma might be able to hold them off or kill them before they become a problem, but we'd be safer if I could cast a shield the instant we need one. I can't do that if I'm carrying Magdalin."

"Let me down, Luke," Magdalin whispered, her ears still pressed back to hear their pursuers better. "I can walk for a while."

"You're still so weak."

"Let me down."

Luke obliged, letting out an involuntary sigh of relief when his magic released. With all the adrenaline, he hadn't realized the magnitude of the strain on his magic. He stretched, taking a drink from his waterskin while Magdalin tested her legs. Luke frowned as Argent urged his horse over to Emma, defending their rear. Frustrated, he looked up the road. Vibrant shades of green filled the arch of trees over the path. The soft rush of water gurgled on their left.

Magdalin started walking, her wing dragging through the mud and debris on the road. Every time it hit a rock or thick stick, she winced.

"Magdalin, there has to be a better way," Luke protested.

She looked up at him, her gold eyes shimmering. "This form is too painful," she admitted. "My wing... it would have been better if they'd cut that one off too."

The breath left Luke. "No, don't say that." He dismounted to crouch before her. "Please, there must be something we can do to help."

She looked at each one of them, eyes finally resting on Emma. "I will turn back into my human form. Then, I can ride."

"Are you strong enough?"

Her eyes flashed.

Luke raised placating hands. "I'm not judging you. I'm worried you'll hurt yourself."

"I have the strength," she insisted, but Luke didn't believe her.

He'd seen her medical projection. Too many of her pain circuits fired in error and the injuries in her wing hadn't healed properly, leaving her helpless. Luke doubted she could defend herself, even with magic, if the direwolves attacked. He called the group to the side of the road opposite the trees. He didn't want to give the wolves a better opportunity to pick them off. "Magdalin's going to try shifting to her human form," he told them, casting a golden shield between them and the trees. It curved around them until their only opening was at the rear, along the river's bank.

Emma paced the line, watching for any hint of a snout peeking beyond the forest. "I'll be able to hit them from behind this, right?"

"Yeah." Luke's shield already felt weak.

William tied the horses to a sturdy branch, fixing the shield on his arm and drawing his sword.

Magdalin rested on her haunches in the middle of them all, her face contorted in pain. Her limbs trembled, her fur rippling like the surface of the water behind her. Her useless wing vibrated as if electrified, and Luke's attention split between his shield and the Olis.

Her features morphed, becoming more human, but the longer it took, the worse Magdalin appeared. The wing stubbornly remained a wing until the rest of her human body was sprawled on the ground. Finally, the awkward limb melted into her shoulder blade, disappearing beneath her torn, rumpled dress.

Luke's heart raced as Magdalin struggled for breath. "Help her!" he cried to Emma.

Magdalin lay still. Emma turned, falling to her knees by the thin woman's form. She pushed Magdalin onto her back, concentrating as she pressed one hand to her chest and shared her strength to equalize what Magdalin had expended.

Luke didn't see the direwolves emerge from the forest until Argent yelled, sword drawn, a mechanical bracer unfolded in front of him.

About as large as Magdalin, the direwolves' thick, shaggy fur covered their muscular bodies in shades ranging from midnight black to heather gray. The wolf in front raked its claws against Luke's shield, sparks flying into its thick fur. The scar across its face contorted with rage. Luke wanted to help Emma but couldn't. His shield was too weak. Argent stabbed through the golden magic, nicking the second wolf across its brown snout before it could rear up to press its full weight into Luke's magic. It snarled, jerking away from them. A third, gray direwolf prowled behind its companions, teeth bared as it surveyed their cornered group. The last two waited in the shadows of the trees.

As if it sensed Luke's weakness, the black wolf raked at the shield again, claws piercing it just enough to show the sharp keratin designed for ripping flesh from bone. Prince Argent couldn't strike well from his position, and for one microsecond, Luke considered letting it down. But it could kill them all if he surprised them by doing so while outnumbered.

Despite his intense focus, the shield rippled, blinking in and out of existence for a moment. Panic tore at Luke's throat. "Emma!" he cried, taking a chance by glancing at his sister. She still knelt over Magdalin's prone form, trembling, her hand clenched on top of the Olis's chest. Emma's shoulders sagged with exhaustion, having given too much of herself already.

Luke would have to drop the shield if they wanted to save both Emma and Magdalin from oblivion. William approached, and the two Pendragons sank into a stance that would allow them to quickly launch an onslaught.

"Now!" William yelled.

Luke wasted no time releasing his magic, spinning to peel Emma away from Magdalin's body. He draped Emma across his legs, blocking the sound of steel and snapping. Emma's pulse felt thready under his fingers. Her eyes fluttered from the effort she'd expended to keep Magdalin away from the brink of death.

"Come on, Emma," he muttered, taking a calculated risk by giving her some of his strength. Exhaustion pulled at his limbs, but he'd given her enough power for her to regain consciousness.

Emma rolled off his lap onto all fours, head hanging for a moment before she took stock of the situation and struggled to her feet.

"Help them," Luke croaked. "I'll do what I can for her."

Emma nodded, her eyes full of apology for nearly taking herself out of the fight. As she assessed the enemy, fire overtook her gaze, her mental gears turning as she decided how best to protect them without killing herself.

Both William and Argent pressed the direwolves back enough to give them space, but it was still three-on-two as the rest of the pack waited in the shadows, as if learning from observation.

Several things happened at once.

Argent landed a lucky strike on the brown direwolf's neck as it lunged, perfectly slitting its throat, a spray of blood hitting Argent's chest. The beast collapsed to the ground, its life soaking the dirt. One of the waiting direwolves, with a mottled coat, immediately leaped into the fray. William kicked the black wolf on the snout. Yelping, it retreated a few paces, right into the path of the incoming beast. The two tumbled over one another, giving William the opportunity to refocus and Emma something concrete to aim at while Argent engaged with the gray wolf.

Emma performed magic that Luke had never seen before. She held out her hands toward two of the animals, closing her fists in midair. The black and gray wolves stumbled, collapsing to their sides, twitching for several moments before lying still. The mottled wolf backed away, staring at them with new fear in its black, soulless eyes until it slipped into the trees with the fifth wolf that had watched the whole fight from afar.

Luke couldn't breathe as he stared at the dead wolves littering the road. Beside him, Magdalin's breath deepened, the energy Emma shared with her doing its job.

Emma doubled over, resting her hands on her knees. Argent knelt beside her, hesitant to touch her but clearly offering some words of encouragement Luke couldn't hear.

His blood rushed in his ears. "What just happened?"

Argent's eyes flickered to his with a silent reprimand.

Luke's temper flared at the Prince, but he aimed his anger toward his sister. "Emma. What did you do?"

Emma straightened and faced him, her face red and splotchy as if she wanted to cry but couldn't. She opened her mouth to say something, but the words never came. Instead, she folded into Argent's side, one of his bloodstained arms wrapping around her waist.

Sound returned. Branches swayed in the wind. Water flowed in a rush toward the Trident. And the horses whinnied nervously, tied to the tree behind him. William kicked the dead wolves, grunting when they didn't move.

Luke checked Magdalin one last time before getting to his feet. He approached Prince Argent and Emma. "What was that?" He did not want to ask again.

Argent's piercing green eyes were hard with layered emotions. "She stole their breath." His attention shifted back to Emma when she went limp in his arms. He dropped his sword, catching her before she could hit the ground. "Em—hey, Emma," he soothed, quickly picking her up bridal style and carrying her back to where Magdalin lay with golden-brown hair splashed against the dirt like a puddle of chocolate.

William appeared by Luke's side, making him jump. "You don't see that use of air magic very often," he muttered, loud enough for only Luke to hear. "Some might see it as... unsavory."

"I didn't know she could do that," Luke said, his stomach churning to the point where he thought he might throw up.

"I don't think she did either, until she did it," William said. He tugged a rag from his pocket, wiping down his blade. It came back stained red.

"I don't know what happened with my shield. It just wasn't holding up."

William shrugged. "I'm not the man to discuss magic with, but it must have taken a lot of effort to carry Skyheart so far, so fast. Running from a pack of direwolves is bound to tire anyone, not just you."

Luke wasn't so sure. "I've held stronger shields under more strain before." As he watched Argent fuss over his sister, fear tightened in a band around his chest. *What will Emma do to protect him if she doesn't know he's a threat?*

"Aye, but perhaps it was a different type of strain." He bumped Luke's shoulder. "Get some rest, eat something. I'll stand watch to make sure those two wretches don't come back."

Luke looked at the bodies, cold washing over him. That was close. Too close.

Finally, he dug through his saddlebag for a biscuit, sitting cross-legged near Magdalin, far enough away from his sister not to strangle Argent if the urge hit. Every time he watched the Prince touch her, whisper in her ear, or do anything that could be construed as trying to get close to her, terror and rage twisted through him, fueled by the belief that no matter what Argent said, he couldn't be trusted.

CHAPTER SEVENTEEN

FAILURE

Emma came to her senses in Argent's arms. The soft fabric against her legs could only be from a bedroll, and the coppery smell of blood filled her nostrils. Her eyes snapped open, focusing on Argent's blood-spattered armor. She tensed for one long moment until he smoothed a hand up and down her back.

"It's not mine," he said quietly.

Emma looked up at him, realizing that twilight approached. Lines of tension pulled at Argent's face, and dark, tired circles stained the skin beneath his eyes. Chocolate brown hair fell in wisps across his forehead, mussed by the battle she'd ended by taking the air from the direwolves' lungs.

She froze.

"It's okay," Argent reassured her, tightening his arms. "You did what you had to do."

"If I can do that to animals," she uttered hoarsely, "I can do it to humans too. I don't want to be that kind of monster."

He bent to kiss her forehead, his lips dry and scratchy. She savored the sensation. "We have talked at length about monsters, Emma. If I'm not one, neither are you. *You saved us.* I don't know how much longer William and I would've lasted had you not done what you did."

"But—"

"Emma."

His firm voice stopped her protest in her throat. He tilted her chin up, meeting her gaze, eyes full of compassion, understanding, and—her heart skipped a beat—love.

"Luke doesn't want us to move until Magdalin wakes. How do you feel?"

She tested her limbs, taking stock of her physical tiredness. "Better. I'm not a wet noodle anymore."

Argent's lips quirked up. He reached behind him, producing a half-crumbled biscuit and a chunk of cheese in a cloth wrap. "Dinner."

She accepted it, suddenly ravenous. "We're still on the side of the road," she said as she sat up, immediately missing Argent's warmth. The beasts' bodies had been moved, their dull fur peeking out from behind some trees on the opposite side of the path. William sat cross-legged by a campfire, poking at the embers with a long stick. Luke stood by the horses with one eye on the edge of the trees and the other on them. "Hasn't anyone passed by?"

Argent shook his head, taking a bite of a sad-looking apple. "People wiser than us stay home. It's too dangerous now. Too many monsters—even on the more trafficked routes between Camelot and the western territories."

Luke turned back to the horses, brushing Crescent's coat hard enough that she tossed her head back and tried to bite him.

Beside them, Magdalin stirred. Her long brown hair tumbled in a halo around her head.

"We cannot stay here overnight." William stared out to the trees where Emma suspected the other two direwolves waited for them. The sun dipped below the horizon. "It's a bad situation either way. We travel during the night, or we remain here with dwindling supplies while trying to fight off direwolves."

"Emma could just—"

A sharp glance from the elder Pendragon cut off the rest of Luke's suggestion.

Magdalin turned her head, drawing the group's attention.

"You almost died," Emma told her, grasping the Olis's hand.

"I shouldn't have tried to change back," Magdalin whispered, wetness collecting in the corners of her eyes. She squeezed them shut, the tears sliding toward her ears. "I've put us all in danger."

"We were in danger before we found you," Argent said.

"Can you stand, lassie?" William got to his feet, one hand resting on the pommel of his sword. Just in case.

Argent and Emma helped the Olis healer to her feet, steadying her when she swayed. "Get me on a horse, and I can ride," she said, closing her eyes. Her brow furrowed. "We must hurry. I can finally feel Sargateth again. He's furious. He knows I've returned, but the King won't let him leave the city."

Argent cursed.

"I'll take her," William said, dumping a cupful of water over the fire. Steam hissed into the air as the flames extinguished, and he kicked the remnants into the river. "You three are more agile than me in a fight."

William and Magdalin mounted the sturdiest horse, her in front, so he could keep her from slipping off if she lost her strength. Emma surveyed their site again, her throat tight as her gaze landed on the pool of blood from Argent's kill. That her fatal magic left no physical evidence behind felt like a small mercy. She jumped when the Prince's hand found hers.

They rode for hours into the night, a crick forming in Emma's neck from continuously looking over her shoulder for direwolves. Argent rode beside her, occasionally asking if she was okay and offering to take watch so she could give her neck a break. The darkness pressed against them like a thick, cold blanket. Three balls of magical light floated ahead, illuminating their way under the stars and waxing moons. Shadows leaped across the ground behind them, their own movement tricking her into thinking the wolves had left the trees.

Emma didn't know what to do about Luke. Since their argument on the first night about Argent, he hadn't talked to her much, and he still wouldn't tell her more about his Vision.

To her right, gray flashed through the trees, drawing her attention. The direwolf matched their speed as they galloped down the road, and Argent dropped back to ride behind Emma. Whether to fight the animal in her place or to defend them from the yet unseen second one, she didn't know.

"Luke, shield, right side!" she called out, frowning when Luke's golden magic flickered so much that it barely withstood the jostling of their horses. "Luke!"

"I'm trying!" he yelled back, frustration lacing his voice. "I don't know why it's not working!"

The direwolf left the woods, now streaking alongside Luke's sputtering shield. Argent rode hard beside the shimmering magic, sword ready to strike.

Emma watched it happen as though in slow motion. The direwolf launched itself toward Argent as the shield had started to stabilize. The beast should have landed against a solid but transparent golden barrier, but instead, the shield winked out of existence. Argent jerked his reins, his horse shrieking in fear as the direwolf raked its claws across the Prince's right side and down the horse's flank. He slumped in the saddle, sword clattering to the ground.

Emma screamed, rearing her horse onto its hind legs before she jumped off.

All thoughts of mercy fled. She reached out her hands, this time welcoming the grim satisfaction as she siphoned the air from their lungs. The wolves collapsed, straining for breath against the crush of Emma's magic. When she finally unclenched her hands a full minute later, blood trickled down her palms from where her fingernails had broken skin.

In the commotion, Luke and William caught Emma's horse and kept Argent from falling from his. Argent whimpered, cradling his arm as Emma picked up his sword and carefully slid it back into its sheath. The horse tried to prance away, clearly in pain from where the claws had pierced its hide.

"Fix them," Emma demanded, pinning her brother with a fierce stare. "Do it, now."

Luke dismounted, his face tense and confused. "I can't while he's on the horse," he said, voice shaking. He gently touched the horse's neck, withdrawing when the animal flinched. They got Argent to the ground, and William did his best to manage three riderless horses with Magdalin in his saddle.

Emma stripped Argent's armor away, revealing long, bloody gashes from where the direwolf's claws broke the chain mail beneath his cuirass. Sweat and blood stained his undershirt, and Luke had yet to do anything useful. "Fix him!" she said again, holding Argent's head in her lap. He'd lost consciousness.

Something snapped Luke from his stupor. He cast a projection above Argent's body, taking a second to assess his injuries before performing any healing magic. "I have to clean the wounds first," he told her, avoiding her gaze.

Within a heartbeat, she conjured a bowl full of steaming water and a rag.

Luke looked at it in surprise. "I meant with magic," he said quietly, his hands hovering over Argent's ragged skin. He pressed one over the open wound on the Prince's arm, the spell glowing a bright green before it faded into nothingness. When he pulled his hand away to check it, the dirt and remnants of wolf fur had disappeared. After that, he worked quickly, cleaning every wound while Emma soaked the rag and laid it across Argent's forehead, not sure what else to do while her brother worked.

With all the wounds clean, Luke returned to the first one, now watching the projection as he closed the injury with soft, flickering light.

"Will it scar?" Emma asked quietly, her eyes on the now healed mark on Argent's arm. Thin pink lines ran the length of it.

"Yes," Luke answered, voice tight.

"Why did you let the shield fail?" Her voice hitched, catching on the last word. She couldn't believe her own brother, her Sentinel, had let the Prince get hurt so badly.

"What?" Luke finally met her eyes, distracted as he finished closing Argent's wounds. His projection flickered once before disappearing.

"Your shield. You lowered it right when the wolf lunged."

"Emma, I don't know what happened. My shields have been off since we got to the Trident. They're not as strong—not as stable. I swear, I didn't drop it on purpose when the wolf jumped. It was just awful timing."

Emma stared at her brother with such intensity that she thought she might pop. After a long, fruitless moment, she sat back on her heels, breathing hard. "Why can't I hear your thoughts?" she whispered, suddenly afraid. Chills that had nothing to do with the cold night air swept down her spine. The rag turned cold in her hands, and she blindly tossed it back into the bowl, water splashing over the ground.

Luke jerked back, his mismatched, fear-filled eyes meeting hers. "I don't know."

Setting that aside for a moment, she surveyed Argent's prone body. "Wake him up. We need to keep moving."

Wordlessly, Luke pressed his fingers to Argent's temple. As soon as the Prince's eyes flickered open, Luke withdrew his hand as if burned, brushing it against his dark brown robes and going to heal the horse. It didn't seem as severely injured as Argent, but it was infinitely more spooked.

Emma cast one more glance toward the trees, trusting Argent's count that all the wolves were dead. She still held his head in her lap, and he gazed up at her, his eyes full of weariness. "I'm sorry. I didn't mean to get hurt."

She burned with anger toward her brother, toward the direwolves, but it lost out to the relief that Argent was alive. She traced the thin scar on his chin, leaning down to kiss his forehead. "We're not out of the woods yet. Literally."

Emma noticed that Luke studiously avoided looking at her as she helped Argent get back in the saddle, and she swung up onto Crescent as if she'd been doing it her whole life. She marveled at how fast she'd gotten used to horseback riding.

William dug his spurs into his horse, starting back down the road at a trot. The rest fell back into formation, Emma's mind racing about Luke's magic problems and Argent's unnecessary apology.

Then, from the back of her mind, a sinking suspicion threaded through her consciousness.

What if Luke can't protect me if I'm with someone he doesn't trust?

At their next camp, Emma woke from a restless sleep, the final image of her nightmare burned into her eyes. Breathing hard, she curled into a ball, trying desperately to stave off tears, glad dawn had not broken yet. She'd cried about these demons so many times already but thought seeing Argent in person again would make them stop.

Empty wishes.

She flinched when a hand touched her back, rolling into a defensive position and ready to attack with her magic—but it was just Argent checking on her during his watch.

He pulled back, a cautious expression on his face. "Sorry," he whispered. "I—"

Emma extinguished her spells, reaching for him. After her nightmare, she needed to touch him again and have solid proof that he was okay.

She hadn't killed him.

And neither had the direwolves.

"Alive," she breathed, her face pressed to Argent's chest. She wrapped her arms around his unarmored middle, warmth seeping through her. His chin rested on the crown of her head, and he stretched his legs out in front of him, holding her sprawled body across his lap.

"Tell me," he asked, his chest rumbling.

Emma took a moment to cast a privacy spell, drawing in a deep, shuddering breath. "It's always the same. We're in the courtyard, and I'm so close to killing you with that last onslaught. Ebony sacrifices herself, but I don't stop. I *can't* stop. You're dead before I can help it—" Her voice hitched, and Argent's arms tightened around her back. "And then my powers are gone. Septim's curse consumes everyone and everything until I'm the only one left alive to watch his army set fire to the city and burn it all to the ground. Everyone I love is dead in front of me." She'd never said it out loud to anyone, not even Bethany, even though she'd once written it out for Argent in their journals. When she finished, she felt lighter but no less drained.

Argent held her for another long minute, letting the silence bleed away her anxiety. "I still have night terrors too. I thought that having Septim's memories would make me dream of the horrible things he'd done during the war, but no…. He tried so hard to have me kill my father that day—and in my nightmare, he succeeds. I watch myself plunge Excalibur into my father's chest, and Septim doesn't let me look away. Almost every night, I watch the light in my father's eyes go out by *my* hand."

"What a pair we are," Emma said, half chuckling with the ridiculousness of it all. She quickly sobered, the restlessness of her sleep catching up with her as she yawned. "Tell me something you liked about your voyage to Helcari," she asked, wanting a distraction.

The rhythm of Argent's steady heartbeat soothed her. One hand moved up to stroke her hair, fingers brushing against where her birthmark stopped its progress up her neck. "The clear, calm nights during the new moons took my breath away," he said, his voice relaxing. "I would sit alone on the prow, the entire sky visible from horizon to horizon, stars like pinpricks of fire. I'd never seen the constellations with such clarity before. Those were the nights I most wished that you could've been there with me, watching as the world turned."

Emma sighed, wishing she had been there too. "We should sail together after this is all over, and you can show me," she murmured, snuggling into his chest even more.

"You're falling back asleep," he whispered.

She gripped him harder. "Stay with me." After a moment, he leaned back to lay next to her bedroll, her body tucked against his side. Her eyelids drooped as a wave of exhaustion swept over her. Argent kissed her forehead, and she drifted into her first nightmare-free sleep in years.

CHAPTER EIGHTEEN
SEND HELP

They made it within a half-day's ride of Camelot by the time the sun set the following day. Magdalin seemed stronger, but she was still not well enough to ride on her own, so she stayed with William, silent except when someone asked her a question.

Luke wanted to know more about Langoth, about Magdalin's experience there, and what it was like stepping foot on a world falling into a black hole. But when they collapsed into a circle around the fire at their last camp of the journey, no one had the energy to talk.

He leaned against a tree trunk, ankles and arms crossed as he watched Emma and Argent cozy up with each other. Despite all the encouragement and evidence set before him, he couldn't shake his distrust. He still resented how Septim tricked them all during their time under his curse, how Argent had trained with them and used Emma, fooling them all. Try as he might, Luke couldn't decouple Septim from Argent. The Prince didn't seem all that different to Luke. Aside from avoiding people more often, he looked and spoke exactly as he had when possessed. *Maybe he never was possessed. Maybe he's been Septim's ally all along.*

The Prince had left on his voyage to Helcari about a year after Emma and Bethany went back to Earth, but even in that year.... Luke tried to remember his interactions with the Prince and surprised himself by not remembering many at all.

With the earthquakes interrupting the effort to rebuild the wall and his duties assisting with the crisis efforts.... He hadn't had time to pay Argent much attention.

But now Emma was back, Argent was back, and even though they had paired journals, Luke couldn't fathom how they had grown so close in those four Earth years.

You and Bethie wrote every day for the same amount of time, one part of his brain told him, unhelpfully.

You knew Bethie for her entire life before then, the other part of his mind answered, feeling justified.

Emma and Argent sat so close together they might as well have been joined at the hip. They held hands, one of Argent's arms wrapped around Emma's shoulders, pulling her closer to his side. Luke felt torn—happy that his sister looked so content, but terrified that it was with Argent. *Even if he's not orchestrating everything, he's definitely involved. Morgan's apprentice wouldn't attack a royal if that royal wasn't compromised.*

Trying to distract himself, he thought of his mother. He had no way of knowing where she'd landed on Talahm or if she was unharmed, let alone safe. Now that they knew about Langoth, he thanked Bethany for remembering the color of the tear. *If Mom had been sucked to that god-forsaken planet, we'd be searching here in vain.*

"Your pack is glowing," Magdalin said, her airy voice like music.

Luke glanced to his side. The journal he shared with Bethany pulsed with light, indicating a new message. He pulled it out, flipping to the last page. He frowned. Bethany's cramped, jerky script was unusual compared to the rest of their writing. As if written in a hurry. He noticed all that before actually reading the words, and when he did, he couldn't breathe.

"Emma!" he yelled, panicking to the point that his hands trembled. He tried to stand, but his legs wouldn't cooperate.

Emma looked at him, her face changing from exasperation to concern. "What?" She scrambled over to him. He handed her the journal, not even caring if she read the other messages between him and Bethany.

As Emma read the book, he could still see Bethany's frantic message upside down. The words burned into his brain.

Send help. We're surrounded. Coven Marks not working, can't talk to anyone. Something is picking us off. Hela and I only ones left. Send help, Luke. I'm scared.

Emma dropped the journal back on his lap, face white as a sheet. "We have to get back *now*," she whispered, her voice strained, cracking like glass. "Tell her we're coming."

Luke frantically rummaged through his bag for a pen, finding an old ballpoint. His hands shook so much that he couldn't write properly for a full twenty seconds.

Her next message came immediately, but—

Hela gone, help—

Her pen dragged down the page as if something snatched the journal from her hands mid-sentence. Luke's heart lodged itself in his throat.

"Bethany's in trouble," Emma announced, hurrying back to her things and hastily throwing them into the bag she'd unpacked less than an hour ago. "William, I know it's a lot to ask of you, but will you get *The Sea Wolf* to Ralador? I don't care what you tell Cordelia. We'll need a way out of Valona once we find Bethany."

"Consider it done," William replied immediately, the glint in his eyes revealing his thirst for adventure. He quickly untied a horse, and within minutes, the sound of his gallop disappeared down the western road.

Luke filled with gratitude as everyone in their little group gathered their belongings—even Magdalin with a blanket held over her shoulders. No one questioned the need to move or complained, nor did anyone ask for just a few more minutes of rest before they rode through the night again.

Luke's heart matched the clatter of his horse's hooves as they galloped toward Camelot, passing darkened farmhouses and sprouting fields. Bethany's words tumbled through his mind, conjuring more and more terrifying scenarios, none of which ended well. Her previous updates had been short, mostly describing their progress into Ralador. A few notes mentioned the active lava flows near the border and the few strange creatures roaming the nearly pitch-black tunnels threading between the two kingdoms.

The change from scouting to fearing for her life happened so quickly....

As they approached the broken city walls, Magdalin gasped. Despite hearing the story from Emma, she must not have grasped the magnitude of the damage. Luke tightened his grip around Magdalin's waist, keeping her from slumping off.

Within minutes, they reached the Trident Gate, manned by two citizen volunteers. One of them must have recognized their party because he quickly shoved the other guard out of the way, waving them through without challenge. It was against protocol, but Luke wasn't about to complain if it got them to the King and back on the road to Ralador faster.

"I should have gotten a Coven Mark," Emma muttered, pinching her lips together.

They raced past unlit homes. Glancing at the moons, Luke estimated the time near midnight, and halfheartedly, he hoped their clamor wouldn't wake the sleeping residents.

At the entrance to the citadel, a witch and a soldier—real ones, this time—blocked their way, staff and claymore ready.

"Let us pass," Argent commanded with an authority Luke had never heard from him before.

It took the guards a moment to recognize the Prince, but once they did, they stepped aside without another word. Distrust flickered across their faces.

The clip-clop of hooves echoed mightily through the tunnel between the courtyard and the inner ward, announcing their entry better than any town crier could at this time of night. Luke dismounted, lifting Magdalin into his arms, not bothering with magic. He barely took five steps toward the infirmary staircase before the doors crashed open, Sargateth Rishon storming toward them, his face an agonizing mix of relief and rage so tightly wound that Luke's heart hurt.

Sargateth leaped over the last six steps, bounding across the enchanted tiles to scoop his wife from Luke's arms. "Mag," he sobbed into her neck. "Oh, Mag, thank the Lord you're alive!"

Luke hesitated to interrupt, but Argent pushed past him, speaking with Sargateth in low tones. Luke couldn't hear what he said, but Sargateth's demeanor shifted almost as quickly as he could change forms. "Follow me," he ordered.

Luke, Emma, and Argent unloaded their things from their saddlebags and hurried after Sargateth up the stairs to the infirmary.

"Is anyone else awake?" Emma asked, jogging to match the Ancient's stride. Magdalin clung to her husband, her face tucked into the side of his chest. A door flew open in front of them, responding to Sargateth's silent magic.

"Just Renault," he said, his deep baritone soothing Luke's frayed nerves, despite the fact they hadn't done anything to help Bethany yet. They entered the main ward of the infirmary, usually Magdalin's domain. It sat mostly empty, occupied by a few sleeping witches and healers who hadn't been conscripted into service.

Renault sat on the edge of a bed, scowling at a healer who dabbed yellow paste on his bruised cheekbone. When he looked up, he shoved the healer away, jumping to his feet.

"Thank God," Renault breathed. "Magdalin."

Sargateth set his wife down on the bed Renault had vacated. "Ren, go wake Tomás and the King. We must discuss a matter more urgent than my wife's return."

Renault stared hard at his uncle but didn't question the order. He ran from the infirmary, the door slamming behind him.

Sargateth's hands trembled as he tended to his wife. Finally, Magdalin grasped his wrists, stilling his motion. "Breathe, my Storm. Breathe."

Luke gave them a moment before he filled Sargateth in on how they had found her, what he'd seen in her initial projection, and her traumatic transformation back into her human form.

Grief pulled at Sargateth's face as he sat heavily on her bedside, her hand in both of his. "You—oh, you haven't been in that form since—since the war," he choked, stroking her hair. Her eyes fluttered shut under his touch. "Oh, my Heart, I am so sorry I could not find you." He bent over her in the protective embrace of a man clearly devoted to his wife. Magdalin's eyes remained closed, a sad smile tugging at the corner of her lips.

"Mountains," she whispered, murmuring her suspicions about her brother's captivity as if the effort to speak exhausted her even more.

Luke, Emma, and Argent sat wordlessly on the bed next to them, watching and waiting, itching with impatience as Renault fetched two of the most powerful men in Renova. Luke fidgeted, opening and closing his journal, re-reading the words and feeling his heart clench and break over and over again. Every glance at Sargateth and Magdalin filled him with longing.

Eons later, the door clicked open again with Renault in the lead. King Aragon swept in, less ruffled than one might expect for someone woken in the middle of the night, and Tomás wheeled himself behind them, face somber. Luke shot to his feet, nervous and hyped.

King Aragon barely acknowledged his son, instead glancing at Argent in the most disappointing show of fatherly affection Luke had ever seen. The Prince shifted on the bed, fingers flexing as if he wanted to touch Emma. Luke forced himself to look away.

"Magdalin Skyheart," King Aragon said, sounding relieved, though Luke couldn't tell if it was genuine. The King's unwillingness to let Sargateth search for her had weakened Luke's opinion of how much he valued Magdalin's life. "Returned at last."

Sargateth sat up, still holding his wife's hand. "Bite your tongue," he said, his words poison between them. "Her survival is a miracle in spite of you."

Luke couldn't breathe. He wanted nothing less than to interrupt a scathing argument between the King of Renova and the Mage once known as Merlin... but Bethany was in danger. "Bethany's coven is under attack, captured, or killed. She sent a message asking for help." Luke held out his journal, again not caring about their privacy if it meant they could send a rescue mission immediately. "We have to leave right now."

King Aragon frowned, his face still twisted in response to Sargateth's bitter words. "Absolutely not," he said without preamble. "I will not risk the Seventh Sorceress *or* her Sentinel on a foolhardy quest into enemy lands."

Luke's heart dropped to the floor, unable to believe the King's decree. "We risked our lives to help the Trident—"

"Silence," King Aragon commanded, his eyes flashing. "You snuck to the Trident without permission, which I could consider an act of treason."

"My girlfriend's *life* is in danger. I can't just—"

Emma gently touched Luke's forearm. Her stony, cobalt eyes glinted with power in the low light as she stared down the King, letting Luke's words hang over them.

Luke suddenly understood exactly how Sargateth had felt for the past eighteen months. While he didn't know why Emma wanted him to stop arguing, he let himself trust her instincts and shut up.

"Father—" Argent rose to his feet, his face an odd mixture of hope and resignation. "Father, please let us—"

King Aragon raised his eyebrows, his eyes widening. "It's *us*, now, is it? Even if I dared approve such a reckless endeavor, I wouldn't allow *you* to put yourself in harm's way with them."

Argent clenched his fists. "Then what was the point of letting me go to Helcari? How could going after Bethany be any more dangerous than storms, tsunamis, and the occasional Kraken?"

Luke heard a gasp from the far end of the ward. Queen Amity had woken up, her blonde hair a wild mess around her thin face. She hurried over to them, wrapping her only remaining son in her arms so tightly Luke thought Argent might object. But the Prince relaxed into his mother's embrace, his jaw clamped and eyes squeezed shut. Amity stroked his hair, rocking him.

"Kraken?" she murmured, and Argent nodded against her shoulder. She held him tighter before pulling away to examine him at arm's length. "I'm so glad to see you whole."

Despite the tender mother-son moment, King Aragon's face hadn't changed, and distaste crawled in Luke's mouth.

Emma took the opportunity to recount their journey, emphasizing all the bad things that happened along the way. While she talked, Sargateth conjured a medical projection above his wife's body, beckoning Amity over to help him make sense of it.

Nerves misfiring, Magdalin's semi-healed injuries still throbbed in constant pain. During a lull in Emma's story, Luke told Sargateth as much, but the Olis nodded, apparently already aware. Magdalin struggled to keep her eyes open, watching the tense group. "It's called psychosomosis on Earth," Luke said, and Sargateth turned to look at him. "Real pain or real healing all coming from the mind. It's a trauma response."

Sargateth's eyes flashed, and he turned to the King as if it was his fault.

King Aragon must have sensed the Olis's rebellion brewing beneath the surface. "Sargateth, Renault, keep these three from leaving the city."

Luke didn't think Sargateth could look any angrier, but his face became downright terrifying, loathing spreading across his normally friendly features. Luke turned toward his father, disappointed that Tomás hadn't disagreed or argued with anything the King had said thus far. "Dad, why haven't you said anything?"

Tomás sighed, shrugging rather helplessly. "I'm so sorry, both of you." He held out his hands, and Luke and Emma took hold, their mutual fear for Bethany's life now tangible. "With three covens gone, I understand the King's hesitance to let anyone else risk their lives searching for them."

Emma actually stomped her foot in frustration. "We *have* to go after them! What if Mom's there? You would leave her to fend for herself, even if whoever is behind this has captured three whole covens?"

At the mention of his wife, doubt crept into Tomás's features. He glanced at King Aragon, whose curt shake of the head was enough to subdue him. His voice cracked. "I'm sorry."

Emma wrenched her hand from her father's, her mouth turning down. Luke sensed her power crackling beneath her skin, and he actually felt sorry for King Aragon. But she said nothing, and Luke wondered.... *What if the woman in purple is in Ralador?*

"Now, if there's nothing else to discuss," Aragon said, challenging them all to speak up, "then we're done here." He waited half a second before he turned on his heel, sweeping out of the infirmary. The door slammed behind him, and the following silence overpowered the room.

"Why is he doing this?" Argent asked, voice ragged. "It's like he wants Bethany to die—like he wants us to hate him."

Queen Amity kissed her son's brow, a sigh of defeat escaping her lips. "He has ceased taking my counsel, Argent. He believes he's acting in Renova's best interest."

"More like *his* best interest," Emma muttered, not bothering to pretend she hadn't said it when Amity frowned at her. She met the eyes of everyone in the room, last of all Magdalin. Finally, Emma seized Luke and Argent, dragging them out of the infirmary without a word.

CHAPTER NINETEEN
ARTHUR'S GROVE

Argent thought Emma was taking them to the Artair Apartments, but instead, she turned into the library, quietly creeping between the stacks and into an alcove by the western tower. As soon as they all huddled inside it, Luke cast an anti-detection ward.

"What's the plan?" Luke asked, side-eyeing Argent.

Argent averted his gaze, the Prophet's heterochromia making him uncomfortable.

Emma took a deep breath. "We get a few hours of sleep. Then we create a distraction so we can sneak out."

Argent's eyebrows rose. "That could work."

She smiled, her tired eyes red with lack of sleep. "I want to get going as much as the two of you, but we didn't stop for long the past few days. It's a miracle we're all alive."

"It would be better to leave under cover of darkness," Luke said, impatient.

Emma rested a hand on his arm, and he stilled. "We won't do Bethany any good if we don't get some rest. We have to gather supplies, anyway. Make a list based on anything you gleaned from Bethany about their path, as well as the fact that we'll be traveling through the lava tunnels for most of the way."

"So, no horses," Luke said, grumpy. "Walking over a hundred miles in the dark is not the fastest way there."

Argent nodded in agreement. "You're right. It's not. But it's the only way to get into Valona undetected. I'll bet that all the covens went missing near the underground borders of the capital."

Luke's eyes narrowed. "And you would know this because...?"

Emma took a step toward Argent as if to protect him. He appreciated it, but he would have to learn how to handle his own subjects sooner or later. He tapped his temple, sick that he had to reveal this to anyone but Emma. "While Septim is dead, he left his memories behind."

Luke recoiled. "You're serious?"

Emma slipped her hand into Argent's, his fingers burning where they touched. Absently, he wondered if she'd created fire unintentionally. "I wish he hadn't. He did many terrible things long before he possessed me. But yes, I know the tunnels that will get us into the dungeons of Valona, if we can make it that far."

"Fine," Luke said, rubbing his stubbly chin. "We'll deal with your *foreign* memories later."

Argent squeezed Emma's hand before she could get into another fight with her brother. "I know a secret way out of the city."

"Not that they're much good while in ruins, but what about the walls?" Emma asked.

Argent shook his head. "The path I'm thinking of leads *beneath* the walls. The entrance is inside the Royal Apartments, and those will be tricky to sneak into if my parents are still there."

"So we can't go tonight," Luke reasoned. "Emma, I hope your distraction is a good one."

Emma rubbed her hands together as if hatching a grand conspiracy. "Let's get some shut-eye and meet back here in about five hours."

Morgan Le Fay barged into the Royal Apartments at close to six in the morning, before the King or Queen usually awoke. Her angry, hawklike voice echoed down the hall, where Argent, Emma, and Luke waited with their traveling supplies, hidden from others under Emma's invisibility web.

"Fool of a king! Never in my service to the Pendragon throne have I been as disgusted with my regent's decisions as I am with yours! How dare you keep my brother from going to his wife as soon as he felt her return? How dare you mistreat our oaths to your forebears? How dare—"

"Morgan, get out!" The King roared.

"Now," Argent urged, and the three of them crept to the open door, slipping inside.

The Royal Apartments were nearly four times larger than the Artair's. A massive common area filled the space between the main door and the rear rooms. On the right, the door to Argent's suite remained closed from when he'd snuck out that morning. The door on the left led to what had once been his brother Adam's room—the room where an assassin had slit Adam's throat, igniting the Valon War.

Morgan stood in the center of the common area, arguing with the King. Queen Amity sat in an armchair by the hearth, weariness painted across her face.

Argent tiptoed to the open middle door. He hesitated before entering, loath to invade his parents' private domain.

If they went through the secret passage, they couldn't come back without the missing covens.

A bed swallowed much of the space inside the King and Queen's room. A recessed alcove shelf ran along the side wall, filled with various trinkets and trophies from Aragon's battles throughout the years. Argent stuck his hand toward the back of the left side shelf, fingers searching for the etched rune that controlled the stone door leading to the escape tunnel. Finding it, he pressed down with three fingers. A tiny green glow shone briefly against the backsplash of the shelf, a grinding sounding behind him.

Argent led them to the wardrobe resting against the far wall, near the curve of the southeastern tower. He opened the wardrobe, pushing aside his mother's dresses until he found smooth wood. He searched for the seam along the side, discovering a tiny latch.

Dim runes lit the stone passage. The hole was big enough for a fully armored man to crawl through, and beyond the gap, a secret staircase led down to their destination.

"In," Argent said. Emma went first without hesitation, disappearing into the hole with her things. Luke gave him a hard look before he vanished into the darkness. Argent carefully closed the wardrobe door, sealing himself inside. While he could shut the rear of the wardrobe, he couldn't close the stone panel without the rune. But it wouldn't matter. By the time his father realized what they'd done—what he'd done—they would be far away.

They sped down the stairs, their breaths the only sound. The air cooled as they entered the underground tunnel, the dirt walls supported by thick metal girders. Every twenty minutes or so, Argent opened a heavy iron door, each of them swinging open at his touch.

"Why are there no keys?" Luke asked after Argent pushed open the second door.

"They recognize Pendragon blood," Argent grunted. He showed Luke his palm, speckled with blood from the tiny razor-sharp spikes that sat in place of door handles. Its coppery scent mixed with their earthy surroundings.

"That's barbaric," Emma said, grabbing Argent's wrist and holding it up to the light in her other hand. "How many more doors are there?"

"Until we reach Arthur's Grove, perhaps two or three more."

"Your hand will be mincemeat by then!"

Argent shrugged. "It's payment. We're not supposed to use this escape tunnel except for major emergencies. Father will never forgive me for using it, but if he were in his right mind, he wouldn't have tried to stop us from leaving in the first place. It's sheer luck that he singled out Sargateth and

Renault last night. If he hadn't, Morgan's vow would have prevented her from helping us." He pulled the door closed behind him, the lock clicking into place.

"Where is Arthur's Grove?" Luke asked, merely glancing at the Prince's bloody palm.

"Three miles beyond the city walls, close enough to the edge of the Valon Forest that we can slip into the trees before anyone sees us."

"And you're sure they won't follow?"

Argent's face hardened. "The only ones who could track us fast enough are the three people he won't let leave the city. My father made his decision... and I've made mine. We both must live with the consequences."

Three greedy doors later, Argent finally let Emma heal his hand. They paused for a moment near a dirt stairway spiraling toward the surface, Emma cradling his raw, trembling flesh while she knit the skin back together. Neither of them asked why Luke didn't do the healing because Argent suspected they both knew the answer.

Argent started. "Luke."

Luke's green and gold eyes glinted, reflecting light from Emma's floating balls. "What?"

"I—" The words stuck in his throat. "Thank you for saving my life. From the direwolf."

He raised an eyebrow, but his face otherwise remained unmoved.

"He says 'you're welcome,'" Emma answered in Luke's place, shouldering past them to climb her way out of the passage.

"Wait, Emma, let me go up first." Argent rushed to take the lead. "This needs payment as well."

She frowned. "Then why did you let me heal you just now?"

Argent grimaced. "It's a different kind of payment but still something only a Pendragon can provide."

"Whoever designed this escape tunnel did not understand the meaning of haste," Luke grumbled. "Every minute we stall is another minute Bethany could get into worse trouble."

Argent heard Luke's silent avoidance of the words *Bethany could be dead*, but he wasn't about to point that out. Privately, he agreed with Luke's assessment. One of his long-dead ancestors—one of the more mentally unstable ones—had commissioned the tunnel, reasoning that even if an enemy ever made it past either entrance, they would get stuck unless they had royal blood. Even so, he could think of plenty of hostage-or-death situations that would provide such an enemy with the necessary blood.

It crossed Argent's mind that his father's paranoia might not be so poorly placed.

Climbing up the staircase, he reached a thatch of thick vines in the shape of a trapdoor. The vines rustled at him, hissing and speaking to him.

Son of Dragon's Blood, the vines whispered, sounding like snakes in his head, *stands bloodless at the gate.*

"What do you require of me?" he said aloud.

A royal memory sacrificed to fate.

Argent frowned. That hadn't been mentioned in the lessons. "A memory?"

"It wants a memory from you?" Emma asked, confused. "I agree with Luke. Whoever made this tunnel—"

Argent quickly shushed her, his finger hovering over his lips. He didn't want to give the vines a reason to imprison them—if that indeed was what they did when insulted. He wracked his brain, considering the stipulation that the memory be *royal*.

"Will I lose this memory forever?" The vines wriggled, and it took the Prince a moment to realize they were laughing.

Seek ye sunlight yon this cage, a potent mem'ry sate.

Argent rubbed his temple. "It's speaking in rhymes and wants a royal memory in exchange for letting us pass." He stepped away from the vines, leaning against the wall of the narrow channel.

"Did you know it would ask for that?" Luke glared at the wriggling vines as if wondering whether he could ask Emma to blast them into smithereens.

Argent shook his head. "I knew that it required payment, but not the specifics. This tunnel has only been used once or twice in the past five hundred years." His eyes turned to Emma.

She stared at him, her eyes wide with fear. "No," she said. "You can't give that up."

"What?" Luke asked, his eyes darting between them. "Whatever it is, we have to get through this thing yesterday."

Argent sighed, running a hand through his hair. *No, Emma, I won't give that up. Not for anything.* "I have few memories that meet the requirements," he admitted, his heart heavy.

He cursed his crazy ancestor and his own rashness for leading here. But only he could pay this price, and they didn't have time to double back. Sargateth and Renault would surely catch them if they surfaced within the city walls.

Before the Valon War, his older brother Adam Pendragon had been the light of Argent's life. He looked up to him, wanted to be like him, and craved his approval. Adam, in turn, had protected him, played with him, and taught him archery.

In his favorite memory of Adam, the two of them perched together at sunset on top of the highest turret over the citadel keep. Adam had snuck them up there after Argent's bedtime, and they shared one of the cook's famous cracked chocolate cookies. He couldn't remember whatever they had talked about, shrouded by time and trauma. But he remembered how he felt that night, leaning against his brother's side, content and safe with the whole western kingdom bathed in the red-orange glow of the sun. Adam, the man who was supposed to be King, loved him more than Argent ever truly appreciated.

With a jolt, he stopped the memory in its tracks.

Potent. Royal.

Could I offer it Septim's death?

Loath as he was to revisit that memory, Argent forced himself to visualize the clearing where Agamemnon Septim had once pitched his white battlefield tent, a testament to his sure victory in the final months of the Valon War.

Heart thundering desperately, Argent wished he could avoid the waking vision, but determined, he pushed on. His companions dissolved, the world shifting around him until he stood inside that accursed tent, surrounded by unnecessary opulence for a front-line command station.

Argent looked down at himself and, one horrible heartbeat later, realized he was experiencing the memory as if he *was* Septim. Until today, that had only happened in his nightmares.

Two men lounged in nearby chairs, biting grapes right off a cluster, the purple juices staining their thin beards. Septim sensed a change in the atmosphere outside, his lips curling into a malevolent grin. He drew his sword, inlaid with pulsing runes as black as his heart. "Ah. We have company."

The tent flap exploded, tattered shreds littering the ground. King Aragon Pendragon charged inside, dressed in full armor, Excalibur already swinging in the close quarters. Septim blocked the strike as if bored... toying with his prey. But the woman who entered next made him snarl. Elaine Artair's short white hair framed her face, a stark contrast to her jet-black armor. Six chevrons marked each pauldron, the triquetra of Renova's Royal Coven pulsing against her throat.

"You brought a *woman* to this fight, Pendragon?" Septim snarled, lifting his shield with more agility than any of his soldiers. Dark, dangerous power surged through his veins, flooding to his fingertips to charge his sword with deadly magic. "Too weak to finish me yourself, are you?" he taunted. His shield took Elaine's blast of magic, rage bleeding through his pores as he traded blows with King Aragon. Each time their steel met, dark stains crept over Excalibur's edge.

Pendragon didn't bother engaging in the conversation. Two more figures entered the tent, and, for a moment, Septim choked in fear. Both Olii—Sargateth Rishon *and* Morgan Le Fay—had ventured beyond the main battlefield to corner him. Septim spat at Aragon, the spittle landing on his rival's cheek.

"You *will* taste this same pain, Pendragon!" His shield cracked under the intense strain of Elaine's magic, now boosted by the Olii's powers. "You will never be free of me!" The shield exploded into a thousand splinters of light; his enchantments overpowered by their sheer force.

King Aragon kicked him to his knees, but the magic stopped. One final swipe from Camelot's ruler sent Septim's sword clattering away, out of reach. Excalibur's cold, sharp tip pressed beneath his chin, forcing him to look up at his conqueror.

Pendragon.

"Your life is *mine*," Aragon snarled, chest heaving.

Septim surged up, evil filling his entire being.

Aragon drove Excalibur down, pain beyond imagining erupting through Septim's body.

His vision swam, and the next thing Argent knew, Emma was holding his face in her hands, her frantic voice subdued as if she called to him from beneath a pool of water.

Slowly, his hearing came back. Argent reached his hands up to touch her wrists.

"Oh, thank God," she breathed, hanging her head in relief. "You—I don't know what happened. You just went out of it."

Luke stood nearby, an impatient look on his face as he tapped his wrist. Argent didn't understand what Luke's wrist had to do with it.

"A memory. Septim's," he muttered. "The last of his own, actually." A small silvery cloud floated from his forehead into the vines, sucked away.

We accept, the vines told him, unknotting themselves and slithering into the earthen walls until a simple wooden hatch appeared.

Argent shook off the odd sensation of losing a memory and carefully lifted the door, squinting and blinking hard, a bright shaft of sunlight blinding him. Adjusting to the light, he crawled through, emerging in the middle of a tight copse. A massive stone sat to one side, covered in a thick mat of green-blue moss, a thin scar the size of a sword's blade near its middle.

Arthur's Grove.

CHAPTER TWENTY

INTO DARKNESS

Argent didn't let them linger. While he had been to the grove a few times, he'd never tried to uncover the secret entrance into the escape tunnel. Regardless, as soon as the trapdoor closed behind Luke, the vines slithered back in place and the vegetation settled into such good camouflage that, if Argent hadn't known exactly where to look, he never would have found it.

But that was the point, he supposed—it was meant for escaping the castle, not entering it.

The edge of the Valon Forest stretched along the horizon about a quarter of a mile away. It was still early, just after sunrise, the city slowly waking up in the distance. This far away, they couldn't tell if anyone had raised the alarm.

"We can make that," Luke said, scanning the fields and distant farmhouses where smoke puffed from the chimneys, the only possibility of someone seeing them flee into the trees.

"Let me make us invisible," Emma interrupted before Luke could take off. She performed the same magic that got them into the Royal Apartments undetected, and they sprinted across the soft grass, the wind whipping at their faces.

Argent was out of breath by the time they reached the trees, and he had to stop. Leaning against a trunk, he pressed a hand to his side, where the direwolf had raked his ribs. Emma and Luke skidded to a halt beside him.

"What's wrong?" Emma asked. She eyed his hand placement, then turned to Luke. "Did you heal him completely?"

"Of course I did," Luke protested. "Want me to double-check?"

Argent heard the obvious sarcasm, but Emma nodded anyway.

Luke rolled his eyes. "Fine." He cast a projection, and Argent experienced the strangest apparition of his life—an outline of himself, standing right next to him, the scars from the direwolf's claws a faded yellow against his frame. Luke frowned. "That shouldn't be there," he said.

Emma's face tightened. "Are your healing skills getting worse, too?"

"Hey!" Luke protested, but his heart clearly wasn't in it. Something else was happening. Argent was sure of it. Despite the Prophet's insistence that he hadn't let the shield down on purpose, Argent sensed a deeper layer of turmoil. "I did my best with what I had on the road," Luke continued. "I can try re-healing you now, but you'll have to let me see and touch your skin."

Argent shook his head. "I'll live with it. We need to get moving."

"If you can't keep up...."

"It won't slow me down. I promise," Argent insisted, gesturing for them to move. "The closest entrance to the lava tunnels is that way."

As Luke scouted, the loamy scent of dirt and moss filled Argent's lungs. Squirrels chattered in the tall branches, a sign of spring emerging, and new buds grew on the deciduous trees more common near the edges of the forest. As they pushed inward, the trunks grew closer together, the path shrinking into a game trail.

Emma slipped her arm around Argent's waist, leaning into his side as they walked. "Do you know which memory the vines took?"

Argent clung to her comfort. "One of Septim's. It's odd—I've had so many night terrors of the day my father killed Septim in these very woods, but now recalling those is difficult. The trapdoor must have taken the source memory." He thought about his next words for a long moment, wondering how to say them. "Septim forced me to almost kill my father in the very same manner. When Father looks at me now, I wonder if he thinks he failed."

Luke glanced over his shoulder. "Are we even going in the right direction?"

Argent pushed his heavy emotions away. "Yes. We're nearly there."

"Is this how Septim's army got here last time?" Luke asked sharply.

"I—yes. It worked so well before."

"Who else knows about these entrances?"

Puzzled, Argent frowned. "I thought *you* did. Besides the soldiers who used them, and the Royal Coven, I don't think anyone else knows."

"They weren't blocked to prevent another invasion?" Luke pressed.

"This one was, yes, after what happened two years ago. I imagine Morgan approved its reopening to send the covens to Ralador. Otherwise, they would be crossing above ground and facing infinitely more danger the closer they got to the Deadwoods and eventually, Valona. There are other lava tubes beneath Renova, but if others are still open, they would be difficult to find." Argent climbed over a fallen log, scanning for the landmarks near the tunnel's entrance. Finding the twisted tree trunk, he pointed. "There. We're close."

They found the tube's opening, a dark cave sunken into the ground, its walls the sharp black of cooled lava.

"Over a hundred miles in there?" Holding tension in his jaw, the muscles in Luke's neck jumped. "What are we waiting for?"

As daylight diminished with every step, Emma conjured balls of light. Three tiny orbs bobbed above them, illuminating their path with long shadows that gave Argent an eerie feeling. She rolled up her sleeves, exposing her incredibly detailed birthmark. Argent knew it stretched up to her neck and across her chest, but it had yet to bleed all the way down her left arm. The black and blue pulsed over her skin, the blue becoming brighter the longer he stared at it. Her white tesseract gleamed, providing another, smaller light in the gloom.

"Never thought I'd be reduced to a glow-in-the-dark lamp," Emma muttered, stepping carefully over sharp rocks and other debris.

"Comes in handy, though," Luke said from the front.

"It won't be necessary the whole way," Argent said as they rounded a bend, leaving them with only the haunting, yellow light from Emma's magic. "Active lava flows still exist near the border. It will get brighter and hotter."

"I've always wanted to see a lava flow up close," Emma said. "Never got the chance on Earth."

Argent shuddered. "I can't imagine why. Too many strange creatures live in or near the flows. When Septim first cleared these passages, he killed more than he could count."

"What kind of creatures? Like the ones from Langoth?"

Argent shook his head. "All native to Talahm. Subterranean creatures differ so much from the ones that live above ground. Just seeing them in Septim's memories is... unpleasant."

They picked their way through the tunnel for several miles, passing offshoots and branching paths until a glimmer of daylight shone onto the ground ahead.

Argent frowned, shifting the pack on his shoulders. "That's not right," he muttered.

"Did we take the wrong tunnel?" Luke demanded, kicking a rock down the tube. The muted clatter echoed back.

"No... but this collapse is new. The earthquakes must have weakened the ceiling enough for the surface to break through." Cracked trees, mounds of dirt, and forest-floor debris had spilled down from the surface, punctured by the shaft of light through the new mouth of the tunnel. The collapse blocked their way forward, and Argent came to a sinking conclusion. They would need to backtrack and find another way through.

"So we turn around," Luke announced, sounding displeased and frustrated. "Take a different branch. They all lead to Ralador, right?"

"Theoretically," Argent said, not sure about his answer. He pointed toward the collapsed section. "This is the path that Septim's army used both times. If we continue south, the tunnels should lead us into Ralador."

"The covens must have made it that far," Emma reasoned, her magic lights washed out by the natural glow spilling into the tunnel ahead of them. "Bethany's coven did, at least. Luke, did she lay out directions when she sent you updates?"

Luke tugged his pack to the front of his body and rummaged inside for the journal. He flipped it open, scanning the last few pages. "A few, but not a step-by-step map." He stared into the distance for a moment. "Can we track the way they went?"

A skittering noise came from ahead, near the debris pile. They took several steps back, hiding in the shadows as Emma extinguished her lights. Argent's heart hammered when a lizard-like creature the size of a chicken came into view, counterbalanced by a long whip-like tail.

"Is that... a *dinosaur?*" Emma breathed.

Argent pushed them back the way they'd come and turned down the first available branch. He tripped in the darkness, stumbling into Luke. The Prophet grunted.

"Lights," Argent mumbled, and the three balls popped into existence again. They shielded their eyes from the sudden brightness. The creature hadn't seemed to follow them, and Argent considered it sheer luck that they'd stumbled through the darkness without killing themselves in the process. Jagged edges loomed all along the walls and ground.

"Argent, *was that a dinosaur?*"

He caught his breath. "I have no idea what a dinosaur is, but I'd love it if you told me. I've certainly never seen that before."

"It doesn't matter, Emma," Luke said. "We're nowhere near Ralador and already off the path we needed to take." He shot Argent a glare, and the Prince's stomach tightened. "Can we track Bethany's coven?"

"Give me a minute," Emma replied, sucking in a deep breath. She closed her eyes, holding the breath for a few seconds before blowing it out her mouth. She held out her hands in front of her, curling them as if around an invisible rope. A moment later, soft blue shimmers blossomed in front of them, turning into a path of footprints.

"You're incredible," Argent breathed in awe.

"We're in the right place, then," Luke said, satisfied. He started down the tube again, and Emma and Argent followed.

"Can you hold this magic for long?" Argent asked, his hand hovering over the small of Emma's back.

"I'll manage as long as I need to," she replied. "This isn't as hard as raising the barriers in the Trident. It's just... different. Honestly, I don't know if I'm making up my own spells or if other witches can do this too."

Argent helped her around a boulder in the middle of the tube, squeezing past the sharp walls. "After this is over," he said, trying to keep his voice low so Luke wouldn't overhear, even if Argent expected him to anyway thanks to the tunnel's acoustics, "I would appreciate it if you and I could find a way to suppress Septim's memories."

"Even if they prove useful for things like this?" Emma asked, frowning.

"They make it harder to separate myself from him," he whispered. "The things he's done.... I don't want those memories corrupting what I do with my life. I don't want to become like him, Emma. I have terrible memories that do not belong to me."

She tightened her grip on his hand. "It'll be more than just sharing thoughts. Are you okay with that?"

Argent nodded, knowing what it would mean. She'd see his most private thoughts, the part of his mind that he tried to avoid entirely. But if she could help, it would be worth it. And if she decided that he was too far gone.... Well, he would deal with that if it happened. For now, he held onto the hope that Emma could help him deal with the aftermath of possession. No one else in Camelot had even offered.

Emma maintained the tracking magic for several hours, but it must have been near nightfall when she finally released all her magic. She leaned into Argent, avoiding the dangerous walls. Her birthmark became their only light source, the darkness beyond them even more foreboding.

"Let's rest for a while," Argent suggested. Even in the dim light, he could see bags under Luke's eyes, evidence of the Prophet's exhaustion despite his determination to navigate all the tunnels in one go. "We won't do Bethany any good if we use up all our strength before we even reach the border."

Luke seemed displeased, but he dropped his pack in agreement, finding a less-uncomfortable spot on the ground where he wouldn't accidentally stab himself on the lava rocks. "Wake me up if any weird underground creatures attack us," he said, closing his eyes.

Argent and Emma sat together a few feet away, leaning against each other. He savored the warmth of her body soaking into his side, each brush of skin threatening to bring him to tears. Six years captive in his own mind had left him starved for physical touch, never experiencing it as his own when Septim had been in control. In the two years since... almost no one wanted to let him get close enough, save for his mother. That Emma actually wanted to touch him, sit next to him, hold him.... He took in a deep breath, trying to calm his emotions.

"When you said you had to give up a memory," Emma started, her voice a whisper, "I thought—"

"I would not give that up for *anyone*, least of all a mat of magic vines," Argent reassured her. He wrapped his arm around her shoulders, her head resting against his chest. He would cling to the memory of his first kiss, their first kiss, forever, as the moment he started to realize that hope existed. "I would not give up what you've given me, even if it meant people knew the truth about what happened with Septim."

He must have startled her into silence. Darkness pressed against them, held at bay only by the gleam of her birthmark. Emma relaxed into him, and soon, he fell asleep, replaying the memory of their kiss in his mind.

CHAPTER TWENTY-ONE
BENEATH VALONA

Emma lost track of how long they'd trekked underground. As they traveled further south, the air grew heavier, wetter, and hotter. Bits of ash floated through the air, and soon entire embers drifted around them. The ones Emma couldn't avoid stung as they landed on her skin.

The floor of the tunnel sloped downward, descending deeper underground as they approached the border between Renova and Ralador. Dull, red light broke the darkness around the bend ahead of them, the tunnel's temperature increasing with every step. The underground network opened into a cavern cut through the middle by a literal river of lava. It flowed sluggishly, magma bubbles popping over the surface before melting back into the stream.

Emma touched her fingers to her throat and willed herself cold, a thin layer of magic drawing the heat away from her body. Without asking, she did the same for Argent and Luke. Their questioning glances were answered when the magic took hold.

Luke breathed a sigh of relief, sweat pouring down his temples. "How do we get across? Another bridge?"

On the other side of the lava river, the darkened entrances to three more tubes branched off into the distance—three more options for getting lost. Emma renewed her tracking spell, but the trail disappeared in front of the river, and she couldn't see the other side. "I don't want to waste strength making a bridge from that." It would take too much energy to force it to cool down fast enough.

"We can't jump it." Luke peered over the edge, backing away when a magma bubble sent up a burst of steam.

Emma lifted herself into the air, the magic almost effortless compared to raising those rocks from the depths of Trident Bay. She flew across the river, enjoying the indignant expression on Luke's face when she landed on the other side.

"Show off!"

"Brace yourselves," she yelled back, lifting her hands toward them. She brought Luke across first, sweating by the time she set him down. "Put a shield over the river," she commanded, thankful when he obeyed immediately. They could barely see the gold membrane between the air and the lava, but her heart skipped a beat when Argent wobbled as she levitated him across. She didn't release her breath until Argent's feet hit the uneven floor next to her.

"Please don't do that again," Luke asked, voice strained. The shield flickered out of existence.

"I will if I have to," Emma retorted. She turned toward the three tunnels, reactivating her tracking spell... but no tracks appeared. Ignoring her brother and the Prince, she approached the entrances, frowning.

"What is it?" Luke asked.

She didn't look at him. "It feels different."

"Magically?"

She nodded, drawn to the tunnel on the right. "I think it's this one."

"Great, let's go," Luke said, striding forward.

"Luke, wait—"

"Come on!" he snapped, adjusting his backpack straps. "We've wasted enough time as it is. Bethany's counting on us—"

The mouth of the new tunnel shimmered with disturbed magic as soon as he passed its threshold. Luke fell forward, collapsing to his knees and rolling onto his side, out of reach.

Emma screamed.

Argent wrapped his arms around her waist to stop her from rushing after her brother. "Emma, no!"

"Luke!"

"Emma!" Argent forced her to look at him, but she could barely see his face, too concerned for Luke to focus. "Are you sure that's the right way in?"

She nodded, choked up. "I have to go after him."

He smoothed her hair, the ridges of his fingertips rough against her skin. "I know. I will follow you no matter what, but I want you to be sure."

Emma took a deep breath, heat from the lava making it through her cooling magic, her lungs protesting. "I'm sure."

Argent gently released her, his hand at the small of her back as they both approached the now-visible magical membrane stretching across the mouth of the tunnel. Luke didn't move except for his breathing, and—she squinted—his eyes rapidly moved beneath closed lids. Whatever had happened, Luke now appeared to be dreaming.

Emma went to the edge of the tunnel, closing her eyes as she searched with her magic for a way to defuse the trap so she and Argent wouldn't have to suffer the same effects as Luke. She found no anchor nor any obvious way to dismantle it.

"What did you find?" Argent asked when she opened her eyes.

"Nothing," she croaked, her voice thick. "I don't know what it is—can't break it or even go around it."

"So...."

She shuddered. "I follow and see what happens." She straightened, throwing her shoulders back in a show of strength. "Don't come through until I tell you to."

"Emma...." Argent touched her shoulder. "I'm not going to stay behind."

She turned to hug him, his leather jerkin warm, absorbing the ambient heat. "It's not to leave you behind. That trap is affecting Luke's mind. Please... if it does to me what it did to Luke, wait until I'm conscious before you follow."

Argent swallowed hard, his arms tightening around her. "If you insist."

She held on for a beat longer, then whirled away from him, marching through the tunnel's threshold before she lost her nerve. She'd walked through Septim's curse over Camelot—she could walk through this.

Almost instantly, her awareness dimmed, and she crumbled to the ground, landing awkwardly beside her brother. Argent paced, his face drawn in panic, one hand pressed against his sore ribs.

Emma tried to pull herself to her feet, but her eyes fluttered shut, and she became captive to her own nightmares.

Her worst memory.

She heard the twang of Argent's bow across the expanse of Camelot's courtyard, the dull thud as the arrow hit her father in the chest. Felt the redness of her anger, the taunts and goading that caused her to snap and channel enough magic to destroy everything in her path. Felt that magic surging through her palms, her fingertips, white hot as it slammed into Argent's shield, her desperate attempt to stop Septim from completing his takeover. She saw Ebony Reva, her teacher and almost-friend, barreling in to take the brunt of the magic, her body unable to absorb it.

Over and over it played, from the moment the arrow left the bow until Ebony tumbled like a ragdoll to the flagstones, her body smoking and damaged, dead before she hit the ground.

Every second reminded her that she had taken a life.

She could barely breathe, stuck in the memory, captive to it, disabled and helpless.

But she had lived this nightmare before. Many times. She knew how it ended—knew how it made her feel. Slowly, Emma found the edges of reality, the hard, sharp ridges of the cooled lava tunnel pressing into her back, the warmth of the air against her face, and the sound of Argent's panicked pacing a few feet away. She stretched her awareness further and heard Luke's shallow breathing, felt her own weight—the heaviness in her limbs. Reality. She grounded herself, and, moment by moment, she pulled herself out of the magic-induced nightmare.

Argent stopped pacing. "Emma!"

She rolled onto her knees. Luke had yet to escape his torment, and she couldn't fathom which of his Visions he might be reliving over and over again. He'd had so many terrible ones.

But Argent.... *Oh no! He has Septim's memories*—she couldn't even finish the thought before the Prince rushed into the trap. He fell to his knees, collapsing onto his side. Emma scrambled over to him, cursing under her breath as she stroked the hair from his temple. "Oh Argent, why didn't you wait?" Reluctantly, she went to help Luke first.

Luke's breathing turned more shallow, more rapid. His eyes darted beneath closed lids, sweat coating his brow. Emma crouched over him, taking his face in her hands, his beard tickling her palms. She bowed her head, closing her eyes and reaching out with her magic. Emma didn't want to see into her brother's mind, but it happened anyway.

She tried to ignore the scene playing in her brother's head, averting her gaze every time Daniel's body hit the concrete floor of the power plant Luke used to work at on Earth. She called out to his consciousness, repeating his name until she sensed him waking up. Luke drew in a deep breath, starved for oxygen, coughing as he struggled for air.

Emma scrambled back to Argent where he lay motionless but for the light rise and fall of his chest, his face contorted in pain, skin clammy. Magic flowed through her fingertips, taking her into Argent's nightmares.

In it, Agamemnon Septim lay half-naked and spread-eagled at the center of a darkened stone chamber lit by a circle of candles. His back arched in pure agony as a tall, lithe woman paced along the edges of the room. She chanted from a book she held open in one hand, her other clenched tightly over a dark red crystal that pulsed in time with Septim's screams. Long, silver hair cascaded over her shoulders, an oddly appropriate parallel to Septim's shaggy gray locks.

Each time she glanced up from the grimoire, the flickering candlelight caught her abnormally youthful face. She reminded Emma of a portrait in Morgan's study, gleaming through the ages. Her glamour faded with each circuit, more and more of her magic filling the crystal. Emma finally noticed a deep cut on the woman's palm, blood feeding the gemstone as well. She left a red trail behind her as the drops splashed to the floor.

Finally, the woman entered the circle, kneeling at Septim's head. She painted a strange mark on his chest, his sweat smudging its edges. With one final chant, she placed the bloody crystal at the center of the mark. Septim's world exploded in excruciating, white-hot pain as magic flooded every cell, knit with his very being, and completed the final Blacksoul Ritual.

Her gift complete, the woman sagged to one side, a triumphant smile on her face. With one finger, she reached toward Septim's temple and let him believe she'd given him everything.

Disturbed, Emma grounded herself in reality, sensing the hard rocks against her knees, her fingers pressed against Argent's skin. Desperate to bring him back, she kissed his forehead, willing the magical trap to release its grasp on his mind. *Argent. Argent. Argent.*

After a minute, it worked. Argent's eyes popped open, and he took a deep, shuddering breath of hot air. He tried to sit up, scrabbling for purchase against the rock and then her. Emma wouldn't let him go, still holding either side of his face.

"Emma." His hands latched around her wrists, gently pulling her away.

They huddled against the wall, occasionally glancing toward the mouth of the tunnel, where the shimmering red glow of the lava filtered through the trap. Emma sat as close as she could to Argent, pressing her side against his. With her face against his chest, she relished the feeling of his arm around her shoulders. Luke sat a few feet away, his head in his hands, shoulders shaking.

Soon, the silence felt too heavy.

"That magic is not in Septim's repertoire," Argent finally breathed. In the silence, he sounded much louder than usual. He stroked Emma's hair, planting a kiss on her temple when she looked up at him.

"Is it in that woman's? Who is she?"

"What woman?" Luke grunted from beside them, hands still buried in his hair, face hidden.

Emma opened her mouth to explain but then reconsidered. She asked Argent with her thoughts. *Can I tell him?*

I trust you.

"He saw Septim receiving his powers from a witch."

Luke finally looked at them, his eyes bloodshot. Soot stained his cheeks. "Receiving? Not stealing from a bunch of acolytes?"

Argent coughed several times, pressing his hand against his wound. "That trap broke whatever block Septim had on the memory. I'd thought this whole time that he'd forced witches to sacrifice their magic for him... but I was wrong. A single, *very* powerful witch gave it to him freely. If she's still around, she'd be more than capable of imprisoning an Olis."

"Who?" Luke asked, scooting closer.

Emma squeezed her eyes shut, trying to remember. "I swear I've seen her portrait in Morgan's office. Younger, for sure, but definitely the same woman." She searched Argent's face for any sign of recognition. "Argent, do you know who she is?"

He shrugged. "No. I know the portrait, but Morgan has never mentioned her name, just that she's a—"

"A former apprentice," Luke finished. "I saw the same picture. Emma, she's the woman from my Vision."

Emma's stomach dropped through the floor. "If she gave Septim his powers...."

Luke's face spasmed, clearly battling something out inside his head. "We need to keep moving. We must be close." Luke's reddened eyes flickered to Argent. "Right?"

"Less than a day's walk," he answered, chest rumbling.

Luke struggled to his feet, pressing his hands against the wall to support his weight.

Emma rummaged through her bag for food and water, pausing at the journal she shared with her father. She'd forgotten about it for the past few days. Tentatively, she opened to the last page, her heart skipping a beat at her father's handwriting.

I know what you're up to. Stay safe. I love you.

Her throat tightened. Their quest was anything but safe, but they had to do it. For Bethany, for the covens, and maybe even for her mom. At that thought, Emma wanted to cry. It felt like so long ago that they'd talked over video, so long since Bethany frantically woke her with the news.

How long had her mom been missing now? She shoved the journal back in the bag, swinging it across her back. They walked into the darkness, now punctured by channels of bubbling lava on either side. A roadway into the bowels of hell.

And for all she knew, that's exactly where they were going.

Luke led, following the footsteps of Bethany's coven that showed up again now that they had passed the mind trap. Emma walked with Argent, wanting to talk about what had happened without making him feel worse. She must have projected her thoughts without realizing, because Argent's soft voice startled her.

"I never suspected someone else held more power than Septim," Argent said quietly, his eyes fixed on the floor, picking his way around the dislodged debris from the ceiling. "She played mind games with him. Explains why he took such pleasure in manipulating us."

Emma huffed in frustration, her birthmark tingling. She held it up like a flashlight. "I hate mind games. Using people as pawns. Breaking trust."

"I have a bad feeling that's exactly what's happened to Bethany," Argent admitted. "Especially if this woman got her hands on Bethany's journal."

Luke stiffened in front of them, but kept moving, squaring his shoulders and increasing his speed.

"We must prepare," Argent continued, his voice loud in the oppressive underground, "for everything we hope isn't true."

Those words rang in her ears for the final hours into Ralador. Each mile they covered brought anxiety, with more branching tunnels leading off into nothingness. The tracking spell kept them straight, leading inevitably toward the citadel of Valona, Ralador's capital. And, in the back of her mind, a thought niggled.

Why hadn't they encountered more of those strange creatures Argent had told them about?

CHAPTER TWENTY-TWO
THE CAPTIVES

"**S**omething's moving up ahead," Luke whispered, holding out a hand to slow them down.

Emma extinguished her magic, peering around the corner of the tunnel but unable to make sense of what she saw. A creature filled the entire diameter of the tunnel, pale flesh creating its own luminescence. Emma couldn't find the creature's eyes, but its mouth opened wide, exposing two massive fangs and a thick, undulating forked tongue.

Luke pressed them back against the sharp wall of the tube, conjuring a shield which, thankfully, stabilized immediately, the gold pane of magic altering how they saw the beast. "Back up," he whispered harshly, and they shuffled the way they'd come, trying to put distance between themselves and the giant snake.

The snake's tongue flickered out, tasting the air. It couldn't oscillate in the tunnel thanks to its size, but it tried. The walls shook, igneous rocks raising a cloud of dust as they fell. Luke extended his shield over their heads, breathing a short-lived sigh of relief when it held.

"I can't even with these things anymore," Emma muttered, not surprised at this point by a giant snake.

"Can you kill it?" Luke asked, muscles straining against his robes as he maintained the shield. The snake tried to wiggle forward, but it must have gotten wedged in the tubes even further. It hissed, a sharp ridge of rocks digging into the creature's neck. Venom dripped from the tips of its fangs, sizzling wherever it splashed. "Any time now!"

Emma held out both hands, trying to choke the air from the beast. Nothing happened, except the snake's venom seemed to leak out faster. Craters formed below the two fangs, and the last thing Emma wanted was for the beast to splatter them with it.

"Try something else!" Luke strengthened his shield as the snake thrashed more, causing cracks to spider along the ceiling.

"I'm going to bury it!" With a great wrench of her hands, Emma pulled the ceiling down on top of the snake, crushing it under the millions of pounds of rock above. Dust clouded her vision, but, remarkably, Luke's shield held, its edges sealed against the ceiling above them. The ground shook with a high-pitched squeal, and then the wreckage settled into silence.

"Great. Now we're trapped," Luke said matter-of-factly.

Emma peered around, shifting some rocks until she reached the wall. "No, we're not. I'm going to tunnel around it."

For the next couple of hours, Emma carved a path around the dead snake, and she wished she could have paid more attention to Luke and Argent as they *finally* had a cordial conversation. But once she breached the wall back into the main tunnel system behind the creature, they all stopped in their tracks.

She'd brought them into a massive underground cavern eerily like the Sal Dorhana, minus the impossible ceiling. Emma could feel the expansive space through her magic. Hundreds of spelled cages filled the room, light purple magic crackling from floor to ceiling as it kept its prisoners contained... and silent. Giant self-sustaining runes pulsed as they anchored both ends of the cages, the energy thrumming around them.

The cage nearest to them flickered with unearthly light, empty. Along the floor, a snake-sized escape tunnel sizzled, the beast's venom still oozing on either side of its former corral.

As they looked around, creatures of every variety thrashed against the barriers of their cages. Some Emma had encountered before, but others she'd thought only existed in Earthly mythology. A group of Fenris wolves in one of the cages snarled as they passed, their fur burned in places where they had tried to press against the magic to escape. In another, feathery serpents coiled and hissed, their plumage puffing when they saw the group.

"Are those dragons?" Emma stared down the long rows of cages where a much bigger enclosure swallowed up part of the cavern. The energy stretched and warped as massive beasts slammed against it, the absolute silence increasing how creepy it all seemed. The captive creatures were bad enough—some of which she had personally fought and killed—but being unable to hear their cries of desperation or anger.... Emma didn't know if she wanted to get any closer.

Luke forged ahead before she could hold him back. The two massive reptilian creatures with leathery wings roared, breathing fire cut off by the magic containing them. A ridge of sharp spines ran along the dragons' backs, three horns sprouting from their heads. On one, blue scales shimmered in the light, while the green of the other's twinkled. The cat-like pupils of their softball-sized eyes narrowed when they landed on the three tiny humans.

"Dragons," Luke breathed, stunned. "It's different seeing them in person. Up close."

Argent drifted over to another cage; his brow pinched in a frown. The animals behind the magic were like hairless coyotes, with wide jaws and pitch-black eyes. "One of these attacked me on Borna," he said, not taking his eyes off them.

"Chupacabras," Luke said distractedly.

Emma groaned.

"I saw a drawing of them in an old library book," Luke continued, glancing at Emma. The dragons thrashed against the cage again, scales sizzling at the contact.

"They're hurting themselves," Emma said, concerned.

"We can't let them out." Argent must have heard her doubt. "Every time we've come across something from Langoth in the wild here, it's done nothing but attack."

"On Earth, too," Emma slowly agreed, thinking of the Fenris wolf again. The image of that girl's prone body came to mind, reminding her what these things could do to the defenseless. "Fine. We leave them like this." She stared for another long moment at the dragons. "Luke, when you had your Vision, the dragon wasn't attacking Camelot."

"As far as I could tell."

She considered the animals before her. "So it's possible they are controlled somehow... besides being put in cages."

"Mind control?" Luke asked, drawing his sword. He poked the magic cage surrounding the chupacabras, pulling back when energy crackled against the steel, the runes along the blade lighting up. "We won't know unless we release them, but I don't want to fight anything in here." He gestured around, indicating the many cages. "Even if they're normally benign, if Morgan's apprentice is controlling them to attack everything, we'd have a hard time holding up against them all."

"We keep moving," Argent said firmly, finally tearing his eyes away from the hairless, slavering animals.

The cavern never seemed to end. They walked down the central aisle, feeling watched in more ways than one, hundreds of eyes staring down at them as if they were dinner.

Finally, they reached another tunnel entrance, the only one available along the flat expanse at the end of the cavern. Emma looked behind them, the illumination from so many magical cages lighting up the underground space like lanterns.

She detected no trap over this new entrance, despite running her fingers along the edges to make sure. Emma cast her magic lights again, sending them down the short tunnel. They emerged into a smaller room, the walls filled with more cages. Emma didn't realize what she was looking at until she focused for a few seconds on the nearest pen.

On the stone ground, a human woman lay curled on her side, dressed in rags.

All thoughts of caution fled. "Oh—Luke, people are prisoners, too!"

Luke grabbed her arm before she could raise it to try releasing them. "Wait," he commanded, the authority in his voice making her pause. "We knew there might be human prisoners. If the animals are victims of mind control, why would these people be any different?"

Argent touched Emma's other shoulder, drawing her attention away from the captive human. The woman hadn't noticed them yet, but Emma sensed that others in the room hadn't missed the sounds of newcomers. "Look there," he said, pointing toward the middle of the cavern. About thirty cages filled the room, clear aisles between the rows. In the cage Argent pointed at, two witches waved at them, faces frantic. Emma took a few steps closer until the tattoos on their throats came into focus—the Coven Mark of Renova.

They still wore their leather armor, two chevrons on each shoulder. "Witches from Camelot."

Luke approached the cage, face wary. "These women are from the first coven sent here," he said. Like the previous cages, these blocked all sound, and each strike of the witches' fists against its walls caused them to pull back in pain.

One of the witches pointed at Emma, then at her own shoulder. Black scuffs marred the chevrons there. Her face filled with relief.

"She recognizes me," Emma said, moving closer. "My tesseract... she knows we're friends."

"Emma—"

But she barely heard her brother's warning. She pressed her palm against the magic of the cage, willing it to disappear. The spell had scarcely vanished before both witches charged, feral expressions taking over any relief they might have felt from being found and freed.

Shouting, Luke cast a shield between himself and the witches, by chance alone protecting Argent but leaving Emma exposed. One witch slammed against the shield without even casting any magic, while Emma was forced to fight the other.

The woman attacked like a rabid animal, completely foregoing her powers as she scratched and hit Emma with unkempt nails, bony fists, and vicious howls of rage.

Acting on instinct, Emma filled her fist with spelled energy and punched the attacking witch beneath her jaw, blood flying through the air. Adrenaline drowned out Luke's and Argent's grunts as they dealt with the other witch.

Emma frantically tried to figure out how to contain the witch without killing her, but the punch to her face didn't seem to slow her down. The option to steal her breath flitted through her mind, but she dismissed it so quickly that it barely registered. That was not a power she wished to use on humans. She formed an energy whip, remembering the restraining magic Renault and Ebony once used. Threads wrapped around the witch's wrists and ankles, trussing her up in the air like a turkey, joints bent at awkward angles. She thrashed, screeching and hissing with such unnatural noises that Emma wanted to cover her ears.

She glanced over her shoulder at her brother and the Prince—just in time to watch as Argent drove his sword into the attacking witch's gut, his face scratched and bloody, Luke's shield gone. The dead witch crumpled to the ground; a look of shock painted on her face. Argent knelt beside her, tears mixing with the blood on his cheeks. He gently closed the witch's eyelids, his hands shaking as the effects of the battle wore off.

Emma tore her gaze away from Argent to figure out what to do with her captive. Closing her eyes, she recalled the feeling of the cage she'd unraveled and focused on recreating it around the threads of restraining magic. When she opened her eyes, the witch glared at her from inside a light blue prison, her chin and chest spattered with blood from Emma's punch. A bruise stretched along her jawline, broken blood vessels reddening her lower eye.

"I'm sorry," Emma whispered, her adrenaline ebbing away with each heartbeat. She helped Argent to his feet, holding him tightly as he trembled, his sword hanging from one hand.

"I didn't want to," Argent muttered into her ear, his voice broken.

"I shouldn't have let them out," she admitted, guilt gnawing at her chest. Argent killed because of her. The thought tasted vile. She pulled away from him, a terrible possibility crossing her mind. She hurried from cage to cage, looking at all the captives' faces for Bethany's. She found more witches from the missing covens and a few older men and women who stared vacantly at them. Some had odd tattoos on their necks and faces, and several had haphazard belongings—bags, rucksacks, blankets—strewn around their tiny prisons. The ones who met her eyes looked at Emma in a way she knew meant they would attack her too.

But Bethany remained absent.

"Let's move," Luke said sharply, casting a significant look at them. "We're close. I know it."

CHAPTER TWENTY-THREE
THE PROPHET'S RUIN

Luke's pack scraped along the ceiling of the next winding tunnel, and he watched as Argent's armor made it difficult for him to move. Luke's heart pounded, but the deeper they progressed into the labyrinth, the clearer his thoughts became and the more he understood where he'd gone wrong. Where he'd failed. If Morgan's former apprentice had given Septim his powers, then Luke's Vision of her throttling Argent in midair suddenly lost the meaning he'd given it since the moment he Saw it.

With a sudden wrench of fear, he realized he hadn't had another Vision since he'd Seen the woman in purple.

Combined with his faltering shields, Emma's inability to hear his thoughts, and his degraded healing skills, Luke finally reached the horrifying conclusion that none of this would have happened if he hadn't been so utterly convinced of Argent's guilt.

And now, woefully underprepared and on the threshold of battle, Luke cursed himself for ruining their best chance of saving everyone.

The tunnel opened into hewn corridors lit by real flames flickering in torches. Smooth, jet-black obsidian lined the walls, etchings of the same mark at the center of each tile. A circle overlaid with a hollow diamond, four crescent moons behind its points.

Argent touched one, his fingertips barely brushing the stone. "This was the mark she used in the Ritual," he said softly, frowning.

"It's not Ralador's coven mark."

Argent tilted his head. "It could be *her* mark. A way to show the magic she used that she was willing to give up power to create the Wraith of Valona."

Luke adjusted his pack, impatient. "That doesn't matter," he said. "Come on!"

"Wait," Emma said, grabbing his sleeve. "We need a plan of attack. You're my—our—shield. Are you going to be able to do that while I fight?"

Luke swallowed his terror. "Of course!"

"Even if Bethany is in danger? Or Mom?"

He could only nod, not wanting to crush Emma's trust in him more than he already had. With Bethany's life on the line, it was all he could do to stop himself from sprinting in guns blazing. Without the guns.

But Bethany wasn't the only one in jeopardy. Their mom could be, too.

Even without proof that Julie ended up here, of all the possible places she could have landed in both Talahm and Langoth, Luke had a feeling. And it wasn't a good one.

The flickering torches reflected off the smooth walls, casting shadows that jumped as they moved down the black corridor. Open doorways branched in new directions at regular intervals, but Luke felt drawn down the main hallway. Emma matched his pace, leaving Argent protected behind them.

A wooden door loomed in the distance, and Luke's mouth dried up. Emma seized his wrist, stopping their progress.

"She's in there," Emma whispered so quietly that Luke barely heard her.

His heart skipped a beat. "Bethie or Mom or the woman—"

Emma squeezed his hand hard, and he bit his tongue. "All of them."

"Argent, if you can, stay out of the way," Luke commanded, knowing it wouldn't help what he'd Seen in his Vision but hoping anyway—for Emma's sake.

The Prince slid his sword from its sheath, face expressionless as he met Luke's eyes. "I'll do my best."

They huddled together on one side of the door, tense with anticipation for whatever came next.

Luke counted down with his fingers.

Three. Two. One.

Emma blasted the door off its hinges, and Luke erected a shield as they swept into the enormous circular stone chamber, vision partially obscured by the wood dust choking the air. Steep walls stretched up to a ceiling so far above them that Luke couldn't distinguish it from the dark. Directly opposite them, a long horizontal window let in a slight, salty breeze, the Sleeping Sea reflecting dimming sunlight as twilight approached. At the center of the room, the remainder of the door lay in kindling by a waist-high obelisk. Luke couldn't shake the bad feeling he got while cataloging the similarities between this obelisk and the ones connecting Renova and Goatfell. Against the far wall behind it, a figure resolved through the dust, slumped beneath the window to the left of a small table holding potion vials.

This is it. This is the room.

They slowly circled the space, moving closer to the figure. The figure lay in chains with tight fetters locked around thick furry wrists and ankles. Iron gloves covered with runes restrained its front paws. Ribs showed clearly through its skin and thinning fur, evidence of malnourishment—for how long Luke couldn't guess. Open wounds covered its sides and flanks, some of them ringed with burns. One long, feathered wing crumpled awkwardly between the wall and its body, the other folded smoothly against its side. The animal twitched, turning its head just so and cracking its eyes open. Two golden irises gleamed across the room, and Luke almost lost his breath.

Mountains Crumble Beneath His Claws.

"Finally," Magdalin's brother breathed, his voice so faint Luke strained to hear him. His front legs tensed as if trying to stand.

Emma glanced at the Olis but didn't give him much attention. Her head swiveled, taking stock of the chamber. Any other occupants would have to be invisible.

Luke took another few steps toward the emaciated Olis, his hands still maintaining the shield. "I'm Luke," he said cautiously, trying to gauge if Mountains was also under mind control. "How long have you been here?"

Mountains' golden eyes fixed on Luke, his pain and weariness evident. "At least a hundred years... if *she's* telling the truth." His gaze shifted over Luke's shoulder.

Luke followed it past Argent. The open doorway shimmered for a brief second before stones materialized over the opening, each *thunk* of rock against rock echoing through the circular room. They all turned around, shivers cascading down Luke's spine as high-pitched cackles rippled through the air.

In front of the now sealed door, the witch dismantled her invisibility spell, revealing herself. Long, thick silvery gray hair cascaded to her waist, framing a smooth face that spoke of a false youth. Dark eyes glittered at them from across the chasm.

"Welcome to Valona," she said, her voice anything but welcoming. Both of her hands curled in the air as if holding invisible ropes.

"Who are you?" Emma demanded, anger ripe in her voice.

The woman took a step forward, her violet dress flowing about her ankles, tiny twinkling eight-pointed stars stitched in golden thread along the hem. Her black corset cinched around her waist, pushing up her breasts and exaggerating her cleavage. A long claw dangled on a cord around her neck, resting against her chest. The invisible leashes she held tugged backward, but her hands remained tense.

"A Vision, a painting, and a memory weren't enough? Should I have whispered my name through your dear brother's sleeping runestone? Breeding paranoia is an *art*," she pouted, the barest hint of a wrinkle appearing and disappearing as her glamour flickered over her face.

"Your name, witch!" Luke barked, strengthening the shield between them. The fact that he'd relied on her device to fall asleep for two years caused nausea to rise, almost breaking his concentration.

"Tsk, tsk, Prophet Artair," the witch scolded, tugging a leash gently with her right hand. "Names are powerful. You can do *so much* when you know a name."

Luke watched in horror as a golden rope of magic materialized, the end of it a noose around Bethany Hawkins' neck. She knelt on the floor; her blonde hair pulled free from its usual fishtail braid. The noose kept her back unnaturally straight. A purple bruise formed around her throat where the rope dug into her skin. Blood and dirt streaked her face. She cradled one arm as best she could with her wrists tied together, the limb bent at an awkward angle, clearly broken. Burns covered her exposed skin where the coven armor and pauldrons had been torn away. The tattoo on her throat was the only clue that she belonged to Renova's Royal Coven.

But her face blazed with defiance, no hint of fear in the hard lines of her jaw, nor in her eyes. She stared directly at Luke, probably having tracked him from the moment they entered the chamber. The noose kept her mouth closed, but Luke could tell she wanted to call out to them—to him.

His fists clenched and every muscle in his body tensed for action. "Bethie," he breathed, her name escaping before he could stop himself.

The witch threw back her head, gray mane shaking as she laughed. "A *pet* name! Even more precious." She schooled her features, piercing them all with her gaze. "She didn't tell you about the memory trap, did she?"

Luke startled, his hand instinctively reaching toward his bag.

"You couldn't bear to burden him by reliving your worst moments, *Bethie*, could you?" The witch tugged on Bethany's rope, the motion forcing her to look up. Hatred filled her eyes. "Shall I tell him?"

"How would you even know?" Luke demanded, rage coursing through his veins.

A feral grin spread across her unnaturally smooth face. "The same way I know *your* worst memory, Prophet. Watching a man fall to his death, knowing it would happen, and doing *nothing* to stop it. How do you live with that guilt, Luke?" Her eyes flickered to Emma. "And you, ooh," she bit her lip in mock pleasure, eyes glancing to the ceiling before fixing again on the Seventh Sorceress. "Delicious, watching you make your first kill."

"Shut your foul mouth," Argent said from behind them, his voice low, angry, and powerful. He pushed between Emma and Luke, standing even with them behind Luke's shield. The protection grew stronger as Luke let his love for his sister and Bethany fill him.

"Make me," the woman snapped. "Your hideous ancestor tried once, when he discovered how I'd thwarted his pitiful attempts to sire an heir. I will not have a Pendragon speak to me with such insolence." Her face shifted into a wild, encouraging grin. "But tell me, Argent, has your darling father started sleeping with the eagle ring he pilfered from Agamemnon's corpse? I'll admit, using that trinket was far easier than everything I'd had to do to set up dear old Hadrian's accident."

Luke sensed Argent using great restraint not to fall for her bait.

"No? Not even a little curiosity about how your grandfather *actually* died? Well, the legitimate grandfather, that is." The witch tsked and shook her head, her hair tumbling around her shoulders. "Pity. It's just as well." She glanced to her left, lifting her hand higher. Another golden rope of magic sputtered into view, speeding away from her like a lit fuse and spreading across a pale white neck marred with thin bruises, lifting another invisibility spell. "You don't want to risk your friends' mother's life, do you? A woman without magic.... Now that's an insult to our kind if I've ever seen one."

Luke's stomach dropped to his feet. He hadn't seen his mother in so long that it took him a split second to recognize the woman with long, scraggly hair and torn clothing as the woman who had raised him. "Mom—"

Julie's face had grown gaunt, her skin whiter than Luke had ever seen. But fire burned in her eyes, determination and tight anger giving Luke a spark of hope. If his mother hadn't broken yet, she could still fight. Like Bethany, the noose kept Julie silent, but she stared hard at her son for a long moment before her eyes darted to Emma.

"Igraine Pendragon," Emma said. "Nice to know you couldn't shut up about yourself to your captives. Thanks, Mom."

"King Arthur's mother!" Argent exclaimed, his hand whitening over his sword's hilt.

Luke jolted, struck by the implication that this witch was yet another ancestor of the Prince.

Igraine's face soured. "Don't remind me of that wretched spawn," she snapped, schooling her features. "I am the Night's Empress, not a *Pendragon*."

"I don't care what you call yourself," Emma snapped. "Unless it's for the peasant marker over your grave."

A smile fixed on Igraine's face. "One of you might care. Perhaps the one I leave alive to take word back to your impotent king. That's if I don't decide to kill you all and tell him myself... before I end the Pendragons once and for all."

Luke barely managed to keep a straight face when Emma's voice erupted in his head, and it was like a breath of fresh air after a smoky day. He'd forgotten how nice it felt to hear her thoughts—how it represented their unity as Sentinel and Sorceress. It was like she convened a military briefing in her head, issuing commands to him, Argent, Bethany, and Julie at the same time. He heard and understood it all, but his only external sign of acknowledgment was an infinitesimal dip of his chin.

Emma's hands moved faster than light. Tiny, crackling balls of plasma shot toward Igraine, veering away from her at the last second to sever the cords of magic in her hands. Bethany and Julie leaped away, and the fight was on.

Several things happened at once, and Luke wasn't quite sure how he kept track of them all.

A whip of fire formed in Bethany's left hand, the end of it cracking as it cut through the rope around her wrists, and she winced as her broken arm jostled. She snapped the whip at Julie's bonds, instantly freeing the older woman.

Julie straight-up tackled Igraine to the ground, punching her once in the stomach—"That's for Bethany—" and twice in the face. "And that's for my gun! I know you have it on you, you steaming pile of—" Julie somehow frisked Igraine without incurring more magical wrath, and she rolled away once she'd extracted the ivory-plated handgun from Igraine's skirts.

Bethany snapped her firewhip at Igraine's flowing dress as the witch scrambled to her feet, the flames smoldering wherever it touched, but the cords slid off Igraine's skin like water.

Julie crouch-ran across the stone chamber, veering around the obelisk to get behind Luke's shield before ejecting the gun's magazine to count bullets. She pulled the slide back half an inch, then slammed the magazine back in, one bullet already in the chamber.

Emma lobbed a variety of magical attacks at the Night's Empress, her onslaught so relentless that the witch could barely shield herself, let alone strike back. Explosions of fire, crackles of plasma, and even sharp spikes of rock pushing through the ground didn't faze her.

Luke strengthened his shield, moving with Emma as she advanced. Finally, their enemy screamed, dark purple strands of magic stretching up her arms as she wrapped them around a ball of energy. It exploded, hitting Luke's shield with such force that he dropped to one knee and bent his head, drawing on all his love for Bethany, Emma, and his mother to fuel it.

But it wasn't enough. His shield cracked and then evaporated, leaving them all vulnerable.

And then it happened.

In a daze, Luke watched Igraine lift Argent into the air with both hands outstretched, kicking over the potions table as she staggered forward. As each vial shattered on the stone floor, déjà vu overwhelmed Luke's brain. It wasn't often he Saw his Visions fulfilled in person. A ship came into view through the long window, Renova's colors out of place in the waters of Ralador. *The Sea Wolf.*

Emma screamed, the sound shredding Luke's soul.

Face reddening, Argent's fingers scrabbled at his neck, his eyes wide and frantic, until Igraine slammed him against the stone wall. "The last of the Pendragons—"

Lightning struck Igraine's back, and she convulsed, releasing her grasp on Argent, who fell in a heap to the floor, coughing and straining for breath. Emma sent another course of electricity into the ancient witch, fury painted on her face. In between bolts, Igraine managed to turn over, catching the next strike in her hands.

Argent crawled toward Luke, and Julie darted to drag him to his feet. Luke shook himself, then re-energized his shield, the golden membrane holding firm this time.

Behind him, snippets of frantic conversation passed between Argent, Mountains, and Julie, but Luke couldn't split his focus to listen in. Instead, he tilted his head to see over his shoulder. Argent fished a wooden disk etched with tiny runes from his pocket, pressing it against one of the iron gloves trapping the Olis's front paws.

The restraint shattered, and Mountains tore off his other bonds with a roar, finally free from the artificial block on his magic. He took a few limping steps before collapsing, chest heaving with the effort.

Luke's knee throbbed where it pressed against the stone floor. Now, it seemed like nothing Emma and Bethany threw at Igraine affected her—she alternated between high-pitched cackles and an ugly sneer. Amidst the loud flashes of magic, there was no time for talk. He pushed his shield further toward the witch, shrinking her field of play to a thin strip between the wall and the golden barrier. Bethany's fire whip sliced through it, wrapping around Igraine's wrist.

"Give it back!" Bethany demanded, her blonde hair wild around her face. "Give my journal back, you self-righteous hag!"

A smirk spread across Igraine's face, and she wrenched the fire whip toward her. Bethany let it go, the magic dissipating without a trace.

Igraine absorbed another bolt of energy from Emma. "Oh, Luke," Igraine mocked, matching Bethany's tone and pitch in a singsong, "I can't wait until I'm in your arms again!"

Angry at the invasion of privacy, Luke poured more power into his shield, pressing the witch against the wall. She skirted around the edge, trying to get behind them, but Luke followed.

How Emma maintained mental links to everyone baffled Luke, but he didn't have time to question it when he heard Argent's voice inside his head.

Move her around the chamber toward Mountains.

Luke assessed everyone's positions, noting how Mountains tracked Igraine with his sharp golden eyes, circling the obelisk in pace with Luke's shield. Emma and Bethany were between Luke and Igraine, moving, fighting, and lashing out with magic from behind Luke's protection. Argent, his eyes red with burst blood vessels, shielded Julie with his body, his sword held at the ready and mechanical bracer unfolded and glowing with enchanted runes. Julie held her gun pointed toward the floor, both hands wrapped around the grip like a vice, index finger ready to enter the trigger guard the moment she had a clear shot.

Luke did as Argent asked, rotating his hands, stepping at an angle to force Igraine to move back and around the edge of the wall as his shield blocked off her retreat. Argent took measured steps backward, keeping Julie doubly protected. For a single heartbeat, Luke felt a surge of gratitude for the Prince, and his shield flared.

"Unlike the Pendragons, I don't keep trophies, *pet!*" Igraine shouted at Bethany, her face ugly with contempt.

Bethany and Emma joined their magic, a bolt of energy blasting the witch in the chest. When the haze cleared, Igraine stood unharmed, a wicked grin on her lips.

"I burnt it like I burned the refuse Morgan calls *witches*," she sneered. "Amazing how fast some things turn to ash."

Bethany roared, holding her good arm out in front of her. A tornado of fire whirled quickly around Igraine, and her gray hair stood on end. Smoke buffeted the witch from all sides, but the flames didn't scathe her. Emma's lightning arced through the stone chamber, but nothing touched the elder witch.

"Why won't she just die?" Luke demanded. His strength waned with each second that passed, but he'd finally learned how to tap into the right emotions to use as fuel. He knew he could never run out of love for Bethany or his sister, but his magic still had limits.

Igraine was now within a few feet of the obelisk, her back to Mountains. "There's more than one way to immortality, you fools! And Septim was the greatest fool! Do you really think I would allow my body to remain weak to the ravages of time? Vulnerable to enemies like you? No one can touch me!"

Get ready to push her in, Emma warned. Mountains stood tall on his hind feet, straddling the obelisk. One paw hovered in midair; a single claw ready to slice downward.

"We don't have to touch you," Emma snapped, and *Mountains Crumble Beneath His Claws* tore through the fabric of the universe with all his weight. A tall purple gash erupted in the air, and almost immediately, Luke stumbled toward it. Mountains dug his paws into the gap, wrenching apart the seams with unexpected strength. Igraine fell backward as gravity increased, her face slack.

Luke pushed out with his hands, his shield forcing the witch to the portal's event horizon until she clawed at the sides, shouting at the top of her lungs.

"You only delay the inevitable!" she screeched, her hands smoking where they grasped at the edges of the universe. Human flesh was not made to touch the razor's edge of the portal, and the longer Igraine resisted the pull of Langoth's gravity, the worse she looked. Her face aged before them, the strength to maintain her glamour now diverted to keeping her alive.

A single shot rang out, Julie's bullet mangling Igraine's left hand.... And then she disappeared, sucked through the tear in the blink of an eye.

Luke released his shield one moment too soon.

A golden noose of magic shot out of the portal, wrapping around Bethany's good wrist and forcing her through the tear between worlds before she could so much as let out a scream.

Mountains reared up, clapping his front paws together over the gaping maw, sealing it shut with a snap. The heavy pull on their bodies suddenly cut off.

Numbness spread over Luke's entire being.

Bethany was gone.

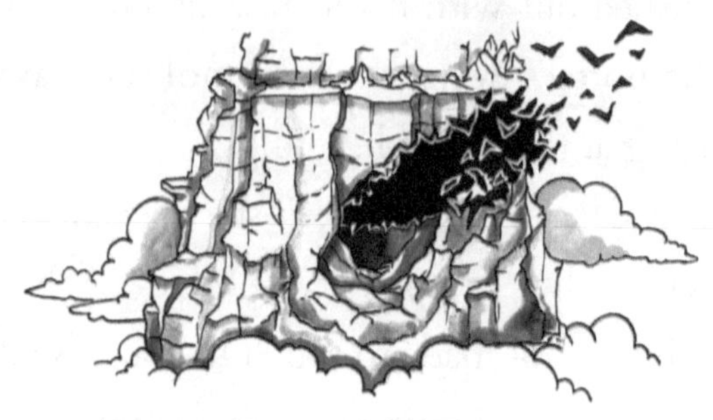

CHAPTER TWENTY-FOUR
MOUNTAINS CRUMBLES

Deafening silence roared in Luke's ears. He dropped to his knees, staring at the jagged purple scar hovering before them.

This is Mountains' fault.

The Olis had landed on all four paws but staggered before finally collapsing on his side, his breath shallow. His shoulders shook, and his tremoring jostled his broken wing, his claws spreading across the floor like daggers. He was missing an entire toe as if it had been cut off.

No... this is my fault.

Julie touched Luke's shoulder, and he flinched. She sank to the ground in front of her son, holding his face in her hands. "Luke," Julie croaked, fingers stroking the white streaks at his temples. "Are you okay?"

Luke took his mother's wrists. "Bethie's gone," he choked. "She's—"

"She's alive," Emma sobbed, locked in Argent's embrace. The Prince rocked her back and forth as they both stared at the portal's scar hanging in midair. "I can still feel her in my head. I can't hear her or talk to her, not at this distance, but she's alive. I don't know for how long."

Luke crawled to the Olis, conjuring a medical projection of his body, and cursed at the number of injuries lighting up the mirror.

Mountains is the only one who knows how to save Bethany.

"Touch my wing and I'll gut you," Mountains panted, grimacing when Luke pressed a healing hand to his flank.

Without warning, Luke put the Olis to sleep, breathing a brief sigh of relief when Mountains' limbs relaxed, including his wing. "Not if I knock you out," Luke hissed, aghast at the Olis's dreadful condition. Consciousness would only make him harder to heal, and the projection already showed multiple failing systems.

"Make him open another one," Emma demanded, her face stained with tears.

"I will the minute I finish healing his sorry sack of bones in Camelot," Luke answered, his voice hollow. "He's going to die if I don't, and we'll lose our only chance to save Bethie." Luke squinted at the projection. The Olis's heart beat sluggishly, long pauses between his shallow breaths. He cast a stasis over the Olis, frowning when it only arrested half of the issues plaguing him. Luke took a split second to consider everything, letting the logical side of his brain suppress the emotions he knew would wreck him if he didn't set them aside.

"I'm going to free all the captives and make a causeway down to *The Sea Wolf*," Emma announced, sounding more angry than grief-stricken. "You're going to take that son of a—"

"Emma," Julie warned, tucking her gun into the leather holster still cinched to her belt.

"—rhymes with witch back to Camelot on a dragon, all right?"

Luke didn't argue with her. It all made sense now. Fatigue pulled at his limbs, and he blindly reached into his pack for a quick bite, shoving the days-old bread into his mouth. The food helped restore some of his strength.

Emma stormed across the chamber, the door reappearing as if it sensed her magical rage and only wished to obey. Argent and Julie followed, and Luke heard as Emma implemented her plan.

Carving a tunnel big enough for dragons. He passed his hands over the largest hollow bone in Mountains' wing, doing his best to heal the obvious breaks and torn tendons that kept the appendage from properly folding against his back.

Shouting.... The captives are free. Luke cleaned and closed the open wounds littering Mountains' forearms and chest—the evidence of countless exposures to Langoth's chaotic portals, and whatever creatures Igraine had forced him to capture for her mindless army.

Screams now—there go the dragons. He tried to calm the misfiring nerves that sent tremors through Mountains' limbs despite his unconsciousness, but much like with Magdalin, it didn't seem like anything was enough.

*A stampede, voices, fear—*Luke helped the Olis's circulatory system keep pumping blood to all the necessary places, and he worried about how he would keep them both on a dragon long enough to fly to Camelot. A colossal tremble shook the chamber, forcing Luke to conjure another shield above them.

"Get ready for your ride," Emma panted, bursting through the door with a flood of refugees and animals behind her.

"It's a dead end!" someone exclaimed, but Emma pushed both her hands out toward the window, using the weak point to blast a large hole in the side of the chamber. Everyone covered their heads.

The sound of flapping wings drowned everything else out as a massive cloud of the missing hawks and other birds erupted from behind them, pouring out through Emma's tunnels and into the rapidly darkening sky.

"Earthwitches, with me!"

Luke could barely see *The Sea Wolf* in the distance, but that didn't stop Emma from leaping into the void. Holding herself aloft, she quickly raised a pillared causeway from Valona's dungeon to their rescue bobbing on the waters far below. The few rescued earthwitches helped shape the pathway.

The refugees and more intelligent creatures crowded to one side when the two snorting dragons nosed into the chamber. Their scales glittered like gemstones. Their snouts glistened with half-healed burns from where they had pressed against their magical cages, and their long, leathery wings stretched to full length in the vast height of Igraine's chamber.

The green dragon bared its fangs and made a beeline for Luke, both of its massive golden eyes zeroing in on him. Its pupils constricted, and Luke felt a foreign presence in his mind. It didn't quite speak, but almost without conscious thought, his Vision of a dragon over Camelot came to mind, the wide forest-green wings of the larger dragon soaring over the high towers of the castle. The presence paused with surprise, slowly finishing its approach.

Luke blinked, looking at the dragons with new eyes. "I hope you're up for a nonstop flight," he said, jerking his thumb toward Mountains. "This one is going to need it."

Luke finished nestling *Mountains Crumble Beneath His Claws* into a divot along the green dragon's back, between two spines as long as Luke's arm. He hoped it sensed his urgency, the stone trembling beneath their feet more frequently. With his bag's strap wrapped tightly around the dragon's spine, Luke seated himself as comfortably as he could on top of the beast.

He peered through the break in the wall, trying to discern Emma's progress. The entire group of refugees, and several creatures, had leapt to the first few pillars, huddling together as Emma raised each ensuing step. With a wrench in his gut, Luke realized he hadn't seen his mother or Argent escape yet. He twisted around on the dragon, staring into the darkened passage behind him, one hand clenching

Mountains' fur for stability. The Olis's time in captivity had left crusty spots on his coat that scratched Luke's palm.

"Come on, Mom...."

Distant footsteps pounded across the stone, echoing in the darkness. Then, suddenly, an orange light shone and a wave of heat blasted against his face.

"Go, go, go!" Julie screamed, bringing up the rear as she, Argent, and two injured battle witches from Renova's Royal Coven burst into the room, a thick stream of lava on their heels. They leaped into the darkness with abandon, apparently fully trusting that Emma had placed the pillars in the right spots.

The dragon followed suit, scrambling to the edge of the stone chamber and launching itself into the night, wings flapping mightily. Luke clung to the dragon's spines as he wildly looked back, fear consuming him as a bright lavafall poured over the edge of the broken dungeon wall, illuminating the path of the pillars down to *The Sea Wolf*. Steam billowed from where the lava met the Sleeping Sea far below, and Luke could barely make out the shadows of the survivors leaping from step to step.

Luke's dragon took them higher, and, in the distance, a pinprick of orange lit the southern horizon, streaking into the air in slow motion. It took him a long second to realize he was watching a volcano erupt. Eyes wide, he clung to the dragon with all his strength, his magic a net around Mountains as the shockwave reached them and buffeted the dragon through the air.

Go north. To Camelot, he urged. *Mountains is Bethie's only hope.*

Behind them, the volcanic eruption lit the horizon with a dull orange that slowly washed out as the sun rose. The multi-day walk turned into mere hours when flying on a dragon. Luke's legs cramped as he clung to the dragon's back, one arm hooked around the beast's spine, his other hand clenching the fur of Mountains' withers. His strength wilted as he tried to keep the Olis alive. Still, he focused on Mountains, his stomach dropping when he could barely feel his life force.

Then, without warning, Mountains' heart stopped.

"No, no, no!" Luke choked, frantically dredging his magic to restart the big cat's heart. Through clenched teeth, he willed a shield of warmth around them. "Live, you wretch, live!" He risked transferring some of his own strength, his own life, into Mountains, feeling lightheaded when it actually worked.

Mountains pulled in a deeper breath than he had for hours, but Luke couldn't allow any time for relief—not with so many of the Olis's systems threatening to shut down again. Distant shouts drew his attention to their surroundings, and this time he welcomed them with relief. Camelot's broken walls looked even worse from above. Farmers shouted in fear, and, after a second, Luke realized none of them could see him on top of the dragon. For all they knew, this was yet another bad event in a long string of bad events.

Luke could only hope that Emma sent a note to their father.

No matter what King Aragon says, I have to make sure Mountains lives, and I have to get Bethie back from Langoth.

The dragon veered over the city, tilting enough for Luke to wave at the citadel ramparts, where Renault's bulky form shouted archers down from their posts. Luke said a quick prayer, thanking God for Renault's sharp eyes.

Down, he thought to the dragon, his arms sore. After a long, weightless moment, it flapped higher, starting its controlled descent, the ground rushing up to meet them. They alighted on the main road leading south, just outside what should have been the Valon Gate. Witches had yet to fix the top layer of stones on the ramparts, and the new iron gate lay useless to one side. Luke searched the thin throng of people for Sargateth, but he couldn't see a single glint of silver in the morning sun. He slid to the cobblestones, sucking in a deep, relieved breath at the solidness beneath his feet.

"Luke!" Renault called out, jogging through the curious and fearful people who had seen them land. "Is that—oh, good, you found him—"

Luke dropped to his knees, weariness finally winning out against the adrenaline he'd experienced the last several days. Or was it weeks now? Renault skidded to a halt, barely giving the dragon a glance as he stopped Luke from toppling face-first to the ground.

"Easy does it," Renault murmured, sounding the least gruff Luke had ever heard him. The half-Olis gripped his forearms, effortlessly lifting him back to his feet.

"No, not me. Save him! He's our only chance to get Bethany back!" Luke swayed, blackness clawing at the edges of his sight. "Save him, Ren."

And then the darkness took him.

CHAPTER TWENTY-FIVE
HEIR TO THE THRONE

"What, exactly, is *that?*" Cordelia Roque's gravelly voice drew Argent's attention from where he sat with Emma on a bench beneath the forecastle deck. After a night with little sleep, Argent and Emma had woken together beneath the stunning sunrise breaching the eastern horizon through the plumes of ash drifting north. Now, after half a day on the ocean, tending to the thirty or forty refugees and nearly a hundred creatures they'd freed from Igraine's mind control, the Seventh Sorceress slept peacefully against his shoulder, utterly exhausted.

"This?" Julie replied, tugging her weapon from the holster at her waist.

Cordelia swooped over like a vulture, plucking the gun from Julie's hands.

Julie snatched it back, masterfully ejecting the magazine and clearing the chamber. "This is a dangerous weapon, not a toy," she admonished, tucking the magazine and free bullet into her pants pocket. "I'm guessing you've never seen a gun?"

"I'm all about dangerous weapons," Cordelia breathed, a gleam in her eye.

Julie patiently showed her the gun, pointing out the customizations and features she was clearly proud of. Argent considered it a miracle that Igraine hadn't melted the pistol into slag the minute she captured it from Julie.

Emma shifted against his shoulder, bringing her left hand up to cover her yawn. Argent gently took her hand, his fingers tracing the birthmark that had now finished its journey down her other arm. "Look over there. I've never seen Cordelia Roque connect with someone like that."

"Does she know that's my mom?" Emma muttered, glancing at the dark clouds filling the sky.

He saw little of Julie in Emma except when the Seventh Sorceress shut down, tamping her emotions. "Doubtful.

Neither you nor Luke look especially like her. The Artair blood is strong in you both."

She shivered, creating a bubble of warmth around them. "I should go see if anyone still needs help," she said, stretching as she stood.

Argent watched her leave, his shoulders tense. Once Emma disappeared among the refugees, he got to his feet, climbing the stairs to the forecastle deck and leaning against the railing, far away from most of the crew. The straps of his bracer pinched the chain mail against his forearm, but he didn't bother fixing it. The pain helped distract him from the pull of Septim's memories. Left unchecked for over two years, the edges of his consciousness bled into what Septim had left behind. It had gotten worse since the events below Valona, but he kept that to himself. He didn't want to give Emma something more to worry about.

A peal of thunder rumbled overhead, a promise of rain in the air. Another scent slipped beneath it, stale and dank, and he couldn't tell if it came from the sea or was conjured by his own mind. He dug his fingers into his arms, trying to resist another one of Septim's horrid memories dragging him under. It wouldn't look good if the Prince of Renova collapsed on Cordelia's ship. He closed his eyes, breathing like Emma had taught him.

In for seven seconds, hold for four seconds, out for eight seconds.

His sense of balance returned, his face relaxing. But approaching footsteps made him snap his eyes back open.

Cara.

The witch Emma had throat-punched.

"Your Highness," Cara said quietly, her voice thready and deep through bruised vocal cords. She sank into a short curtsy.

Argent's stomach roiled at her address. "Miss Fletcher." He didn't know what else to say. Didn't know if he should apologize.

Cara hesitated as if choosing her words deliberately because of who he was. "We don't blame you for what happened to Eloise," she said, so softly Argent strained to hear her over the sound of the bow carving through the ocean. "We all—" She closed her eyes, schooling her features. "We all were under that wretch's thrall. You saw what I endured." She lifted her chin, giving Argent the full measure of the bruise mottling her skin. "I got lucky facing the Seventh Sorceress like that."

Argent swallowed, his throat scratching like sandpaper. He looked at the deck's planks instead, avoiding the pity in Cara's eyes.

"We forgive you," she said, and Argent's gaze snapped back up to hers. "*I* forgive you. Eloise was my battle sister. You are my Prince. You did what you had to in the worst of circumstances."

Argent sensed she wasn't only talking about Eloise's death. For a moment, hope blossomed in his chest—that perhaps Emma, Tomás, and William weren't the only ones who trusted him at his word. But he didn't know what to do with forgiveness. So, he gave her a curt nod, not trusting himself to speak without coming apart at the seams. Septim's dark thoughts pulled at him, extinguishing hope and replacing it with worthlessness.

Cara drew her lips into a sad smile, and she left, her hand coming up to brush against the bruise on her neck. A few feet away, she glanced over her shoulder, expression clearly showing compassion that he didn't think he deserved.

He swallowed hard, his Adam's apple scratching as it bobbed up and down. He turned around to face the open sea, needing the space, the physical distance between him and the witches who dared forgive a monster.

When he looked inward, he couldn't tell where his memories ended and Septim's began.

"Argent," Emma's voice whispered behind him.

The Prince looked around at her gentle call, relief flooding his chest at the sight of her. He offered her his hand.

"Emma," he finally said when she took it, his voice cracking. "I'm so sorry about Bethany."

Emma nodded, sucking in her cheeks. "We'll find her. I don't know how, but I will get her back."

Argent hugged her, both of them relaxing a little bit more at the contact. A flash of lightning lit the southern skies, and a moment later another roar of thunder rumbled toward them.

"What did Cara want?"

He took a deep breath, his exhale long, and told her. Forgiveness was a foreign concept to Septim, and it took Argent a moment to remember to separate himself from the stain Septim had left behind. "I don't deserve it."

Emma stroked his breastplate, reminding him of their reunion in the Trident. The contrast of that memory with the darkness he currently felt turned into a splitting headache that he barely managed to hide behind his well-worn mask.

"Isn't that the point of forgiveness? That we don't deserve it?"

He shrugged, the pounding behind his eyes getting worse.

"Hey, are you okay?" Emma touched his cheek, her black-and-blue birthmark remarkable as it stretched down the fingertips of her left hand. "You don't look so good."

Argent clenched his teeth. "It's his memories. They're—they're getting stronger." His hands curled into fists. "They've been getting worse since Igraine's memory trap."

She caressed the rough stubble along his jaw, her brow furrowed in contemplation. "Come with me."

Without hesitation, Argent let Emma lead him back down to the main deck, then around the edge to his familiar perch on the bowsprit, where he'd last read her beautiful message in the journal now at the bottom of the Sleeping Sea. They sat together, Argent struggling to stay present, stuck with the maelstrom in his mind.

"Let's do it now."

He blinked. "What?"

"Purging him from your head. Let's do it right now."

He'd asked days ago, but it felt like a lifetime. His head tipped forward in relief, Emma's hand coming up to cup his cheek. The next breath of air felt different. Lighter. "Thank you, Emma. For everything."

"Don't thank me quite yet," she murmured. "I don't know what to expect going into your mind." She loosened her embrace to look him in the eyes.

He wanted to kiss her again. "I trust you," he said. Another peal of thunder burst across the sky, and the first patter of raindrops landed on his uncovered head.

Emma shifted, taking Argent's face in her hands. Her thumb brushed against the scars across his cheek and chin. She closed her eyes, leaning her forehead against his, and the world fell away as she slipped into his mental landscape.

A chaotic storm ravaged his sight. Clouds of malevolent emotions roiled along the edges, dead, dark threads of things left behind by Septim's soul when Ebony's sacrifice tore him from Argent's body. Amidst it all, he felt Emma there, a stable anchor in the middle of the squall.

Purge it all, he told her, his own words ringing through his mind.

I won't erase you.

He reached for her, and when their consciousnesses touched, he couldn't distinguish where he ended and Emma began. He and Emma were one, and when she flinched, he knew that she finally experienced Septim's memories as he did.

Everywhere.

All at once.

Suffocating.

He felt her experience his desperation as if it were her own, the overwhelming desire to flee from something he could never escape. Once trapped within his mind by Septim's soul, he was now trapped with what Septim left behind in his death.

Oh, her mind exhaled.

The effort to push back, to define the lines between himself and Septim, to resist the sheer *familiarity* of the memories... finally, she understood.

This wasn't just a fight for Argent's sanity—his entire identity teetered on the precipice. For over two years, he'd woken up every day actively reminding himself that his imprisonment was over.

This wasn't a dream.

He was himself again.

And yet... with those six years lost, Argent didn't know who he was *supposed to be*.

Help me, he asked, the words as much hers as they were his. *I don't know who I am anymore.*

Their hearts filled with every memory of their journal entries, Emma's experiences with Argent, who she believed he was meant to be—his heart ached at her visions of his future—how much she loved him....

Her magic wrapped Argent Pendragon in purifying mental fire, and he held onto her belief in him, the anchor keeping him from perishing alongside his grandfather's memories. At the edges of his awareness, Septim's dark taint dissolved, stripped away by the overwhelming *goodness* that countered everything he'd stood for. Argent's soul brightened as the foreign influence dissipated, the tattered wisps of dark scenes purged like he'd asked.

Argent didn't know how long they stayed like that on the ship's prow, their eyes closed and foreheads pressed together, her hands holding his face while he gripped her waist like a drowning man holding on to his only hope. The rain picked up, soaking his hair until it plastered against his neck.

He came back to himself, taking stock of where they touched before blinking his eyes open, finding himself immediately locked in her cobalt gaze.

"Who are you?" she asked, the corners of her eyes crinkling with genuine curiosity.

He glanced up at the sky, closing his eyes against the rain and grinning as it helped wash away the remnants of his past, leaving him feeling like a brand-new man. When he looked back at her, he laughed, his tears of relief mixing with the rain as he cupped her cheek. "I am Prince Argent Pendragon... future King of Renova. And I'm hopelessly, completely in love with you."

She met his kiss halfway, the bliss of it ten times stronger than it had been in the Trident. His arms wrapped around her shoulder and waist, and he lifted her up, unable to contain the ecstasy caused by his freedom and the fact he felt truly accepted by a woman who loved him for who he was—not who everyone else thought he might be.

Shouts of dismay tore them away from the little world they'd created. As they climbed up to the forecastle deck, Cordelia forced an elderly refugee at sword-point from the navigation room onto the sterncastle. "Just because you've gained freedom doesn't mean you have impunity for spying on my ship's charts! You're only here because I indulged my First Officer, not because I wanted to ferry your sorry flesh to safety. I ought to keelhaul you!"

Long white hair plastered against the old man's skin, a shocking dark blue tattoo covering the entire right side of his face. Argent leaped back to the main deck, racing across the planks to intervene before Cordelia could follow through with her threat. Unsheathing his sword, he shoved his way in front of the refugee, knocking Cordelia's weapon to one side. He'd never felt so strong before. "Swallow your worthless tongue, Roque," Argent snarled.

Cordelia laughed hollowly, clearly unimpressed. "You can't fool me, little Prince. I've seen your broken spirit pacing the deck of this very ship for too long. Still mourning your precious diary?"

Argent stood tall, drawing his shoulders back. "By my authority as Prince of Renova, I order you to stand down. You will not threaten anyone on this ship."

Cordelia bared her teeth at him. "I should dump you all overboard this very minute. You can swim back to Camelot for all I care," Cordelia snarled, wind and water whipping around her face.

"And delay a reunion twenty years in the making?" Argent needled, jutting his chin toward Julie, who stood hugging Emma behind the captain. Next to them, several more refugees and crewmembers were gathered, all with angry looks on their faces. William Pendragon leaned against the mizzen mast, arms crossed over his barreled chest, his bushy beard unable to hide his frown.

Cordelia glanced over her shoulder. "What—"

"Julie *Artair*. Pleased to meet you," Julie deadpanned, giving a sarcastic wave.

Captain Roque's jaw dropped; shock plastered across her sharp features. A moment later, she drew herself up again. "Lock this pretender in the brig," she ordered, pointing her sword once again at Argent's face.

He swung his sword up in a fast arc, knocking hers clear across the deck. In the brief spate of silence, he slid his weapon back into its sheath, squaring his shoulders and staring Cordelia Roque down like he wished he could have months ago. "I am in command of this ship now, Miss Roque. They don't answer to you."

CHAPTER TWENTY-SIX
TOMÁS SEES

Emma pressed her cheek against Argent's armored back, tightening her arms around his waist as he directed their shared horse east down the River Road toward Camelot. She smiled into the steel, giving herself a brief respite from her panic about Bethany to enjoy the fact that Argent was now completely free of Septim's hold at last, and that her mother had weathered her rough introduction to Talahm better than anyone had expected.

Many of the refugees trailed behind them, some on horses and others on foot. A few had remained in the Trident to help rebuild, much to Elijah Cade's relief. The

Lord of the Trident had wasted no time finding them horses and supplies when Emma explained what had happened in Ralador and their urgency to get back to the city. He must have sensed a change in the Prince, since Emma had seen them shaking hands and smiling before they'd set off down the River Road.

Soon, they emerged from the Valon Forest, the western side of Camelot looming in the distance. The soon-to-be-setting sun cast deep orange brushstrokes across the sky, light winking off the windows of the tallest towers.

Julie pulled up short beside them, her voice tight. "Your father—"

Emma's heart lodged in her throat. They hadn't had a good chance to catch up on *The Sea Wolf*, and now they were within a few miles of returning home. At least she'd remembered to send Tomás a quick note the first night on board, warning him to expect Luke arriving on a dragon. "Leaving us was the hardest thing Dad ever did," Emma said matter-of-factly. "But he did it to help save what we have here, now."

Julie swallowed, tapping her heels to the horse's flanks. "It's been over twenty years."

"Mom, there's another thing you should know," Emma said, desperately wishing she didn't have to say it. "Dad.... He's paralyzed from the waist down." She told Julie about the poisoned arrow, Tomás's narrow escape from death, and the aftermath the Tears of Nightshade had wrought on his body. She left out that Argent had been the one to draw the bow. Emma didn't dare trying to read her mother's mind now, thinking that this would all be too much even for someone who hadn't just gone through a traumatic captivity. "I'd hoped he'd be cured by the time I got back."

When Julie turned her head to stare into Emma's eyes, her dark hair cascading over her shoulders, Emma could see the spark of the woman her father had fallen in love with nearly thirty years ago. "Paralysis or not," she said softly, "there has only ever been one man for me. It's always been Tom."

Emma's heart almost burst with the love she felt for her parents. As if Argent sensed it, he urged the horse into a trot, then a canter, until he, Emma, and Julie drew ahead of the rest of the refugees, speeding across the fields toward the Trident Gate. Emma surveyed the broken walls, knowing now that the slow progress of rebuilding had less to do with the crises caused by Igraine, and more to do with King Aragon's poor decisions while under her influence. She knew without a doubt that King Aragon could restore Renova once Argent tore away every remnant of Septim and every trinket tied to Igraine.

Their minds must have remained more connected than she thought because his posture changed in front of her. He sat taller in the saddle, shoulders back and proud. For a moment, the image of William Pendragon standing in a similar pose at the helm of a brigantine sprang to mind. Argent glanced at her from over his shoulder, his lips drawn into a smile.

They rode right through the Trident Gate, grateful for the lack of a welcoming party. Even though Emma had kept her father informed during their journey home, she had worried about subjecting her mother and the Fifth Travelers to the stares of Camelot's people. A few minutes later, they approached the citadel, and two soldiers with crossed halberds blocked the gate.

"Let them through!" Tomás shouted from the courtyard, leaning heavily against Renault. He wore a metal exoskeleton around his legs, the struts glowing with runes. Emma wondered when Luke, Renault, and Sargateth had found the time to design and enchant the contraption, but she couldn't care less now that he could stand, albeit with difficulty.

The soldiers uncrossed their weapons, stepping out of the way as the two horses clattered into the training grounds. Julie swung down, her hands dangling awkwardly at her sides as she took tentative steps toward her husband.

As he dismounted, Argent's boots cuffed the flagstones, the sound oddly loud in the following silence. He offered his hands to Emma, lifting her by her waist and gently setting her on the ground. She clung to his arm, unable to take her eyes off her parents.

"Julie," Tomás breathed, his mismatched eyes shining, features slack with so much emotion that, for the barest second, Emma wished King Aragon was more like her father. For Argent's sake.

"Tom." Julie's voice trembled, her façade of strength crumbling as she rushed forward to cling to Tomás, sobbing into the loose folds of his robes.

Emma thought everything was going fine until Julie started beating her fists against Tomás's chest. "Uh, Mom—"

But Tomás held his wife, tears streaming down his face, taking the beating as if he deserved it. Which he probably believed he did.

"How could you leave us?" Julie's muffled voice cut through the air like a knife. "I thought you were dead! I grieved for you every day!"

"I can't say anything to take away that pain," Tomás murmured into his wife's hair, stroking her back, his wedding ring catching the sunlight. "But I promise to spend the rest of my life hoping to earn back your trust." Over Julie's head, he mouthed, *"Thank you,"* to Emma.

When Julie had exhausted her tears, which hadn't taken long, she sniffed, wiping her nose with her ragged sleeve.

"Is this the custom Glock 19 I gave you as a wedding present?" Tomás asked softly, pointing at the white grip of Julie's holstered gun.

Julie smiled, and it shifted her entire demeanor. She drew the pistol, tracing the engraving on the slide with one finger. "'For when life gets a little too risky. With eternal love, Tom,'" she read.

Emma snorted, turning her face into Argent's chest.

"Delightful," Renault interrupted, his gruffness pulling them back down to reality. "As much as I'd love to sit back and watch your little family reunion, I have a half-dead Olis in the infirmary, and your son refused to answer my questions until you lot got back."

"You'll have to wait a bit longer, I'm afraid," Argent told him, a glint in his eye. "I must first speak with my father."

Argent hesitated at the doors of Pendragon Hall, a muscle jumping in his cheek. Emma stood next to him with her fingers threaded through his. "Ready?"

He tipped his chin in a curt nod, pushing the doors open with both of his hands, his entrance much more grandiose than anyone inside would expect from him—flighty, timid Argent. He brushed the hair away from his eyes. That version of him was gone, flushed away with the sour reminder of his evil grandfather.

A few people sat at the tables in Pendragon Hall, and all of them looked up the moment he swept inside. King Aragon lounged on his throne, a cup of tea in one hand and a book in the other. The King glanced up, eyes stony across the length of the hall, and snapped the book shut.

"Everyone, out," Argent commanded.

Emma felt a rush of satisfaction when they all scampered without complaint.

When the door closed, Argent took a single step forward, only for King Aragon to lift a finger in warning, his features hard and angry. Argent ignored the feeble attempt to stay him and stormed toward his father, pointing at the green-eyed eagle wrapped around Aragon's finger. "Take off your ring."

Aragon got to his feet, leaving the cup of tea balanced precariously on the arm of his throne. "How dare you—"

Argent's nostrils flared, and Emma sensed his courage. "I said, take it off, Father. Or I will force you to." He held out his hand, and a long moment later, Aragon's eagle ring dropped onto his palm.

"What is the meaning of this?" King Aragon demanded through clenched teeth, gray eyes cloudy with anger. His hand closed into a fist, the tan line from the ring stark against his sandy skin.

Argent ignored him, handing the ring to Emma. She closed her palms around it like a nutshell. A searing white light shone through the spaces between her fingers, and a sharp pop rent the air. When she opened her hands again, the ring was gone.

Fury arced through the King's eyes. "Explain, now!"

Argent squared his shoulders as he clasped his hands behind his back, the picture of royalty. A rush of attraction coursed through Emma. "Igraine Pendragon used that ring to influence Septim his entire life. And you picked it up as a trophy. She's been using you this whole time, Father. The King who led us through the Valon War wouldn't lock his best fighters behind broken walls."

The King looked confused. "Igraine? Arthur's mother?" Aragon rubbed his mouth, beginning to pace. The gold of his crown glinted as it caught the magical lights lining the hall. "You are mistaken," he decided, jaw clenched. "She died when Arthur was only thirteen. This is an attempt to distract me from the fact that you directly disobeyed me, boy!"

Emma watched Argent relax. "If you are so disappointed in my decision to save the lives of the people—*our* people—now crowding the infirmary, then by all means... disown me."

Aragon stared at Argent in silent shock.

Emma's heart sped up as Argent's next words tumbled out. "How many times now have you looked at me and seen only Septim? How many nightmares have you woken from where Emma doesn't stop him from executing you like you executed him? How many—"

Aragon held up his hand, turning his face away from Argent. "Stop."

But Argent pressed once more on that tender wound. "How many nights have you wished that Septim would've just killed me, too?"

"I said, stop." The King's gray eyes shone, the paleness of his face stark.

"It can't have been more times than me." Argent sucked in his cheeks. Emma slipped her hand into his, offering her strength and support for him to borrow. "Do you think I wanted any of that? To be remembered for regicide, for patricide? To live with that kind of guilt? That was his plan all along. To force me into murdering my own father, and I could do nothing about it."

Aragon sat back in his throne, slouching over his knees, placing his face in his hands. The teacup teetered on the edge before tipping over and shattering to pieces when it hit the floor, brown liquid spilling across the stones. The smell of bergamot filled the air. One of the King's hands crept to his crown, hooking under its edge. Slowly, he slid it off until he held it in both hands, despondent. "Every night," he croaked. "And every time I look at you," he continued slowly, as if each word made one more cut among the thousands he already bore. "It was easier to let the rumors spread than to admit that I didn't know how to love you again. To admit I had failed to protect my heir... again."

Emma and Argent watched the King with bated breath, not daring to look away for fear of missing a single admission.

King Aragon's eyes flickered up, meeting Argent's with more compassion than he had in the last eight years combined. "I was foolish. I am still foolish. I have no one to blame for the state of our kingdom but myself," he said, and Emma sensed the words were more for himself than for Argent. The King cast his eyes back to his crown and turned it in his hands, his fingers tracing the ridge. "If I keep Renova but lose my only remaining son, I am nothing but a failed regent."

Argent knelt in front of him, looking up into his father's eyes. "I never wanted the throne. But my duty is to you, my King. To this crown. This country. If one day I sit where you sit now, my only wish is that it be because I had no other choice than to take up your mantle." He reached up to touch his father's hands, the edge of the crown brushing against his skin. "Our ancestors had an enemy they didn't know about. But we do. And together we are stronger than she ever anticipated."

They heard the shouts before they even reached the infirmary, but when the King pushed the door open, the entire room fell silent.

"Half-dead or not, can he open a portal to Langoth yet?" Emma demanded, marching over to Mountains' bed.

Luke stared down the King, a pained look on his face. "We need to go after Bethany, now."

"I must understand the whole situation first," King Aragon replied, his voice sounding weary and thin. His gray eyes weren't as stormy now, as if the fury behind them had drained away with the destruction of the ring. Queen Amity swept over to her husband, fussing as she took his arm. He stopped her with a placating hand on her waist. "Starting with how Igraine Pendragon is still alive and well enough to target her descendants with corrupted magic."

Emma could've heard a pin drop in the silence following those words.

Renault interrupted, eyes black as night. "Are you sure it was Igraine? Not one of Septim's witches? Or Septim himself playing some elaborate scheme—"

Mountains laughed, the sound guttural and scratchy against Emma's ears. The Olis had finally woken.

Argent spoke before Mountains could finish laughing. "It's her. I've studied my lineage extensively, and there's a portrait of her in Morgan's office. She knew me. But how can she be alive? It's been hundreds of years since Arthur. How could she have come here at all? The Gateway did not exist until Arthur lay on his first deathbed—"

Morgan's velvet voice was cracked and uncertain. "She was my first apprentice. One I did not treat as well as I now wish I had. Igraine went down darker paths than I would lead her, and our differences forced me to end her apprenticeship when she bore Arthur. Clearly, she continued searching for magic not meant for mortal minds."

Mountains cackled. "Oh, she gloated about her sway over the Septims, and oft complained of you, *Purifying Fire of Darkest Night*, and the plans she has to pay you back in kind."

It took Emma a moment to catch Morgan's startled expression. *Her true name, then.*

"She made the Septims into the monsters she loosed on Renova. She perfected her Blacksoul Rituals on his ancestors until it worked perfectly on dear, old Agamemnon, with barely any cost to herself."

"She's your problem too, moron," Luke growled. "If she survived the trip to Langoth, and she probably did, she has a way back here. Your stupid claw."

Mountains reflexively tensed his paw, the missing appendage obvious in its absence. He flinched when Magdalin climbed from her bed to kneel next to his, hands trembling as she reached for her brother. "Don't touch me, traitor," he spat.

Emma watched the situation spiral downhill. Sargateth pulled his wife out of Mountains' reach, and Morgan's fingers went white as they tightened around her staff, eyes flashing in ancient anger.

Renault took a menacing step forward, his hands balled into fists. His muscles jumped in his neck, and he clearly wanted to blast Mountains with his staff. By some miracle, he restrained himself. "I would flay you to an inch of your life if it would do us any good. But it won't. Nothing but the Lord's will can change the impenetrable opinions of someone as stubborn as you and your ilk." The room quieted with each word, everyone hanging on the promise of learning more about the Olii than ever before.

The sneer on Mountains' face deepened until Emma wondered if the beast had ever experienced an emotion other than contempt—he wore it like his own fur. "You must be Fire's half-breed spawn. Still throwing tantrums over decisions made by beings far greater than yourself, let alone your pitiful human sire."

Renault's hands turned blue. His rage was so intense that Emma felt the hostile magic radiating off him in waves. A window cracked, the noise breaking through the intensity in the room.

Morgan finally moved, putting herself between her son and Mountains. "That will do," she snarled, flames dancing in her eyes—a hint of her true nature, and perhaps the reason for her native name. The amethyst on her staff flared bright purple before going dark again. "Now is not the time for petty differences of opinion over how the Council makes its decisions—" She glared at both her son and Mountains "—regardless of whether the reasons behind those decisions still affect us. At least one of my battle witches is lost on the third world, currently beyond our help."

Luke made an undignified choking sound. Julie wrapped her arms around his waist from behind, finally having left the comfort of her husband's side.

"She'll stay lost for now. I can't indiscriminately open a gateway to Langoth," Mountains said, using one of his remaining intact claws to pick at his teeth. He ignored the outrage around him. In fact, he seemed to revel in it, and Emma wondered how much that century of captivity had addled his brain. How much Igraine had influenced him despite his many injuries. "Unless you want all of Camelot sucked to the dying lands."

Despite her shock at the Olis's revelation, Emma shot Luke a sharp glance before he could respond. *We're not getting Bethany back today. We'll have to make a plan... and Mountains must be part of it.*

The Prince released Emma's hand and barked for their attention. "My father's question remains unanswered. How is she alive?"

Both Sargateth and Morgan shrugged helplessly under the Prince's steely gaze, making it apparent that neither had an answer for him.

"It doesn't matter at this point," Morgan finally said. "She survived, and she's a threat. Now that we have a true common enemy, I suggest we determine how to deal with her."

Luke couldn't hold back his frustration any longer, ignoring Emma's projected thoughts. "Have none of you been paying attention? She's on *Langoth*. With *Bethany* as her captive! We can't do anything from this useless hunk of rock, so if any of you are really committed to handling this, why aren't you opening a portal right now?" Julie's arms tightened around him, grasping her other wrist to keep him from breaking free.

Emma's heart broke for her brother. He'd lost enough control over his emotions that tears shone in his eyes, and she knew he did not want some people in the room to see him like this.

"If it was Emma, you wouldn't think twice about going after her," Luke accused. "But because it's Bethany, just a *girl from Earth*, she's not worth it. Is that what you think of her? The witch whose magic is second only to Emma and the Olii?"

"Luke—"

Luke shook his mother off, taking another step toward the Ancients, clearly at his wit's end. "She's a hundred times better than you, Mountains. A thousand times. And I will do whatever it takes to get her back."

Tomás hobbled over, touching Luke's back and drawing him from the fray, making him sit on one of the infirmary beds. Emma went with them, Argent close behind.

"This is all my fault," Luke whispered, pressing the heels of his palms against his eyes.

"Tell me," Tomás said gently, the perfect picture of a compassionate, supportive father.

"I made so many mistakes, Dad...." And then Luke admitted everything. Even though the enchanted sleep device had left him at Igraine's mercy, it had only strengthened his existing doubts and paranoia. He told them about his Vision of Igraine and his belief that he'd save the kingdom by leading Argent to his death. Luke bared his entire ruin, ending with his failure to keep Bethany safe.

Emma wrestled with the myriad of feelings in response to her brother's revelation, leaning on Argent for strength and sanity. In trying to expose a traitor, Luke became a traitor himself. Not just to Renova... but to Emma. He'd failed in his duties as Sentinel, and, as a result, his magic worked against him—against them all.

He deserves forgiveness as much as I did, Argent thought to Emma, his hand tightening over hers.

She nodded, brushing the tears from her cheeks as she knelt in front of her brother, reaching up with both hands to clasp his face. She closed her eyes, pressing her forehead against his, letting him know her own pain, as well as the forgiveness and peace she knew he didn't think anyone would offer him.

"We will get her back," she reassured Luke.

His hands wound around her wrists, reconnecting them as Sentinel and Sorceress. "I'm so sorry," he breathed.

"The witches of Renova aren't afraid to get hurt," Emma said, echoing something Bethany had once told her. "And Bethany is a witch of Renova."

Finally, Luke gave a wet laugh. "She's taking all the pain that's offered."

For one long, peaceful moment, brother and sister found hope in Bethany's tenacity.

And then—

"Tomás!" Renault's urgent cry jolted Emma's soul.

She looked up at her father, rigid where he sat on the bed, his muscles straining as his hands clenched the blankets until they tore. One of his leg braces broke, the metal pin skittering away. Renault caught him before he fell forward onto the flagstones, gently easing him to his side until the throes passed. Emma shuffled over, unsure what to do.

Julie rushed to Tomás's side, her hands shaking as she knelt by Emma. "He still has seizures?"

Luke rested a hand on his mother's shoulder. "He must be—"

Tomás's mismatched eyes fluttered open, finding Emma's. His hand gripped hers hard enough to hurt. "Twelve Olii fly across the Glass Channel to confront the Night's Empress at Perga's Scepter. She frees herself from the tides of Langoth, but it costs us all." His gaze turned to Mountains. "We need him. And if we fail…. No." Tomás squeezed his eyes shut, shaking his head. "I've never Seen a Vision with two possibilities. We must not fail."

Emma's heart hammered in her throat. "Dad? What will happen?"

"Igraine Pendragon will rule Talahm until its bitter end."

CONTINUE THE STORY
TIDES OF FATE

Nothing is more important than saving Bethany from The Night's Empress.

In the aftermath of losing Bethany to Langoth, Emma's magic fails with every effort to rescue her. Desperate to save her best friend, Emma and her brother Luke will stop at nothing to bring Bethany home.

With an eclectic band of allies, they set sail across the portal-riddled ocean to Perga's Scepter, an island in the far north with the last stable obelisk. From the highest mountain's peak to the depths of The Shadow Star library, it's a race to save Bethany and sentence Igraine to the black hole on the verge of consuming Langoth.

But time isn't the only thing against them.

When Luke starts having Vision-like nightmares right as the journey gets underway, he doesn't know who to trust besides his family. As the threads between the Pendragons and the Artairs start to unravel, Bethany's ultimate fate hangs in the balance.

In the struggle between heart and kingdom, one is sure to lose.

Get Book 3 at https://talahm.com/tides-of-fate or by scanning the code below:

ALSO BY COLLEEN MITCHELL

THE CHRONICLES OF TALAHM

Main Series

Book 1: *Mark of Stars*

Book 2: *The Prophet's Ruin*

Book 3: *Tides of Fate*

Book 4: *The Last Horizon*

Companion Stories

The Orphan's Gambit

Visit talahm.com for the latest reading order and available books in the Talahm universe.

ACKNOWLEDGEMENTS

All praise, honor, and glory go to my Lord and Savior Jesus Christ. This, the second book in *The Chronicles of Talahm*, is a result of the gifts my Creator bestowed upon me to use in service of His Kingdom.

To my husband Tim, thank you for every opinion, idea, brainstorming session, and encouragement along my writing journey.

Jeannie, my best friend, my back-of-the-choir-class partner in literary crime, thank you for everything you've given me.

Mom & Dad are the best parents a T1D writer could ask for. I got Mom's creative gene (but none of her painting skills) and Dad's imagination and ingenuity for out-of-the-box ideas. The first book in this series was dedicated in part to my dad, who passed in November 2019. I could not have asked for better parents.

The second woman in my dedication is my Grandma Marilynn Van Hise. Grandma Van passed away in December 2019, just fifty-three days after my dad. Grandma had two speeds: fast, and fast forward, until she slowed down in the last years of her life. While she never would have understood (or particularly enjoyed) what I write in *The Chronicles of Talahm*, she nevertheless was an example of commitment and faith—both qualities essential to the life of a writer. Grandma Van too was a stickler for grammar and did not hesitate to share her opinions in letters to newspaper editors. We miss her energy and presence but draw comfort knowing she is celebrating eternity with her Savior Jesus.

Karen Walker, my sister, thank you for your continued excitement about my writing. I'm tickled that you like it enough to immediately ask, "when's book 2 coming out?" after finishing book 1.

I could not have finished *Mark of Stars* or *The Prophet's Ruin* without the incredible 60 Day Novel Writing Challenge and the authors who keep coming back to write with us. Community among writers is so important. Being able to bounce ideas and get feedback makes the whole process way less lonely.

Special thanks and gratitude go to Lauren Willitz, who never ceases to encourage me.

Thank you to my coaches and fellow Life Coach School graduates for your support and coaching of my dramatic brain: Erin Woodruff, Thais Glenn, Pete Tidwell, Emily Bui, Karen Boville, Kimberly Nichols, Lisa LeBlanc,

Lincoln Kinkade, Kanwal Akhtar, Racquel Murray, Dave Moreno, Mariana Fávero Bonesso, Cheryl Bennett, Nadège Saysana, Dele Downs Kooley, Shideh Shafie, and Pete Beskas.

The Prophet's Ruin went through six beta readers: Shanna Lowe, Christy Boring, Chris Helgeson, Lauren Hambrook, Megan Bass, and Joe Barber. Thank you so much for your feedback!

My amazing editing team: Halie Fewkes Damewood, Lauren Loftis, and Anne Staver, thank you for each of your special skills in coaxing out the best plot, tightest sentences, and proper commas.

Thank you to Angelique Modin for the fabulous cover, and to LeighAnn Lopez for the incredible chapter headers. I'm continually blown away by the quality of LeighAnn's illustrations. I am so completely in love with all the chapter headers and the maps she's done for this series! I did end up naming a city after her and put it in such a place that cannot ever be flooded.

Like many writers, I can pinpoint a moment in time where I tipped from "writing is cool" to "I can write, and this could turn into something...." For me, that moment happened in high school, during Gwen Mansfield's creative writing class. I am also forever grateful to Victoria Stamp for her love of English and making me fix sentences without using semicolons.

And lastly, to you, my reader, I thank you for picking up this book and reading it all the way to the end. No matter how you found it, you're now part of Talahm.

To sign up for updates on future books in the series, visit www.talahm.com.

See you in Book 3!

About the Author

Colleen Mitchell finds it oddly satisfying to tug on reader heart strings, which started in Fanfiction and bled into her original works. She's been writing since age twelve and spent a good chunk of choir class ignoring the teacher to trade stories with her best friend in the back row.

She lives in Montana with her husband Tim and their cat Luna.

You can visit Colleen online at talahm.com, or on Instagram @colleenmitchellwrites.